Mark of the Cobra

By

Herbert Grosshans

Published by
Melange Books, LLC
White Bear Lake, MN 55110
www.melange-books.com

Credits

Copy Editor: Sherry Der Wille
Line Editor: Nancy Schumacher
Format Editor: Mae Powers
Cover Artist: A.Bratt

About the Author

Herbert lives near Winnipeg, Canada. He spends his free time spinning tales about imaginary worlds and the strange creatures inhabiting them. His first published story `The Anniversary Gift' appeared in `Sweet Revenge' published by Midnight Showcase. Even though he writes in other genres, his love is Science Fiction. He enjoys building alien worlds and societies. Most of his stories contain an element of Erotica. All of his books are available from Melange Books.

Website: http://www.hegro.shawwebspace.ca
Blog: http://hegro.blogspot.com

Mark of the Cobra
Herbert Grosshans

When his company sends Peter Hartmann to meet a new prospective client, he is obliged to do more than just sign some contracts. After being arrested for a crime he didn't commit, his violent past catches up with him and takes him on a roller coaster ride filled with danger and sexual encounters.

* * * *

Visit Herbert's website:

http://hegro.shawwebspace.ca
http://hegro.blogspot.com/

Works also by and including Herbert Grosshans:
Stars In Chains 1, Slave
Stars In Chains 2: Liberator
Stardogs 1 & 2
The Xandra Trilogy
Cliffs of Time
Orion the Hunt
Beyond the Stars Digest
Orion: Symbiont of Passion
Men of Eros
The Spider Wars, Books 1, 2 & 3

See more of Herbert's books on sale at
www.melange-books.com

Chapter One

The gate opened. Peter Hartmann drove down the winding driveway toward the large house. Through his open window, he smelled the fragrance of flowers and trees in bloom. The noise of a lawn tractor made him aware of the immaculate lawn and the neatly trimmed shrubbery.

He parked his car and walked slowly to the huge front entrance. Thick pillars held up a large canopy so high it made him feel dwarfish. As he approached, the door opened, and a black girl in a maid's outfit asked him to come in. "Mrs. Liebman is waiting in the library," she said. "This way, please."

She walked in front of him. He took great enjoyment watching her plump buttocks roll inside her tight short skirt. She had nice legs, too.

The woman who sat at a small round table got up when Peter walked in. She was fairly tall, slim, and middle age. Early fifties, Peter estimated. Her black hair was tied in a tight bun behind her head. The black, high-collared long dress she wore clung to her body, revealing a nice, curvy figure.

"Hello," she said with an enchanting, beautiful smile, shaking his hand. "I am Rhonda Liebman."

"Hi. Peter Hartmann." He held her hand for a brief moment, feeling the urge to bend down and kiss it. Something about this woman radiated class, almost royalty. "I hope I'm not too early."

He noticed the diamond-studded earrings, the necklace of delicate woven gold strands, and when she pulled her hand away, the sunlight from the large window caught in the multifaceted diamond she wore on her third finger.

5

This woman represented money and power. He would have to tread very carefully.

She laughed. "With my husband, everybody is always early. He's been held up at a meeting, but that's fine. I am his silent partner. You can discuss business with me."

"All right." Peter fumbled with his briefcase, but Mrs. Liebman held up a hand. "There is time, Peter." She smiled and walked over to a small couch. When she sat down, the slit in the front of the dress parted and exposed two long, well-formed tanned legs. "You young people are always in such a hurry to talk business."

She crossed her legs and patted the seat beside her. "Come, join me for a drink and tell me a little about yourself. I like to know more about the people I do business with."

Speaking to the servant girl, who had been waiting patiently by the door, she said, "Two glasses of white wine, Rita."

"Yes, ma'am."

Peter sat down beside the older woman, feeling somewhat awkward and apprehensive.

"Can I ask you a question?" he asked.

"Sure."

"I recently met a Delta Liebman. Are you by any chance related to her?"

Rhonda laughed. "You've met Delta? Yes, we are related. Through marriage. My husband and her husband are brothers." She paused a little. "Delta and I don't always see eye to eye."

"It happens. My girlfriend and her sister aren't exactly friends, either."

"So you're not married?"

"No, I am not, but Kathleen and I have been living together for five years."

"She is younger?"

"Yes. Eight years." He felt as if he were on trial. "She's very beautiful," he added.

Mrs. Liebman laughed. She had a captivating laugh. "I'm sure she is. A handsome man like you would never settle for an ugly one. Children?"

Peter shook his head. "No."

"Any reason?"

"We're not married."

"That is not a valid reason. People have children without getting married."

"I guess they have." He hesitated. "It's medical. Low sperm count. I'll probably never have children."

The maid brought the drinks, interrupting their conversation. Peter almost emptied half the glass. Catching himself, he put the glass onto the small table beside him.

Mrs. Liebman just sipped hers. Looking at him over the rim of her glass, she said, "That's too bad, but I'm sure there are compensations."

He chuckled, somewhat embarrassed, guessing what she meant, but he feigned ignorance. "Like what?"

Smiling, she put down her glass. "You ever cheat on the woman you live with, Peter?"

He looked into her hazel eyes, a sudden flash of heat creeping up his neck. He didn't know how to play her game, and he knew she was playing with him. Like a cat with a mouse. I'm the mouse.

Her eyes were cool, almost cold, her face unreadable.

Don't blow this one!

"My job takes me away from home a lot," he said carefully. "A week can be a long time, and it gets quite lonely sometimes."

She drained her glass and got up. "Would you like to go for a swim?" she asked.

"I don't know," he said, his voice sounding flustered. "I mean…sure. I'd like to, but I'm not prepared for a swim."

"No trunks?" She chuckled. "We'll find you a pair."

Rita, the maid, brought him a pair of swimming trunks and led him to a change-room outside. When he emerged, he saw Mrs. Liebman already waiting by the pool. She must have worn her outfit under her dress.

Peter tried not to stare but failed. This woman had the body of a twenty-five year old, and she displayed it liberally in her string bikini and a tiny halter that barely covered her nipples.

She noticed his staring and smiled, studying him in return. "A bodybuilder," she commented.

"I used to, but lately I've been neglecting my workouts a bit," he said.

She gave him a cryptic smile. "I believe in workouts myself. What do you do?"

"Martial arts, mainly, and some weightlifting."

"You'll have to show me some of your moves sometimes," she said. "Maybe I'll show you mine." She laughed softly.

"You're into martial arts?"

"Not really. It's more like acrobatics." She looked at his trunks and smiled. "You want to cool off?"

His eyes had been feasting on her luscious body. He couldn't believe this woman was over fifty. She certainly didn't look like the tough old bird his boss had called her. Her waist was maybe not quite as tiny as that of a younger woman, and her hips a bit too fleshy, but her belly was flat and trim, her buttocks and breasts looked firm and solid. His loins were beginning to pound, and his penis came to life in his borrowed trunks.

Becoming aware of his erection, he didn't answer, just turned and dove into the pool.

Damn! If he could only be sure what she expected of him. The signs were there, almost too obvious, but did he read them correctly?

Coming up for air, he saw her dive after him. Her legs were straight as she entered the water with barely a splash.

She swam right up to him under water and rose in front of him, her body rubbing against his. Laughing, she began to splash water at him. "Are you competitive, Peter?" she asked.

"To a certain degree, yes, I am."

"Let's race then."

She swam away with strong strokes. He went after her but couldn't catch her.

Suddenly, she ducked under water and swam back toward him. Her hands gripped his trunks and pulled them down. Coming up for air, she spit out water and laughed. He noticed that she had removed her top. Her naked breasts bobbed above the water.

"Am I shocking you?" she asked, still laughing.

He treaded water in front of her, looking into her hazel eyes. "What is it you want from me, Mrs. Liebman?" he asked bluntly.

"Isn't it obvious?" She smiled. "I want you to screw me, Peter, or don't you find me attractive? Am I too old for you?"

"I find you attractive and very desirable," Peter said, carefully, "but I can't afford to blow this deal."

"Screwing me is part of the deal. So if you want to do business with my husband, you'll have to do more than just deliver some papers to him. I expect delivery first." Her hand reached between his legs. "And from what I can see and feel, you have all the necessary equipment."

He put his hand behind her head and pulled her to him, his mouth closed over hers and she opened it to let his tongue probe the cavity. When they broke apart, she gasped, "Outside," and slipped from his embrace.

She climbed out of the pool and ran across the tiles toward the grass. There she lay down, removed her string bikini and waited for him. Her chest was heaving, and her breath came fast, and it wasn't because she had exerted herself.

Peter flopped down beside her, and then he rolled between her spreading thighs. Just watching her running in front of him had aroused him tremendously. His penis was hard and throbbing, and, with a groan, he pushed it into her welcoming sex-organ.

She cried out when he slid into her and pulled her knees higher to let him in deeper. She moved with great passion underneath him, her soft tight sheath rippling the length of his penis.

Peter didn't feel hurried. He knew he had to please this woman and rushing it was not the way to do it. Moving slowly between her fleshy smooth thighs, he brought her to several orgasms.

When she requested it, he let her move on top. He admired her solid breasts, sucked on their large nipples when she offered them and let his hands trail down her wide suntanned hips. He saw no wrinkles on her flat belly, and she used her pussy with greater expertise than a younger woman ever could.

He noticed the tattoo in the image of a coiled cobra around her navel, but then his eyes focused on the black fuzzy triangle between her legs. Looking at her curvy body, Peter found it quite a challenge not to come inside her squeezing softness.

"Let's do it doggy-style," he suggested. She slid off him and got on her knees in the soft grass, pushing up her ample posterior.

Her buttocks were round and well shaped, with a fleshiness that made them very erotic. He ran his hands over them, and then he got in position behind her and put his hard mast between those soft cheeks.

She spread them with her hands, but he moved the tip of his penis lower. He'd never done it that way and probably never would. Sliding back into her creamy pussy, he grabbed her smooth hips for support. Then he began slamming his belly into her soft buttocks, fucking her hard and furious until she cried out and pushed her buttocks forcefully into his groin.

"Now!" she cried. "Now!"

He exploded inside her clutching sex-canal. When he was finished, she collapsed and lay on her belly, breathing hard, Peter on top of her, his penis inside her. After a while, he started moving his still erect member slowly in and out. She gasped and began contracting her inner muscles.

He rolled onto his back, keeping her on top of him. Revolving her hips and grinding her buttocks into his lap, she stayed like that for a long time. He held on to her breasts to keep her from rolling off.

He let go of her breasts when she sat up and leaned forward, presenting her tanned buttocks to his hungry eyes. Watching his pole disappear inside her sex-organ and her smooth cheeks descending again and again was a sight he could watch forever.

Aware of nothing else, it came as quite a shock when a woman's voice spoke beside them.

"Now, there is something I wouldn't mind doing myself."

Looking up, he saw a fat woman standing a few feet away, a big smile on her pudgy face.

Mrs. Liebman didn't even bother to slow down. "Oh, hi there. I didn't hear you come."

The fat woman chuckled. "I haven't yet, but if I could borrow that handsome stud of yours for a bit, maybe I can come, too."

Mrs. Liebman laughed and slammed down hard, her laughter turning into a loud gasping moan. She took Peter deep into her pulsating sheath. He felt warm liquid trickle down the insides of his thighs.

"I can hear you coming." The fat woman laughed at her own joke.

"You can have him now," Mrs. Liebman said, lifting off. Kneeling beside Peter, she tried to catch her breath.

He hadn't come, his penis stood like a lonely pole. The fat woman pulled down her panties and lifted her thin dress. The mound of her womanhood was thick and sparsely covered with brown hair. Straddling Peter, she hovered above him for a moment, and then she lowered herself, her descending pussy sheathing his rigid mast.

He slid into a moist hot inferno. She had fat but strong thighs. She never put her full weight on his body and moved her big torso with surprising agility. Despite his slight distaste for fat women, he was immensely turned on. Her pussy was as soft and tight as any other pussy that had ever swallowed his rod.

The first time she experienced an orgasm, she gave a little shriek and sat in his lap, her body shaking like jelly. Then she lifted off and lay down in the grass, her legs wide open.

Peter was quite aroused and didn't need any encouragement. He got between her fleshy thighs and pushed his manhood back into her creamy pussy. He began to move with slow steady strokes, pushing as deep and hard as he could. His hands moved under her thin dress, and when he climaxed, he dug his fingers into the soft globes of her breasts.

Groaning loudly, he filled her insides with his spurting warm liquid.

Her fat arms went around him, clutching him to her. She wheezed and breathed like a steam engine, and he feared she might pass out. When her breathing became normal again, she let go of him.

"You are some kind of man," she commented. "I don't believe we've been properly introduced."

"Peter Hartmann," he said lamely, giving her a lopsided grin. "And who might you be?"

"I am Mary Jane," the woman answered, smiling. "A nosy neighbor."

"Now that we all know who we are," Mrs. Liebman said, "how about a cold drink?"

"Sounds good to me," Mary Jane said. "How about you, Peter?" Her eyes twinkled behind fatty folds. "Or do you have other plans?" Her inner muscles had been gently milking his penis, and he found himself growing inside her.

"You do have other plans." She laughed delightedly.

Lying between her cradling meaty thighs and on top of her soft belly felt so comfortable. Sighing, he began to snap his buttocks back and forth.

Her vagina muscles tightened and gripped him with gentle force. Laboring between her clutching thighs, he brought her to a couple more wet orgasms, but his own climax, when it came, was quite dry and somewhat disappointing. There was only so much juice in him.

Sweat covered his body, and Mary Jane's dress was plastered to her massive body. Gasping, they finally broke apart and lay exhausted in the grass.

"You could give a woman a heart attack," Mary Jane whispered hoarsely. "I've never met a man with your stamina. Maybe I should hire your services. You could become my personal instructor to help me lose weight."

"Always trying to give my best." Peter grinned and accepted the cold drink Mrs. Liebman handed him. Looking at her, he said, "Maybe there is a bonus in it for me."

Mrs. Liebman smiled over her drink. "You can be certain of that."

Mary Jane was still breathing hard when her overweight body flopped onto one of the lounges. Mrs. Liebman gave her a cold drink and watched as the exhausted woman gulped it down. "You don't look too good," she said, concern in her voice. "Are you okay?"

"I feel a little faint," Mary Jane said, wiping her forehead. "Maybe it's the heat."

Peter looked at her and had to admit her face looked somewhat gray.

She sat up suddenly and gulped for air, and then she slumped back into her seat. Her head fell forward and to one side.

Mrs. Liebman picked up Mary Jane's hand and searched for a pulse. "Shit!" she exclaimed. "I think she is dead."

"Maybe we should call a doctor?" Peter suggested.

"No doctor," she said sharply. "This sure messes up things. Damn!"

She whirled around to stare at a young man who had just come through the patio door. "Who the hell are you?" she demanded, almost angrily.

"I'm sorry if I startled you," the man apologized. "The maid let me in." His eyes riveted on her nude body. Staring at her genitals for a moment his gaze finally settled on her breasts. "I am from Beta

12

Research, and I was supposed to meet Mr. Liebman." He looked clearly uncomfortable.

"You are from Beta Research?" Mrs. Liebman asked and turned to look at Peter. "I thought...never mind." She gave the man a sharp look. "Mr. Liebman is not here. I am his wife. You can leave everything you have with me. I will make sure my husband gets it."

"I don't know. I was supposed to give the papers directly to Mr. Liebman." He hesitated, still staring at her breasts.

She smiled. "Maybe you want to join us, young man. You'll have to take off your clothes, though. There is only one thing...my husband is a jealous and violent man. He may take offence, finding you naked with his wife."

"I think I'll leave everything with you then, ma'am," the young man stuttered. Opening his briefcase, he took out a large padded envelope and handed it to the woman. Sighing, he gave her one last look, glanced at Peter, and then he turned and left.

Mrs. Liebman put the envelope on a small table and looked at Peter. "I have a bit of a problem here. Who the hell are you?" she asked, her voice dangerously low.

"I am Peter Hartmann. I work for Computer Regeneration Development. I thought you knew. You've been expecting me, Mrs. Liebman."

"Well, I guess it is my fault. I assumed you were from Beta Research. By the way, I am not Rhonda Liebman. She is." She pointed at the lifeless woman in the lounge.

"Now I am confused." Peter shook his head. "Mind telling me what the hell is going on?"

The woman poured herself another drink. "I work for the Federal Government. I am here to intercept these documents." She held up the envelope. "We believe that Mr. Liebman has dealings with a Middle East country, selling military secrets. That's all I can tell you."

"What about her, the real Mrs. Liebman? How does she fit in?"

The woman shrugged. "She's probably innocent. We told her that we expected her husband to be the victim of an extortion attempt. She agreed to let me assume her identity in order for us to apprehend the extortionists." She stared at the still body. "But this complicates things."

13

"I don't see the problem," Peter said. "Sure, the woman is dead, but you're the law."

"Mr. Hartman...Peter," the woman said, exasperated. "The coroner will certainly detect semen in her vagina. Your semen. How are we going to explain that? With the truth? She fucked herself to death? You fucked her to death? Nobody is going to believe that." She stared at him. "You are in big trouble, mister."

"Why me?" It was Peter's turn to stare. "I didn't rape her."

"Who will believe you?" She looked thoughtful. "There is only one way. Leave it to me. I think you should leave now. No one will ever know you were here."

"My boss knows. He sent me here."

"I'm sure you can think of an excuse why you couldn't make it."

"How about the maid? She's seen me."

"The maid works for me, so does the gardener. The original staff has been given the day off." She smiled. "We are quite efficient, Mr. Hartmann. Better go now."

Peter glanced one last time at the dead woman on the lounge. Then he went into the change room to get dressed.

Chapter Two

Kathleen wasn't at home, only a message on his answering machine.

"Hi, Honey. I've decided to stay over at Evelyn's place. Ed is out of town, and she feels lonely. There's food in the fridge. See you tomorrow. Pleasant dreams. Love you."

He ate the food listlessly, the image of the dead body of Mrs. Liebman, the real Mrs. Liebman, spoiling any other fantasies he might have entertained. He drank a beer with his meal, and then he flopped into his big chair and turned on the TV. Waiting for the news, he sipped on a drink he found in the fridge.

Suddenly tired and his head buzzing, he decided to go to bed. His sleep was plagued by strange nightmares. He dreamed of snakes and hooded women who tried to seduce him.

He awoke feeling groggy, but after a cold shower, he felt refreshed, and the memory of the nightmare slowly faded away. He'd just finished dressing, when the doorbell rang. Wondering who it could be, he opened the door to face two men wearing trench coats and dark glasses.

"Peter Hartmann?" one of them asked.

"That's right, and who are you?"

They flashed a couple of shiny badges and pushed him into the room.

"We have a warrant for your arrest, Mr. Hartmann."

He shook away their hands and moved back, ready to strike, if necessary. "Arrest for what?" he demanded. "Besides, I'd like to get a closer look at your badges."

The bigger of the two shoved his badge into Peter's face and growled. "For the murder of two of the most prominent citizens of this city, Mrs. Rhonda Liebman and her husband J. J. Liebman of Liebman Electronics. As if you didn't know!"

A cold hand gripped Peter's insides. "I don't know those people...not personally," he said.

"He's a cold-blooded killer," said the other one. "Maybe even an assassin."

Peter shot him an icy look. "I didn't kill anyone."

The big man walked over to the table, took off his sunglasses and picked up Peter's briefcase. After opening it, he looked at Peter. Then he pulled a pen out of his pocket and reached into the briefcase.

Peter stared at the gun dangling from the pen. "That's not my gun," he blurted out.

Letting it slide into a plastic bag, the detective gave him a hard look. "I bet your fingerprints are all over this gun. I also bet that the bullets that killed the Liebmans came from this gun. Let's go."

They read him his rights, and then they cuffed him. Peter was too stunned even to think about resisting.

The ride to the police station didn't take long. After taking his picture and fingerprinting him, they took him into an interrogation room.

"Before you say anything," the smaller of the detectives told him, "take a look at this. I found it on my desk this morning."

He shoved an envelope in Peter's direction. There were pictures inside. Peter stared at them, his face beginning to burn, but his insides going cold.

"You sick bastard!" the detective snarled. "First you raped her, and then you murdered her."

"That's not me, just someone who looks like me. I was never there," Peter said, looking at the fat woman and the man between her spread legs.

Another picture showed a car with the license plate clearly visible, the big mansion in the background.

"Your car. Your license plate," stated the big detective. "We checked it out." He stared at Peter. "You're going to fry, you son-of-a-bitch. They were good people."

"So I was there. That doesn't prove I killed her," Peter said. "And I didn't rape her. I admit we had sex, but it was mutual consent. She wanted it, after watching that government woman and me. It wasn't really my fault. She died of natural causes..." He finished lamely, realizing how ludicrous it sounded.

"With a bullet in her brain?" the detective said ferociously. "Come on, you have to do better than that. Why did you kill them? Who paid you to do it?"

"I told you, I didn't kill anyone," Peter said, frustrated. "I know nothing about her husband. I never met the man. I left before he came home. You see there was this government agent there. She pretended to be Mrs. Liebman. They had set up a sting operation to catch an extortionist. That's all I know."

"Wow!" The big detective wiped his brow. "A sting operation! That explains everything. Was this government agent by any chance a woman?"

"That's right."

"And you fucked her also?"

Peter nodded, smiling crookedly. "You're putting it somewhat crudely. We made love. Actually, at first, I didn't know she was a government agent. As I said, she let me believe she was Mrs. Liebman."

"I see." He stared at Peter, and then he suddenly smashed his fist on the table. "Mr. Hartmann, you must think we are a couple of morons. You really expect us to believe that ridiculous story? It doesn't even make sense. Come one."

"It is true." Peter had to admit it did sound ridiculous. He leaned back and folded his arms across his chest. "I'm not saying anymore. I want an attorney."

The big detective handed him a cell phone. "Go ahead, call your attorney," he sneered. "No big-talking lawyer will get you off, you insolent bastard. You're guilty as hell."

"I don't have an attorney."

"Then you'll be provided with one."

"No." Peter took the phone. "I'll call my boss. He'll get me one."

He dialed Robert Palmer's private number.

"Robert, this is Peter. I'm in trouble. I need your help."

* * * *

They put him into a cell for a couple of hours, and then they hauled him back into the interrogation room. A middle-aged, distinguished looking gentleman sat at the table, studying a magazine. He looked up and smiled thinly when Peter walked into the room.

"I'm Thomas Turner," he said. "Your attorney. Seems you have a bit of a problem."

Peter told Turner his story in detail, leaving little out. The attorney listened quietly, making notes into a small notebook. When Peter finished, Turner cleared his throat and looked at him over a pair of narrow reading glasses. "Plead guilty to involuntary manslaughter. With good behavior, you'll be out in a couple of years."

Peter stared at the attorney. "You haven't heard a word I said, have you? I only had sex with that woman. I didn't know she had a bad ticker. I'm not taking any blame for that. Besides, I didn't rape her. She wanted it badly."

"Mr. Palmer gave me some background on you, Mr. Hartmann." Turner's voice sounded cool. It didn't show any compassion. "You have a reputation."

Peter sighed. Maybe it hadn't been such a good idea to ask his boss for help.

Turner got up and handed Peter a card. Peter glanced at it.

Thomas B. Turner, Attorney at Law.

That's all it said. And a phone number. Golden raised letters on black, velvety background.

When Peter turned the card around, he noticed the picture of a scorpion in one corner. Dropping the card into his shirt pocket, he said, "Thanks for the advice, but I can't take it."

Turner shrugged. "Under the circumstances, that's the best advice I can give you. The police have evidence. I've seen the pictures. If they find your fingerprints on that gun, and I have a feeling they will, your chances are worse than a snowball's chance in hell. Pardon the cliché."

"I told you, I have no idea how that gun got into my briefcase. They won't find my prints because I never touched that gun."

"That's no proof. You could have wiped it."

"I didn't."

"So you say. I don't know, Mr. Hartmann." Turner shook his head. "If this goes to trial, the prosecutor will take you apart, and more than you are willing to share will be made public." He stared at Peter, his lips curving into a tight smile. "But then I guess it won't matter anymore. The jury will find you guilty, and you'll get the chair, so what does it matter what will come out at the trial."

18

Peter hated the man at that moment, hated everything about him, his callous, uncaring remarks, his cold eyes and face, his smug smile.

"What kind of attorney are you?" he asked. "You have found me guilty and already sentenced me without a trial. You're supposed to be on my side. I don't like you, Mr. Turner."

"I'm just giving you the facts, Mr. Hartmann. That is the way I see it, and I am on your side. You may have a slight chance if you could produce this mysterious woman." Turner turned toward the door. Before he reached it he said, "Take my advice, and spare us all a lot of grief."

Peter stared at the closing door. "Fuck you," he murmured.

Putting his head between his hands, he sighed.

He was in deep shit. And that might possibly be an understatement.

When he heard the creaking hinges of the opening door, he looked up. A couple of burly guards came in to take him back to his cell.

He didn't sleep well that night. The bunk was hard and continuous noise came from a neighboring cells.

Kathleen came in the morning. They weren't even allowed to be alone. A female guard sat by the door, watching them. She was a squat woman and ugly to boot. Peter resented her sneering face.

Kathleen was understandably upset. "Why didn't you phone me? I was worried to death. I had to read it in this morning's paper." She stared accusingly at him. "They say you raped the woman before you shot her. Is that true, Peter? Did you have sex with that…that fat blob?" She broke into tears. "How could you? How do you think that makes me feel?"

"That's what bothers you? That I might have had sex with a fat woman? Would it make a difference had she been skinny?" Peter shook his head in disbelief. "Do you realize the trouble I'm in? I'm accused of murdering two people. If I'm found guilty, they will send me to the chair. I'm going to die! Now there is something to worry about."

Her green eyes were large and shiny with tears. "Did you do it, Peter? Did you kill those two people? Shoot them with a gun? I didn't even know you had a gun."

"I don't have a gun. I didn't kill anybody. Somebody framed me." His voice sounded bitter. Looking at Kathleen, he realized how beautiful she was, and he wanted to take her into his arms, kiss her tearstained face. But they had been told no touching.

He cursed silently, guilt washing over him. This was the punishment for screwing around. Kathleen was more than enough woman for any man. How could he have been so stupid!

"I love you, honey," he said quietly. "Whatever happens, never forget that."

Kathleen said nothing, just looked at him. Suddenly, she smiled, but with sadness in her eyes. "I love you, too. I hope you can forgive me." She stood up and without looking back she walked out of the door, leaving Peter to puzzle over her remark.

Back in his cell, he spent most of the day lying on the hard bunk, thinking about his plight. Once in awhile, he got up to do some exercises. The night was long, he lay there thinking about the last few weeks. How the hell did he get into this mess? It all started when he accompanied Linda, the wife of his boss, to a charity event…

Chapter Three

"Charity begins at home. Before we send more money to all these third world countries, we should look in our own backyard first. There are millions of people who go to bed hungry each night right here in the good old USA, the Land of Plenty." The speaker took a sip of water from her glass, waited until the few people who applauded stopped clapping.

"We sent relief money to Haiti when their country was destroyed by a hurricane, to Thailand after the tsunami, and to countless other places. Our boys are in Afghanistan and Iraq, dying for a cause many Americans don't believe in. They should be at home, helping our own citizens. Over a million people were homeless after a hurricane destroyed New Orleans, and many died because help didn't come fast enough. We're always there for the world. Has the world ever been there for us?"

Peter Hartmann was more interested in the speaker's appearance than in what she said.

I wonder what she's like in the sack.

She was tall, at least five foot ten, with a sturdy built. Good-looking, the form of her body hidden by the loose dress she wore. Her short platinum hair framed a tanned face.

This woman spends a lot of her time in the sun. Most likely by the swimming pool, like all these rich broads.

Looking around the room, he saw mostly women. All of them well dressed, expensive clothes, lots of jewelry. The few men at the tables with them looked bored. Peter couldn't blame them. He hated these charity drives. He studied the woman across from him.

Linda Palmer. His boss's wife.

He didn't know exactly how old she was. He figured in her late thirties. She looked quite attractive in her gray business suit. She had taken off her blazer and draped it across the seat beside her. The blouse she wore was loose, but her large breasts strained against the thin fabric.

"Who is that woman?" Peter whispered across the table.

Linda leaned toward him. Peter could see the top of her creamy breasts and stared at her deep cleavage. "That's Delta Liebman, Senator Liebman's wife. You've heard of him?"

Peter shook his head. "Can't say I have," he said, still staring at her breasts.

Linda saw his look, smiled, leaned closer. "I can see you're bored. How about getting out of here?"

"Don't you have to leave some kind of contribution after the speeches are over?" Peter asked.

Linda shrugged. "You're right. I wanted to talk to Mrs. Liebman anyway. Robert told me to give the check to her personally." She leaned back into her seat, smiling. "We don't have to stay long after that."

Peter nodded, turned his attention back to the speaker on the stage. It seemed she was just finishing her presentation. "Thank you very much," she said, closing her folder. "I'm told there are refreshments available. Good evening."

Peter watched her descend the steps, wondered what she looked like underneath the dress. She walked easily, like a cat. Looking at her wide shoulders, he would have bet she was an athlete.

She headed straight toward his table.

Peter stood up when it became obvious she was going to join them. He pulled out a chair, held it.

Mrs. Liebman smiled. "A gentleman," she said, taking the offered chair. "A rare animal these days." She looked at Linda. "Who is your escort? Your lover?"

Linda laughed. "He's Peter Hartmann. One of our reps. Robert couldn't make it. You know how it is."

"Pleased to meet you, Peter," Mrs. Liebman said. "I hope you enjoyed my speech."

"It was quite interesting," Peter said. "I especially liked the part about 'charity begins at home'. Do you really believe that crap?"

The woman stared at him for a short moment. Her blue eyes seemed icy, but then she laughed and pointed a finger at him. "You're quite outspoken, Peter Hartmann, and not afraid to say what you think. I could use a man like you. It would be refreshing to have a man around who is not an ass-kisser." She chuckled. "About my speech…let me put it this way: It makes for good publicity. My husband is in politics. I have to support him, you know."

"I understand," Peter said, smiling. "I meant no offense."

She studied him, her blue eyes steady and unblinking.

Like a predator sizing up its prey, he thought.

"Of course, you didn't," she purred, her voice low and husky. "Tell me, have you always been a salesman?"

"Not always," Peter admitted. "But most of my adult life, yes."

"Somehow you don't fit the typical description of a salesman," Delta mused, almost talking to herself. "You look more like a government man to me. FBI. CIA. Under-cover-agent…?"

"Not a very good one if it is that obvious," Peter chuckled. "Rest assured, I am a sales rep. Been with Computer Regeneration Development for five years now."

"I can vouch for that," Linda broke into the conversation. "Peter is one of our best. The Best." She pushed an envelope across the table. "By the way, here is a small contribution toward your cause."

Delta took the envelope and got up. "Thank you." She glanced at Peter and then gave Linda an inquiring look. "I'm surprised your husband trusts you with a handsome hunk like Mr. Hartmann. I hope you can keep your hands off him. I couldn't." Smiling, she turned and walked over to another table.

Linda chuckled and looked at Peter. "Come on, handsome hunk, let's get out of here."

They had come in Linda's car, but Peter slipped into the driver's seat. Linda leaned back in her seat and lit a cigarette. Blowing the smoke through her nostrils, she pulled her lips into a pout. "It's still early. What do you say we drive to the office? There is something I want to check out."

Peter glanced at her, finding her suddenly very alluring. Shrugging, he said, "You're the boss. I have nothing planned for the rest of the night."

"Won't Kathleen expect you?"

"She's out of town. She won't be back for a couple of days." He started the car and backed out of the parking space. A few minutes later, they were on the freeway. He turned on the air-conditioning and opened the window slightly. The cigarette smoke didn't really bother him, but he liked fresh air.

After a while, he closed the window again. The hot outside air smelled humid, promising rain.

"How long have you and Kathleen lived together, Peter?" Linda asked.

"Five years," Peter answered.

"How come you two never got married?"

He shrugged. "Maybe we're just too comfortable with the way it is."

"Like an old married couple, huh?" Linda chuckled.

"Yeah, like an old married couple."

"You don't sound happy. Is everything all right between you two?"

Peter sighed. "Not really. Sometimes I wish things could be better."

Linda stubbed out her cigarette in the car's ashtray. "Why? Not enough sex?" She laughed and threw him a sidelong glance.

"That's not it," Peter said. "It's hard to pin down. Little things, like criticizing me when that's the last thing I need, complaining I don't do enough around the house. Too much on the road, when I should spend more time with her…"

"Come on, Peter, you have to admit, you men are sometimes too laid-back about those little things." She touched his arm, a seemingly casual touch. "You've been together only five years. Robert and I have been together for fifteen. What should I say?"

"That is different. You're married."

"There is no difference. Fifteen years is a long time to spend with another person. Things sometimes change."

Peter turned his head and looked into her eyes. "What are you saying?"

Linda reached for another cigarette. "Nothing, Peter. Forget it."

They drove in silence for the rest of the way. It had begun to drizzle slightly when Peter entered the underground parking lot of the fifteen-story office building. There were a few cars still in their designated stall, cars that belonged to supervisors, managers, or dedicated employees who needed to catch up with work.

"Number eighty-seven," Linda said.

Peter drove down the ramp to the next level.

A dark blue BMW occupied stall number eighty-eight, the spot next to Linda's. It belonged to Robert Palmer, his boss.

"I thought Robert was out of town," Peter said.

Linda shrugged. "That's what he told me. Maybe he was delayed."

"Or maybe he took a taxi?"

They took the elevator up to the ninth floor. When they walked down the thickly carpeted corridor, Peter noticed a faint strip of light under one of the office doors.

Linda's office.

"Wait here," Linda told him. She tried the doorknob. Found it locked. Searching through her purse, she took out a key and opened the lock. Then she slipped into the office. She came back a few minutes later, a strange expression on her face. She looked grim and at the same time triumphant.

"I suspected," she hissed. "Now I know."

"What?"

Grabbing his hand, she pulled him toward the elevator. Inside, she punched the button for the tenth floor, and then she put her hand behind Peter's neck and kissed him. When the elevator door opened, she let go of him, grabbed his hand again and dragged him along.

She stopped in front of Robert Palmer's office, opened the door and pulled Peter inside.

After dimming the lights, she stood in front of Peter, her hands on her hips. "Now I want you to fuck me, Peter, and no arguments, unless you want to lose your job." She kissed him again, hard and demanding. Her tongue pressed against his teeth, forced its way into his mouth.

She tasted of tobacco and alcohol. He could feel her heart pounding against his chest. Her mouth still glued to his, her fingers unbuttoned his coat, his shirt, and then she undid his belt. Unzipping him, her hand went down to his groin, found his already reacting penis.

Then she let go of him, breathing hard. She stepped back and began to undress. "Naked!" she commanded.

Peter shrugged off his jacket, took off his tie and shirt.

Her eyes widened when she saw his muscular upper body. She stepped out of her black lacey panties, exposing her thick thatch of brown hair. Then she came back into his arms, ran her hands across his broad shoulders, caressing his deep chest. "I knew you were built," she said huskily, "but I had no idea."

Her arms went around his neck and captured his erection between her smooth thighs. Rubbing her pussy on his rigid shaft, she soon started panting. She pulled him toward a leather chair and pushed him into it. Climbing into his lap, she bent her knees, grabbed his stiff penis with one hand, held it and slid her wet and hot sheath over his hard pole. Gasping, she sank down and took him deep into her.

Moaning, she began to rock in his lap, faster and faster, her large breasts hot and soft against his chest.

Peter groaned. His rod was a hard piston in the softness of her pussy. He grabbed her fleshy buttocks, slowed her down, not wishing to erupt too soon. She stopped moving, quivered and cried out, dousing him with her warm discharge.

Peter held her against him and stood up. Then he walked with her clinging to him to the sofa and put her on her back. Cradled between her strong but soft thighs, he moved with powerful steady strokes on top of her.

With every deep thrust, she let out a suppressed cry. Climaxing a few more times, she finally gasped, "Have your climax now, Peter. I'm drying up."

He had held back, but now he let the waves of pleasure overtake him. Grunting like a mad bull, he came inside her clutching love-sheath, filling her thirsty interior with his hot gushing liquid. Then he collapsed into her arms, flattening her soft breasts.

After regaining his breath, he asked, "Mind telling me what that was all about?"

Linda looked up at him, her brown eyes shiny and distant. "Right now I don't care. I've never been fucked like this before. You are an extra-ordinary man, Peter. Maybe I should thank Robert for this incredible experience."

"What does your husband have to do with this?"

Linda's eyes came back into focus. Looking at Peter, she smiled. "Had he stayed faithful to me I might never have done this."

"Robert is cheating on you?" Peter propped up on his elbows. Still inside Linda, the gentle milking of her vagina walls made his penis swell again.

"With that bitch Helga, my own secretary. I should fire her," Linda said, but somehow her voice didn't sound angry. It had a dreamy quality to it. "This is unbelievable," she gasped and began moving her lower body. Her creamy pussy walls rippled the length of Peter's hard shaft.

"Let me be on top," she whispered.

Without uncoupling, Peter swung her on top of him. She sat up and crouched in his lap. He watched her solid, well-formed breasts bop up and down as her lower body gyrated above him.

He studied her features in the dimmed light. She looked quite beautiful with her large brown eyes, her flushed face and her slightly open full lips. He could tell she didn't color her hair. It shimmered with the same brown hue as her pubic hair. She had a flat, smooth stomach and round, firm breasts with fat pink nipples.

Watching his penis slide in and of her thick bush, he enjoyed the warm, soft grip of her creamy vagina walls.

Suddenly reality seemed to hit him in the face with a hard fist.

He was fucking the wife of his boss!

As if reading his thoughts, Linda said with a breathless voice. "I guess you never thought you'd be screwing your boss's wife in his own office?"

Peter smiled. "I have to admit, it was never one of my goals in life."

She slowed her movements for a moment, gasped, and closed her eyes. Peter felt the contracting of her inner muscles, felt the tightness around his penis and the warm liquid running down the inside of his thighs.

Opening her eyes again, she smiled. "That was a nice one." She increased the speed of her rotating hips. "If it's any consolation, it was never mine, either. Had I realized though that you were such a hunk, as Delta Liebman put it, I might have sampled you a long time ago. Robert can screw that dried-up prune Helga as often as he wants. I think this is the beginning of a beautiful relationship between you and me, now that I've discovered you."

She stopped moving and lifted up. Peter found his erect penis suddenly unoccupied, but he wasn't finished yet. Linda smiled when she noticed his disappointment. "I'm not done," she said, and then she walked over to the big desk. Leaning over it and spreading her legs slightly, she presented her round rump to Peter's watching eyes, her pink cleft clearly visible below her plump cheeks.

"Come on," she crooned. "What are you waiting for?"

Peter got off the sofa and joined her at the desk. Stepping behind her, he guided his penis between her white cheeks and found the slippery entrance to her pussy. His hips snapped forward, and again the soft walls of her hot vagina closed tightly around his aching member.

He grunted and began to move slowly in and out of her. His penis appeared to be much more sensitive after his first climax, and the bliss of being inside a warm, moist pussy felt much greater.

Fucking the wife of his boss on his own desk added even more to the enjoyment.

Spreading her arms, Linda gripped the edge of the big desk tightly, whimpering as Peter slammed into her from behind. He clamped his hands around her wide hips to hold her in position. Looking down, he saw his pole disappear between her fleshy white cheeks, like the well-oiled rod of a machine. Holding back as long as possible, he felt the built-up deep inside him. When he couldn't suppress it any longer, he rammed into her, holding her tight as his penis pumped precious liquid into her.

Linda squealed, pressed her face against the polished oak of the desktop. Her pussy walls milked him until he stopped jetting.

He stood behind her for a moment, enjoying her warm tightness one last time. Then he regretfully pulled out.

She sighed and slipped off the desk, getting to her feet with sluggish movements. "Wow!" she exclaimed weakly, stepping closer. Looking up into his face, she said, "You told me you had some problems with your partner. It certainly can't be the sex."

"I never said it was."

"Well, whatever it is, Kathleen should consider herself lucky. She's got something not many women have…a man who knows how to satisfy a woman." She sighed. "And I am satisfied. I also must look quite a mess. I'm going to take a shower."

Peter had to admit, she did look a mess, with her hair disheveled, plastered to her head and her mascara running down her flushed cheeks. He still found her quite attractive and watched her as she walked toward the door to the private bathroom. She had nice round and fleshy buttocks, firm and solid but not overly large.

Peter liked women with a nice ass, and Linda certainly had one.

He sank into Robert's black leather chair. Looking at the floor, he saw a picture, which Linda had knocked off during their lovemaking. Bending down, he picked it up and put it back onto the desk. The picture showed Linda in her wedding gown. She had been a beautiful bride. But then what bride wasn't on her wedding day? He wondered if he and Kathleen would ever get married. She'd make a beautiful bride.

Thinking of Kathleen brought on pangs of guilt. This was not the first time he cheated on her. He was away a lot and those cold hotel rooms got lonely sometimes.

He pushed his thoughts of guilt away and leaned back in the chair, put his feet on the desk. The leather felt cool against his naked butt. Studying the picture of Linda, he couldn't think of a reason why Robert would cheat on her. He just didn't seem like the kind of guy.

Especially with Helga. Flat-chested and big-assed, she lost hands down to Linda in the 'good-looking' department.

She must be in her fifties. An old spinster.

A 'dried-up-prune', as Linda put it.

Not so dried up, obviously.

Peter smiled, imagining his boss screwing the living daylights out of Linda's private secretary. In Linda's office.

Well…now she screwed one of her husband's best employees…in his office. There had to be some kind of justice in there somewhere, if not a great deal of irony.

Linda came out of the bathroom. She looked fresh, her make-up immaculate, as always, her hair a little more curly than before, but otherwise ready to go and join a crowd.

Except…she was still naked.

Peter whistled. "You look ravishing. Robert doesn't know what he's got."

"Well, thank you, kind sir," Linda said with a fake English accent. "If you're done with me, I think I will get dressed now." She did a little pirouette. "I'm glad you like what you see." She dropped the accent. "I wish Robert would look at me the way you do. I know I've gained a little weight over the years, and I always thought that might be the problem, but now I don't understand it. Compared to Helga I'm skinny. Look at her ass."

Peter laughed at her outburst. "And look at her tits," he said.

"What tits?" Linda lifted her breasts. "These are tits. Helga doesn't have any. She's flat."

"She must have something Robert likes."

"What can she have that I don't have? A tighter pussy? I always thought women loosened up as they grew older." She gave him a crooked smile. "You've been inside me. Am I still tight?"

Peter chuckled. "Any tighter, you'd be closed, baby. That 'loosening-up-thing' is probably just a myth. Maybe he likes her ass?"

She slipped into her black panties. Looking up, she said, "I never thought of that. You know he's tried several times to enter me that way, but I don't like that. I'm not a pervert."

Peter shrugged, his eyes on her breasts. "It must be something about her that attracts him." He rose from his chair, walked around the desk and crossed the few steps separating them. Taking her face between his hands, he looked into her large, brown eyes. "Sometimes men cheat on their partners. If asked why, they don't know the answer. Don't blame yourself. It happens, just like what happened here tonight between us. You know the reason for that…revenge. You were hurt, and you wanted to get even."

He let his hands glide down her back, stroked her buttocks, and cupped the soft globes.

Linda giggled suddenly when his rising penis poked her belly. "You are something," she said, her breath catching in her throat.

"No, you are," Peter said. "You're beautiful, sexy, and smart. A great combination. Turns me on."

"I thought most men liked the 'dumb-blonde' type?" Linda murmured, closing her eyes. "That feels nice," she whispered. "Do you want to do it again?"

"I do," Peter said, "but I feel a little jittery here in Robert's office. What if he decides to come up to check on something?"

She shook her head. "Not this late, and besides…he's busy with his hussy."

"This long?"

"This long." Linda nodded. "He does have stamina."

"I thought he was no good in bed?"

"He doesn't have finesse. He's too mechanical." Linda kissed him on the lips. "Maybe you're right. We should go."

She gave a little yelp of surprise when Peter lifted her up by her buttocks, and then she gasped as he slid into her. "You're sure about this?" she asked, moaning loudly.

"I'm sure," Peter grunted and walked toward the nearest wall, with Linda clinging to him. Pressing her against the wall for support, he fucked her furiously. She dug her heels into the back of his thighs and wrapped her arms around his neck.

"You're crazy, you know," she gasped into his ear. "At least you should have let me take off my panties. You'll stretch the leg-opening."

"I'll buy you another pair." Peter kissed her hard as she shook in the throes of an orgasm.

Then he felt his own climax approaching. Thrusting deep into her, he held her soft body immobile against the wall. Her buttocks quivered in his hands as he filled her up again.

When Peter finally put her down, she sighed deeply. "You can't be human, Peter Hartmann. No normal guy can have this much vitality and such endurance. What are you? Some kind of 'love-machine'?" She touched her silk panties. "Might as well take them off, they're sopping wet."

Peter chuckled. "Are you sorry now?"

"Sorry?" Linda smiled. "Are you kidding? I'm sore but not sorry."

She stepped out of her panties and wiped herself with them. Then she put on her bra and her blouse. "I'm ready for another shower, but I think I'll skip it," she said, reaching for her pants. "No man ever brought me to the point of being sore." She shook her head and stared at Peter. "But I've never been this satisfied, either. How about you, Peter?"

He grinned. "I'm okay."

"Don't tell me you could still go on!" The look of incredulity in her brown eyes showed clearly.

He shrugged. "I could, but that doesn't mean that I'm not satisfied. It was terrific. You were terrific. I'm not always this horny."

Linda finished dressing and then watched Peter get into his clothes.

"Something wrong?" he asked, when he noticed her scrutinizing look.

"No." She smiled. "I was just thinking. Maybe we can do this again...soon?"

"Maybe," Peter said.

Linda straightened out a few things in the office, looked around and walked with Peter out of the door.

Robert's car was still in its spot.

Linda gave Peter a quick kiss, and then she got into her car. Waiting until she left, he walked over to get his own car.

Driving home, he suddenly felt quite tired.

Thinking about the evening's event, it didn't trouble him too much. Linda seduced him. That was all there was to it. Could he have refused her? Maybe, but she was the wife of his boss and used to getting her way. He only hoped she would be discreet about what they'd done. It wouldn't do to have Robert find out, but he felt certain Linda would not tell him. Of course, she might search him out again, probably would, but he would handle that possibility when it happened.

Kathleen wasn't home.

Too tired to take a shower, he decided to take one in the morning. Stripping naked, he took the time to fold his clothes neatly, but then he flopped into bed.

Chapter Four

Pulling into the driveway of his home, Peter looked forward to a quiet and relaxing evening. After spending three evenings in a hotel room, it was nice to be home again.

He heard Kathleen laughing as he opened the door. The sound of another woman's laughter made him wonder who it could be. Kathleen must have heard him, because she came out of the living room to greet him.

"You're home early," Peter said, "I didn't expect you yet."

Smiling, Kathleen came up to him and molded her slim body against him. "I've missed you," she murmured, pressing her full lips on his.

Peter tasted liqueur. "Entertaining?" he asked when they broke the kiss.

"Just a friend." Kathleen pulled him into the living room. "Meet Sue Lin." Kathleen shook her long auburn hair and laughed when she observed his stunned look.

"Hello, Sue Lin," he said, staring at the woman's exposed breasts, momentary lost for words. He looked at Kathleen.

"I thought we needed a little spice in our lives," she said. "Our sex-lives." With that, she lifted the hem of her dress and pulled it over her head. Wearing only a black, transparent skimpy outfit, she struck a sexy pose in front of him.

"You never cease to amaze me." Peter shook his head. "What brought this on?"

"Well…with you so much out of town it seems the romance has gone out of our lovemaking."

"Another woman is supposed to bring romance?" he asked, baffled.

She laughed and hooked a finger into his belt. "Maybe. Doesn't the prospect of making love to two women at the same time excite you?"

His gaze lingered on Sue, who had begun to push her miniskirt past her slim hips, revealing a tiny thing that barely covered her pussy. "I think I need a drink." He walked over to the liqueur cabinet, where he poured a large glass of brandy. When he turned, he saw Kathleen and Sue locked in a deep, passionate kiss. Sue had one hand on Kathleen's ample breast and the other one between Kathleen thighs.

Suddenly he was tremendously aroused. The two women broke apart. Kathleen saw him watching and smiled. "Come, don't be a stranger, join us on the couch."

He finished his drink and poured another one. Noting the almost empty bottle of wine and the glasses on the table, he knew the women had been drinking.

They made room for him on the couch. Kathleen began unbuttoning his shirt. "You don't look comfortable," she said. As she leaned over him, her elbow touched his crotch. "Oh my." She giggled and put her hand on his erection. "That looks promising." She got up and said, "I'll go get another bottle of wine from the cellar. You keep our guest entertained."

Suddenly left alone with an almost naked attractive young woman he'd never seen before, his hard penis straining to jump out of his pants, Peter felt a bit uneasy. "So…how do you know Kathleen?" he asked.

Sue smiled and stroked his chest. "We've been friends for a long time."

"Why has Kathleen never told me about you?"

Shrugging, she let her finger trail down to his belly. "Maybe you two don't communicate as much as you think you do," she said.

"Or maybe it's because Kathleen hired you?" he said bluntly.

Sue laughed. "I'm not a hooker, if that's what you're implying." Very casually, she pulled down his zipper and freed his penis. Putting her head into his lap, she slipped her lips over his hurting cock and sucked it into her warm mouth.

Surprised by her boldness, Peter almost lost control and nearly came inside her mouth, but he had learned to suppress that urge. Moaning, he closed his eyes and enjoyed her gentle tonguing. When she lifted up, he felt a moment of regret.

Sue sank to her knees in front of him. Then she pulled off his pants, leaving him naked. "That's better," she said, giggling. Reaching for her glass, she looked at the tiny amount of wine in the glass. Pouting, she said, "Wonder what's keeping Kathleen? I am quite thirsty." She looked at Peter with half-lidded eyes. "She told you to keep me entertained. I'm bored. Come on, entertain me." With that, she bent over. Kneeling on the soft carpet, she pushed up her buttocks.

Peter downed his second glass of brandy, feeling the heat go down his throat. He dropped to his knees behind her. Pulling off the thong to expose her shaved pussy, he put his finger into her slit, found it wet and slippery.

Sue moaned, pushed back against him. "Don't tease," she gasped. "Give me your big cock."

He didn't need another invitation. Grunting loudly, he shoved it into her and began to move in and out of her with powerful thrusts.

He became aware of two arms embracing him from behind and a warm naked body pressing against his back. A pair of soft breasts touched his skin.

"Shoot it into her, Peter. She likes that." Kathleen's breathless whisper added to the excitement he felt. Her hot breath caressed his neck as she moved with his thrusts. "Let me know when you do," she breathed into his ear.

It was too much. He couldn't hold it any longer. "Now!" he called out harshly. "Now!" With a hoarse shout, he let go. His penis seemed to pump forever. With every pulsing throb, he growled deep in this throat, like a savage animal.

Sue Lin arched her back and pressed her pussy into his groin. His shaft was buried to the root inside her sucking sheath. He was only dimly aware of her cries of pleasure.

Clinging to him, Kathleen ground her lower body against his quivering buttocks. When he was finally spent, Sue Lin fell forward, freeing his penis. Kathleen's hand reached around him and curled her fingers around his mast, stroked it gently. "You're still hard," she breathed. Turning him around, she pushed him into a sitting position and straddled him. With a cry of pure delight, she sank into his lap. Her dripping pussy closed over his penis and sucked him deep into her.

His hands gripped her soft buttocks, held them tightly as she snapped her lower body back and forth. Arching away from him, she thrust out her lovely shaped breasts. He could see her rippling flat belly as she milked his aching penis.

He pulled her to him, crushed her breasts against his chest. Then he kissed her hard.

Her hips never stopped thrusting, and her hot pussy never missed a stroke as she moved it along his rigid shaft.

She cried out, quivered in his lap, her body shaking in the grip of a powerful orgasm. The warm liquid of her gushing discharge flooded his pubic hair. He held her tight until she relaxed. Then he stood up, carried her to the couch, his penis still lodged inside her. She wrapped her long slim legs around his torso and laughed into his ear.

"Fucking Sue Lin surely brought out the stud in you, lover. I haven't climaxed like that for a long time," she whispered.

He just grunted and fell with her on top of the couch. Her legs flew open wide as he began thrusting deep into her. He never stopped until she had another earth-shattering climax.

After she calmed down, she whispered, "I'm getting exhausted. Maybe you should make love to Sue Lin again."

"Fine by me," he said somewhat hoarsely and pulled his stiff member out of her pussy.

Sue Lin, who had been lying right beside them on the floor, smiled and spread her thighs. She was completely naked now, her pale body curvy and beautiful. Peter moved between her smooth thighs and, without any preliminaries, he shoved his hard penis into her welcoming sheath.

She felt tight and creamy, like Kathleen…and yet different. The way she rippled her inside muscles along the shaft of his sex-organ spoke of training and experience. Peter studied her beautiful oriental features. She had such a young and innocent look about her; she was probably no older than twenty. How would she get all that experience? Maybe it was talent.

He suddenly realized he was actually having sex with another woman with Kathleen's permission, who lay right beside them, watching.

He looked at her. She smiled and reached out a hand to touch his face. "Enjoy," she whispered, her eyes bright with excitement.

And enjoy he did.

Where he found the stamina, he didn't know. He was probably working on pure adrenalin. Sue Lin writhed and whimpered beneath him, as he fucked her with powerful strokes. She climaxed several times. He would have come a long time ago, but every time he felt his climax approaching, she did something to him to prevent it. Her slim fingers pressed into the root of his penis and touched other parts of his body. Even though he didn't climax, the pleasure was almost constant.

He'd never experienced anything like this before. When he finally came, it was with tremendous force, and as his sperm shot into the womb of this lovely woman, he was overcome by total and unconditional love. For this strange woman and for Kathleen, who had made him this gift.

Exhausted, he collapsed into Sue Lin's arms. Too tired to pull out of her, he fell into a deep slumber, cradled by her arms and warm thighs.

When he awoke, he was still lying on top of Sue Lin, his penis inside her. Light filtered in through the window, and he saw her face more clearly than at night in the dim glow of a couple of candles.

Lying there and asleep, she appeared even more beautiful.

Just looking at her and feeling the soft warm curves of her body underneath him, made his penis react. It became hard and solid. Slowly he began to ease it back and forth inside her extremely tight pussy.

Sue Lin moaned in her sleep and responded. Her lower body moved in rhythm with his slow thrusts. He fucked her gently at first, but after a while, he pushed harder and deeper. Her pussy felt creamy, soft, and responsive. Even though she had her eyes closed, she met every thrust with great passion.

He long legs wrapped around his torso, and her heels dug into his taut buttocks. She never fully awoke, only when he burst inside her, she opened her eyes. He wondered briefly, why they were blue, but then the tremendous force of his climax swept him away.

When he was finished, she was still staring at him. Smiling sleepily, she murmured, "That was nice," and then she closed her eyes again and went back to sleep.

His cock still inside her, Peter propped himself up on his elbows and studied her delicate features again. Her slightly slanted eyes were closed, and her chest rose and fell with her even breathing. He looked at her breasts. They were not very large but round and firm, with small pink nipples. He bent down, kissed one of the gently.

Her long black hair spilled across the pillow someone must have put there, framing her beautiful face like a lacey veil.

"She's lovely, isn't she?" Kathleen's voice brought him back to reality, and he looked up with a guilty expression. She stood in the door to the living room. He had never noticed her absence.

Nodding, he got off Sue Lin, acutely aware of the soft 'plop' his semi-erect penis made as it slipped out of her vagina. "She is lovely," he agreed, smiling crookedly. "So are you."

Kathleen laughed and came closer. She still wore that black lacey outfit, even her stockings, and she did look very sexy. Looking down at the sleeping girl, she said, "She has what I lack, Peter. That innocent beauty only youth can give you. Is that the problem? Am I getting old?"

She crouched down beside him and looked into his eyes. "I love you, Peter. Tell me, do you love me as much as you did five years ago?"

He reached for her, pulled her down on top of him. "As much, if not more, sweetheart." He said it, and he meant it.

She laughed when she felt the growing hardness of his penis and reached between them. Her legs parted, and then she gasped as he slid into her.

When Peter said, "I want to look at your breasts," she sat up. Her breasts were cone-shaped, perfectly formed. He'd always loved her breasts. Touching them, he squeezed them gently.

"You have beautiful breasts," he told her.

She smiled and closed her eyes. "And you have a beautiful cock." She began snapping her hips back and forth. "Beautiful and hard and I love it."

He watched her breasts jiggle as she writhed above him, watched her face contort in the grip of an orgasm. She moaned, clamped down hard.

Opening her eyes, she lifted up and slid off him. On her knees, her shapely buttocks sticking up high, she beckoned to Peter. "Come on...fuck me like you did Sue Lin."

He knelt behind her. With deliberate slowness, he let the swollen shiny glans of his penis touch her thick labia. Her pussy was dripping. She was totally turned on. Moaning loudly when she felt his touch, she pushed backward. Her pussy-lips opened, slipped over the slick head, but he pulled back slightly, teasing her.

"Let me have that cock, Peter," she moaned. "I need it badly."

He grabbed her slim waist, steadied himself, and snapped his hips forward. The shaft of his hard penis slid deep and easily into her liquid hot interior. She cried out and arched her back like an angry feline, swallowing his penis up to its base.

Peter began to rock back and forth, his hard belly slamming into her soft fleshy buttocks over and over.

She let out a loud moan every time he slammed into her. "Now, Peter, now!" she cried out, shaking beneath him, her buttocks quivering against his groin.

Erupting with the force of a geyser, he flooded her sucking pussy with his hot discharge. His loud moans blended with her ecstatic cries. Both of them spent, they toppled over like a pair of rabbits, gasping for breath.

"You two can surely wake up the dead," said Sue Lin's voice beside them. Sitting up, she rubbed her eyes. "Boy, did I sleep well. I must have been exhausted. What time is it?"

"Time for another piece of tail, maybe," Peter said, chuckling.

Kathleen laughed and turned to face him. She reached down and touched his limp penis. "I think not," she said, "unless Sue Lin has some kind of magic potion to bring this fellow back to life."

"Even if I had, I think I would have to decline the offer. My pussy is just a little bit sore." Sue Lin smiled and stood up. She stretched her lithe nude body, and Peter couldn't help but stare.

She has the body of a goddess, he thought, his eyes glued to her naked form.

Tall and slim, narrow waist with gently flaring hips, legs long and slender, buttocks fleshy and round, and her breasts perfectly molded, she would delight and inspire any artist.

Her face was so beautiful it almost hurt to look at it for too long, because he wanted to cover it with hot kisses, and he knew she was out of his reach.

Oh sure, he fucked her, and he may do so again, but she would never be his, could not be his.

He ached for her, more than he had ever ached for any woman, even Kathleen.

However, there was a difference. He loved Kathleen. He lusted for Sue Lin.

He sighed and watched her as she went through a series of exercises, unaware that his penis had grown between his legs, as unaware as he was of Kathleen's watching eyes.

He never saw the thoughtful expression on her face.

* * * *

"How old are you, Sue Lin?" Peter asked her at breakfast.

"Why do you want to know?" Sue Lin smiled coyly. "Not knowing the age of a woman adds to her mystery."

"It's just… you look so young," Peter explained his curiosity, "and last night, the way you…" he hesitated.

Sue Lin laughed. "Say it. The way I fucked? Well, I guess it is my Chinese upbringing. My father was an American, but my mother is Chinese. She comes from a long line of courtesans. She taught me how to please a man, how to prolong his pleasure and everything else a woman needs to know about sex."

"You'll make some man very happy some day." Peter smiled crookedly.

Sue Lin's laughter teased him. She touched his hand. "Did I make you happy last night?" she asked.

Peter looked at Kathleen then back at Sue Lin. "Yes, you did," he answered. "That is not what I meant, though. We had sex, and it was very gratifying, but there is more to a relationship than good sex."

He reached out and took Kathleen's hand into his. "Even though lately our sex-life seems to have been lacking in excitement, we have one thing that is also very important: We love each other."

Kathleen smiled, her fingers curled around his hand. She seemed to have trouble with her eyes, but Peter wasn't fooled. He looked at her. "What you did was very admirable, honey, and I appreciate it. Sue Lin here is a beautiful girl, and I enjoyed having sex with her, but that's all it was, a sexual encounter. I love you, only you."

Sue Lin clapped her hands. "Bravo, Peter, a very noble speech. But isn't love between a man and a woman nothing more than sexual attraction?"

Peter shook his head. "I don't believe that. There can be love without sex."

40

"I know." Sue Lin held up a hand. "I'm not talking about love between siblings, parents and children, or between friends. That's a different kind of love. I'm talking about what happens between a healthy man and a healthy woman when they fall in love. Let's face it, the main reason couples get married or move in together is the sex, the rest develops later."

She stood up and opened her robe, completely naked underneath. "Do you desire me?" Her voice sounded husky, her face looked a little flushed, and her blue eyes stood wide open. "Do you want to fuck me, Peter? Right now? I am ready."

Peter's eyes flickered to Kathleen who gave him an innocent smile. "You know I want to," Peter said hoarsely. "But I can't. Not under these circumstances."

Sue Lin closed her robe and sat down again. "I believe you when you say you love Kathleen. But how strong is that love? How quickly do you forget about it when faced with an opportunity? What happened to your love for her last night when you pushed your big cock into me? Or did you do it out of love for her?"

"Hey, wait a minute!" It was Peter's turn to hold up a hand. "That's not fair. You were the one who surprised me by giving me a blowjob. I am a horny guy at the best of times. I couldn't help myself. Especially after Kathleen already told me to fuck you. I was seduced."

Laughing, Sue Lin leaned back in her chair. Her robe fell open, and Peter stared at her creamy breasts. "You did help yourself, lover. I didn't mind, and I enjoyed it immensely. And yes, I seduced you, but it was Kathleen's idea, not mine. I also believe that she did that out of love for you."

Tearing the gaze of his eyes away from Sue Lin's exposed breasts, Peter looked at Kathleen. "I know. How can I make it up to you, honey?"

"It was a gift, Peter. No strings attached," Kathleen said. "By the way, Sue Lin and I are going into the country to visit one of her friends. We'll be back Monday night."

"Oh, so I'll be alone for the weekend." Peter finished his coffee and got up. "Maybe I'll go to the movies."

"I have a better idea." Sue Lin handed him an envelope. "Go to this address. It's my sister's place. Give her this envelope, okay? And don't ask too many questions."

Chapter Five

Connie was her name. An older version of Sue Lin, tall and beautiful, with a radiant smile.

After reading the contents of the envelope, she looked at Peter. Her eyes were black, not blue, like her sister's. "She didn't tell you anything about me?"

"Nothing," Peter said. "She told me to give you this envelope."

"Come in, then." Connie smiled. "By the way, I am a professional masseuse."

He followed her down the hall. The shape of her body was hidden under the loose flowing robe she wore, but by the gracious way she walked and the sway of her hips, Peter had a pretty good idea what she looked like.

She led him into a dimly lit backroom. "Get undressed and lie down on this table," she told him.

"You're giving me a massage?" he asked.

"That's what I do for a living." Connie gave him a questioning look. "Did you expect something else?"

"I had no idea what to expect," Peter said, somewhat embarrassed.

Connie chuckled. "Yeah, that's my little sister all right...full of mischief and always mysterious. Just to let you know, this will be a complete massage. So take off everything. Relax while I get ready."

She left the room. Peter undressed, folded his clothes, put them neatly on the floor. Then he lay down on the low padded table, face down. Closing his eyes, he listened to the soft music coming from speakers in the ceiling.

He must have dozed off. Startled by the touch of a pair of soft hands on his back, he almost sat up, but then he relaxed and let the gentle massaging fingers put him into a state of complete relaxation.

Very gently, almost like a lover's touch, the fingers moved across his back, stroked his buttocks, his thighs, his legs, kneaded his toes.

"Turn around and close your eyes," said a soft voice. Connie's voice.

He obeyed and shivered with delightful pleasure, when those soft hands massaged his belly then his groin area, the inside of his thighs.

"Have you ever had a massage, Peter?" Connie asked softly.

"Sure I have but never one like this," Peter murmured.

"This is just the beginning," Connie said. "Just listen to the music, and let things happen."

She stopped massaging. "I'm going to cover your eyes. It will enhance the experience."

She put a dark cloth over his eyes, tied it behind his head. Her fingers traveled across his chest, his belly, to his groin. Touching his scrotum, she squeezed it gently. He became aware of a throb in his penis, felt it swell.

"Let it happen," a voice whispered.

Soft warm fingers encircled his penis, started a gentle massage. It didn't take long before he had a tremendous erection.

Something soft and creamy touched his swollen glans, closed on it, slipped down a little further until an incredibly soft and tight sheath of hot flesh enveloped the length of his hard penis.

Slowly at first and then progressively faster it began to spin around his mast, like a greased wheel around a stationary axis.

His penis was the axis.

Heat was generated. Pleasure built up. It felt glorious.

His whole mind and body concentrated on his sex-organ. No other sensation existed.

The spinning motion stopped suddenly, the bodiless pussy sucked him in completely. He felt the momentary touch of a pair of soft buttocks, and then they were gone again.

With agonizing slowness, the slippery, but extremely tight pussy moved up and down on his throbbing organ. Again, no other sensation, not even the touch of the buttocks.

A couple of times he felt that almost ghostly vagina quiver and contract, squeezing his penis even tighter. Both times he became aware of some warm liquid running onto his groin, down between his buttocks.

He wanted to release his own pressure, but every time he thought he couldn't hold it any longer, soft fingers touched the base of his penis, below his scrotum, pressed gently, and kept him from coming.

He had three orgasms without losing any fluid. The fourth time he felt it building up he knew it would be explosive.

This time, no pressing fingers held him back. It rushed up from deep inside him, and with a loud roar he pushed up, deep into the floating vessel above him. He erupted several times inside the greedily sucking pussy. He couldn't remember the last time he experienced a climax as intense as this one.

When he was finished, he felt the weight of a light body descending into his lap. His penis was still gripped tightly, and it was still tingling.

He undid the blind and removed it. Connie stood beside him and smiled down on him. She was naked, and her body looked as expected. A little fleshier in the hips, her breasts a little larger, but otherwise a copy of Sue Lin.

However, it had not been Connie who fucked him. He inhaled sharply when he saw the girl sitting in his lap.

She smiled. "Hi," she said sweetly. "Was it good?"

Peter let out his breath. "Yes, it was," he said, his voice a hoarse whisper. "But you're just a kid."

"Not really," she said. "Just turned eighteen a couple of months ago, but I'm as good, if not better, than any older woman you ever had sex with."

"You don't look eighteen. I don't know if I should believe you. This could earn me a trip to the penitentiary," he growled, studying the girl. He corrected himself. Young woman!

She was thin, her breasts small, but her face was most exquisite. Her black slanted eyes sparkled mischievously as her lower body slowly gyrated in his lap. She laughed when she felt his penis respond. "You're a horny old man." She snapped her slim hips back and forth.

He clenched his teeth and grabbed the padded sides of the bench. "And you're a little bitch," he grunted.

She stared at him as she milked his swollen organ. "You have a big cock," she said, fiddling with something in her hands. Suddenly, she seemed to float above him. The weight of her body was gone, only her sex-organ was joined to him.

Then he saw it. She was strapped into a contraption hanging from the ceiling. With a remote control device, she made it go up and down.

Fascinated, he watched his penis disappear in her tight hairless pussy, as she lowered herself down, then slowly appear again, as the contraption lifted her up.

"Pretty neat, isn't it?" She gave a childish giggle. "And it is automatic. I do nothing." She pressed another button, and she began to swirl around in a circle, his penis the center of the circle.

The sensation it created was incredible. After a while, she stopped and hovered above him. Her face looked flushed. "I admit it makes me a little dizzy." She lowered herself, sank into his lap. Then she undid the straps holding her in place. The bottomless seat moved up, hung close to the ceiling.

In his lap, the spry young woman began moving her hips. She snapped them back and forth, slowly at first, but with ever-increasing speed. Her dark eyes were glued to his. "I will make you come again," she promised, "and this time it will be even better."

Peter held back as best as he could, determined to last as long as possible. In her soft, tight sheath, his organ seemed to be on fire. Waves of pleasure radiated constantly through his body. He stared at her delicate exquisite features, lost in the depth of her dark eyes.

She smiled, milking him hard.

It was too much.

He almost lost consciousness from the pure pleasure and the length of his orgasm.

This is just a little girl. She may be eighteen years old, but she looks like fifteen. She doesn't even have breasts to speak of. How can she make me feel this way?

When it was finally over, he felt spent, tired. All that time, the gaze of her eyes had never left his face. "You're done," she said, lifting off and freeing his limp penis. She knelt down beside him, took it into her hands. "Look at him," she said with a childish tone. "I fucked the life right out of him. Poor thing."

He should have been a little shocked to hear this language coming from her, but the way she said it, it sounded natural and clean.

Bending down, she kissed his penis. "There, that should make you feel better." Looking at Peter, she said, "I hope he recovers soon. I think my mother has plans for him." With that, she turned and rushed out of the room.

Peter watched her pert round buttocks as she walked away.

"Her name is Julie." Connie spoke softly beside him. "Isn't she a treasure?"

"She certainly is," Peter agreed with an ironic twist of his lips. "A real jewel."

Connie produced a basin with water and began sponging his groin area, stroking his penis slowly and lovingly.

"I think you're wasting your time," Peter apologized and sighed. "You daughter squeezed every last drop out of me."

"Don't complain." Connie held his limp member up and dropped it. "Yep, this little feller has had it. But don't worry…we'll have him up and in action in no time." She put on a robe and handed one to Peter. "Here, put this on. I've ordered some food. I hope you like 'Chinese'?" She smiled, aware of the pun; her slanted black eyes sparkled with mischief.

Peter slipped on the robe and chuckled. "I love Chinese, and not just the food."

Julie had already set the table. There were cartons with steaming food and a bottle of red wine. She looked sweet and innocent in the overly large t-shirt she wore. It covered her cute little behind but rose up when she bent down, exposing her naked buttocks.

Connie noticed his look.

"You like little girls?" she asked.

He felt heat rise up into his face. "No, I don't. I've always considered them jailbait. Besides, it is morally wrong."

Connie shrugged. "I know, the law in the western world is not favorable to men who have sex with, what the law considers, underage girls, and that age varies from country to country. And it can change any time, depending on the lawmakers. However, there are societies where it is acceptable. I myself see nothing wrong with it. Biologically, a girl becomes a woman when she gets her periods."

She poured him some wine. "You don't seem to be quite as shocked as you perhaps should be, after having sex with a girl who looks underage. Who may possibly be underage. You only have her word."

"If I may say something in my defense," Peter said. "I didn't know. I was blindfolded, remember?"

"I am not judging you, Peter. I am just trying to make a point. You're right, you had no way of knowing, but rest assured, Julie is eighteen years old. She just looks so young. Many oriental girls do. Maybe you're not quite as moral as you think you are. After you took off your blindfold, you saw a young girl in your lap. Why did you keep your pecker inside that young tight pussy?" Connie looked at him over the rim of her glass. Her eyes were large and shiny.

Peter felt a gentle throbbing in his loins. He wanted this woman. Something about her turned him on immensely. "I was practically raped," he said, his voice a soft whisper. "Just as you are raping me now…with your words and eyes."

Connie laughed. "You are very perceptive and extremely virile. Sue Lin told me much about you in her letter. She wrote that you are the best stud she ever had sex with." She took a sip of wine, ran her pink tongue along the rim of the glass. "She also said that you are easily seduced. And you have no inhibitions. That's why I let my daughter play with you. I knew you wouldn't object."

Peter gave her a silent look. "You know, you are very much like your sister. The way you talk, the things you say." He looked thoughtful. "A long time ago I knew someone like you, for a very short time. There is a similarity between you and her. She was about Julie's age when I met her. But it was on the other side of the globe."

"All Orientals look alike." Connie smiled. "Let's finish our dinner. Chinese food is best when it is still hot."

Julie joined them. She didn't say much, just ate her food and sipped on a can of pop. She seemed almost shy. Yet…when she glanced at him, her eyes smoldered with a hidden fire. He remembered that fire and the incredible fuck she had given him. However, this time he wanted Connie.

If the daughter screws like that, how much more can the mother give?

When they were finished eating, Julie got up and started cleaning the table. Peter watched her as she moved gracefully through the kitchen, enjoying the view she presented when she got down on her knees to put some stuff into the cupboard.

She had the most beautiful little cheeks, and her hairless pussy was clearly visible between them.

"Do you have children?" Connie asked. He tore his eyes away to look at the older woman. She knew what he was looking at, but she didn't comment.

"No," Peter said. "It's me." He chuckled. "What irony. As you already observed, I am quite virile. Some people might say I am oversexed. I'll probably never have children. My sperm count is too low, almost non-existent." He chuckled. "It does have some advantages. Won't get a woman pregnant, and I never have to worry about wearing a rubber. Don't like them anyway."

He took another gulp of wine. He knew he shouldn't, he could feel it go to his head. Looking at Connie, he grinned. "Julie said you had plans for me."

"I have, but all in good time. I don't like to rush things." She refilled his glass. "Have some more wine."

He drank some more, his eyes again watching the play of Julie's naked buttocks as she reached up to get a glass from an upper shelf. "So, where is your husband?" he asked, his voice a little slurred.

"I was never married," Connie said. "I got pregnant with Julie when I was twenty. Her father was already married." She shrugged. "I was young and foolish. I loved him, and he told me he would leave his wife and marry me. It never happened."

He chuckled grimly. "That's an old story. Repeated over and over. How do you make a living?"

"I told you, I am a masseuse." She laughed suddenly. "Oh, I know what you're implying. No, I am not a prostitute. My massage parlor business is legitimate. And I don't screw every customer either, only some."

She looked at him with lowered eyelids. "I don't consider you a customer. You're a special guest, recommended by my sister." Studying him, she said, "I have another reason." She reached out, and as if by chance, she touched the tattoo of the snake on his right forearm. "I will give you special treatment…at no cost."

Peter grinned. "Just getting laid by that pretty little daughter of yours was quite a special treat already. What else have you got in mind?"

"You'll see." Connie stood up. "The night is long."

As she walked away, she shook the robe off her shoulders. It slid to the floor, leaving her stark naked.

Peter stared after her, gulped as he watched her fleshy but round solid buttocks move under smooth skin. Looking back over her shoulder, she asked, "Are you coming?"

Grinning, he got off his chair. His own robe fell open, exposing his suddenly rising penis. "I hope not," he joked, "at least not yet."

"Very funny." Connie smiled. "Come on."

He followed her into the backroom. There she instructed him to lie face down on a low padded bench. Before he lay down, he removed his robe. As he stretched out on the cool leather, he noticed an oval hole in the bench top. His penis and scrotum hung through it.

"Relax," Connie said and spread oil over his body. Then she began rubbing it in. He closed his eyes, just concentrated on her soft, gentle hands.

When a hand touched his penis underneath the bench, he knew it wasn't Connie.

Julie…that sly little vixen. He smiled, hardening almost immediately under the gentle milking of the small soft hand. A pair of warm moist lips closed over the swollen head, slid up further until his entire penis was inside a hot mouth. He felt the head touch the back of her throat. Then very slowly, the soft lips moved back, small teeth grazed along his shaft, a warm tongue darted against the tip.

His penis was freed completely, and then the procedure repeated.

His mind concentrated on only one thing.

Warm lips touching the head…opening…sucking him into a hot mouth…letting go.

When he thought he would explode, a finger pressed into the root of his penis, preventing him from coming, leaving only exquisite pleasure.

Connie never stopped her gentle massage. It only enhanced the pleasure.

Suddenly, the mouth was gone, and his aching penis cried for a warm place. He didn't have to wait long.

Something hot and moist began slipping over his rigid mast like a tight envelope, something soft and smooth. Slowly, the warm sheath engulfed his organ, and soft muscles began contracting with a gently rhythm, while thick lips tightened like a vice around the root of his penis to hold him prisoner.

Even though her vagina felt small and tight, Peter knew it wasn't Julie. This woman was much more experienced.

While he was being fucked from below, Connie straddled him, sat on his buttocks, her thick pubic hair tickling his skin. Her weight pushed his penis deeper into the other woman's vagina.

He opened his eyes, curious to see the woman under the bench, but he only saw a pair of slim, dark-skinned thighs sticking out on either side of the bench. They formed a horizontal line, attesting to the flexibility of the woman underneath him.

She lay perfectly still, only her vagina seemed alive. He had a few orgasms, but he never came. Each time he came close, Connie seemed to sense it. Her finger moved between his buttocks and pressed down gently. He climaxed without releasing any liquid.

After what seemed like an eternity of heavenly bliss, the vagina underneath him stopped rippling. The tight grip eased, and he felt the woman's body move lower. His penis almost popped out, but then she began to move her pelvis up and down, while slowly rotating it.

He couldn't move his own body, because Connie sat on him, keeping him immobile. Her hands gently massaged his back.

The woman below dropped away. Connie lifted up. "Turn around," she said softly.

He did.

As soon as he lay on his back, she lowered her body, impaling herself on his rigid shaft. The moment he entered her, she doused him with her discharge. Crying out, she dug her fingers into his forearms. She felt incredibly soft and alive. Writhing above him, she cried out repeatedly, slamming her thick vulva into his groin, taking his solid mast deep into her each time.

This beautiful woman possessed a wild passion he had only encountered once before, a long time ago. He studied her lovely face as she rode him from one orgasm to another. Her raven-black hair, thick and shoulder length, fell into her face, covering her black eyes as she bent forward. Pressing her soft breasts against his chest, she kissed him deeply.

Then she leaned back again, thrusting out her breasts. Her slim but strong thighs clamped tightly against his hips as another orgasm gripped her.

Peter feasted his eyes on her lovely breasts, let his gaze travel to her narrow waist, her flaring, thrusting hips, down to the thick black triangle of her pubic area. He watched his penis disappear inside her black thatch, felt the clutching liquid walls of her vagina swallow it to the root and watched it appear again as she lifted up. Just for a short moment then she took it deep into her again.

He held back, kept from climaxing inside her demanding hot pussy. Mesmerized by her incredible beauty, by the way her lovely body writhed above him, the way she used her sex-organ, he wanted this moment to last forever.

"Come inside me," she breathed, slamming her body against his. "I'm ready for you. Don't hold back."

She came again and let out a series of little shrieks. Then she collapsed on top of him.

"You didn't come," she said accusingly, gasping for breath.

"No," he said. "I want to fuck you my way now."

She smiled and lifted off.

He made her lie down on one of the thick rugs that covered the floor. She groped for a pillow and put it underneath the small of her back. He lay down beside her, touched her breasts, her belly, played with the thick black patch of her pubic hair. He stroked her swollen labia and pushed one finger into her.

Moaning, she clamped her thighs around his wrist. Slowly, he finger-fucked her until she came. Then he gently pushed open her thighs. She pulled up her knees, opened wide.

He moved between them. Slowly and deliberately, he eased his rigid organ into her hot moistness until he was lodged deep inside her clutching vagina. Then he proceeded to fuck her with slow, deep thrusts.

"You must be the most beautiful woman I ever made love to," he said, looking deep into her black, slightly slanted eyes. She looked so much like her younger sister Sue Lin; the shape of her nose, her lips, and yet…there was a vast difference. Even though older and more mature, there was a side to her that was wilder, more passionate, and more serious.

51

Her beautiful smile struck the depth of his being. "I must be?" she gasped, digging her fingers into his upper arms. "You're not sure?"

"I'm sure," he groaned, fighting another urge to come. She pulled down his head and kissed him gently, her tongue snaking into his mouth. He felt it coming then from deep inside him, building up like a tidal wave, and then it rolled over him. Clasping Connie to him, he pushed his spurting member as deep as he could into her desperately clutching vagina.

She came at the same time, mixing her fluid with his. Her fingers dug painfully into his clenching buttocks, pressing him tightly against her trembling body.

All too soon it ended.

They lay in each other's arms, gasping for breath.

"I love you," he said after a while. "Nobody ever made me this happy."

"Not even your lover?" Connie asked.

Peter sighed, feeling a little guilty. All this time, he never even thought of Kathleen. Wonder what she is doing right now, he thought, but then he chuckled, remembering the way Kathleen and Sue kissed each other.

Who knows what else they did.

Suddenly he didn't feel quite as guilty. "Not even my lover," he said.

Connie smiled. "You don't love me, Peter. You are infatuated with me, because I gave you a most satisfying fuck, but that's all. How can you love me? You know nothing about me."

"Love at first sight?" Peter grinned.

"Right." Connie gave his penis a hard squeeze. "Love at first fuck is more like it."

"By the way, who was the dark-skinned girl?"

"That was Giavanna, one of my girls." Connie smiled. "I wouldn't exactly call her a girl. She's almost forty. Just small for her age."

"Like Julie?"

She nodded. "Like Julie."

Chapter Six

"Have you made any plans?" Connie sipped from her glass of wine, looking at him from lowered lashes.

Peter shrugged. After sleeping most of the afternoon in her bed, he felt quite rested. "Not really. Kathleen's message on my answering machine was not too specific. She and Sue might be gone until next weekend. Maybe I'll take a few days off myself."

"And do what?" Connie leaned forward. Her robe opened, and Peter stared at her shapely breasts.

He grinned. "I know what I'd like to do now."

She smiled. "I can guess, but you'll have to take a rain check." She laughed when she saw his mock-disappointment. "How would you like to go to a costume party with me? It'll be fun."

"All right," he said, his face not showing much enthusiasm. "I have no costume to wear."

"No problem. You can go as a secret agent. Your suit will do just fine." Connie got up. "I'm going to get dressed now. Maybe you want to take a quick shower?"

He showered and shaved with an electric razor he found in a drawer. When he came back into the family room, Connie waited for him already. Peter whistled softly when he saw her. "Wow!" he said.

The red long dress she wore clung to her body, leaving nothing to the imagination, and making it obvious that she didn't wear any panties underneath it. The dress went up to her neck, but her breasts thrust out through cutouts in the front. The fine, lacey cloth covering them might as well have been absent.

She had thrown a black cape around her shoulders and a red mask over her eyes.

"Do you like?" she asked, turning around in a circle.

"Like?" Peter almost choked. "I want to rip it off your delectable body and ravish you right here on the floor."

"That's nice." She laughed and handed him a pair of sunglasses. "Here, put these one. They'll make you look more mysterious. Besides, all under-cover agents wear them."

Peter offered her his arm, and she took it. "Let's go," he said. "Adventure awaits us."

He suggested they use his car, and Connie didn't object.

The trip took almost one hour. When they arrived at their destination, Peter was impressed when he saw the huge house, hidden among tall conifers at the end of a long, winding driveway.

A number of cars were already parked in the large parking lot. Whoever lived here obviously had a lot of visitors on a regular basis.

They walked right through the open entrance door into a large vestibule. No one greeted them, but Connie seemed to know the way. Walking down a wide staircase, Peter heard the sound of laughter and music. Another open door and they stepped into what looked like a scene out of a fantasy movie.

A crowd of people dressed in a variety of costumes, some of them more than others, filled an immense room. Peter saw a lot of bare skin. A girl in a skimpy maid's outfit offered them a drink. Connie picked a glass of wine, and Peter took a mixed drink.

"Have fun," Connie said to him, and before he realized it, she disappeared in the crowd.

He shrugged and started walking toward a table heaped with all kinds of food, fruits, and vegetables. Picking up a serviette, he put a few pieces of cheese and some grapes on it. When he turned, he bumped into someone beside him. "Sorry," he mumbled, looking into a painted face.

"Oh, hi, Handsome." The voice could have belonged to a man or a woman, but from the shape of the figure, Peter saw it was a man.

"Are you alone?" the man asked.

"No…yes. I came with someone, but it seems I've been abandoned." Peter chuckled. "Quite a party."

"Sure is." The painted lips smiled, displaying a row of white even teeth. "Maybe we can make it even better. How about you and I looking for a quiet place?" He closed one eye in a slow wink.

Peter noticed the long painted lashes. He smiled back. "I don't think so," he said politely. "I don't swing that way."

The painted lips pouted. "Too bad. We could have had so much fun. But maybe you can do me a favor and look after my two friends for me."

Only now, Peter noticed the two women on either side of the man and wondered how he could have missed them.

One of them was dressed from head to toe in a black outfit entirely made out of a net. It was so tight, it showed every tiny muscle and bump on her beautifully formed tall and slim body. The nipples of her breasts were clearly visible, and so was her well-developed mound of Venus.

The other woman, a little shorter than the first one, but just as shapely, was completely naked, except for a tiny string bikini bottom and two flower petals pasted on top of her nipples. Both women had short dark blond hair, tied back into a little ponytail. Their eyes and lips were painted black, as were their fingernails.

"How about that quiet place?" asked the one with the bodysuit. "Or can't you handle two girls?"

Peter grinned. "Let's find out," he said, his voice suddenly a little hoarse. "You girls just lead the way."

They moved to either side of him, hooked onto his arms, and almost dragged him out of the room. Climbing up the stairs, they ended up in a small room, the only piece of furniture a large bed in the center. A wall-to-wall mirror covered one wall, and when Peter looked up, he noticed the large mirror on the ceiling, above the bed.

The women giggled and began to undress him. Before he realized it, he stood completely naked.

"Wow!" the one in the bikini said, running her hands over his chest and biceps.

"You can say that again," breathed the other one and touched his already reacting penis. She pressed herself against him and kissed him on the mouth.

Peter put his arms around her. Letting his hands travel down her back, he cupped her fleshy buttocks. Her skin felt soft and smooth, and it dawned on him that she was nude, the net nothing but paint.

She laughed and lifted up her legs to wrap them around his torso. His rigid penis nestled between her buttocks.

He walked her to the bed, turned around and sat down. Sitting in his lap now, the woman lifted up. Her hand grabbed his penis, held it and then he felt the wonderful sensation of a soft, moist pussy taking him deep inside. Her full tits rubbed against his chest as she began to move.

"I needed this badly," she gasped into his ear, pumping her lower body back and forth. It didn't take long before she clamped down hard and cried out, "I'm coming. Sweet Mother, I'm coming."

And she did. Peter felt the warm liquid matting his pubic hair, and he crushed her to him. Even though he didn't climax, just the thought of making a woman come that fast, felt exhilarating.

The woman lifted off, but there was no rest for Peter. The other one pushed him onto his back and straddled him. She had removed her bikini bottom and he watched her hairless pussy hover above his standing member but not for long. She came down hard, swallowing him up to the root. Then she began whipping her shapely bottom with furious speed.

Peter dug his fingers into her breasts. Looking at the ceiling, he could see the image of her white buttocks moving in his lap.

She experienced a couple of powerful orgasms, but he controlled his own urge. After her third climax, the woman stretched out on top of him, pressed her breasts against him, and gave him a long kiss. Then she rolled to the side.

Before Peter could move, the painted woman sat on his chest, smiled, and moved higher. Pushing her slit onto his mouth, she said, "Lick it up."

He pushed his tongue into her, tasting the salty flavor of her pussy. A mouth closed over his penis, and he groaned when a soft tongue began teasing his glans.

The woman sitting on his face moaned deeply and dug her long fingernails into his arms. Opening his eyes, he looked at her quivering belly and her jiggling breasts. Staring at those lovely breasts, he concentrated on the soft mouth working his penis.

His control began to slip and then he just couldn't hold it any longer. He wanted and needed this climax and he came with explosive force in that sweet mouth.

His hands grabbed the painted girl's hips and held her immobile until he was finished.

She looked down at him and smiled. "Did you have a good climax?" she asked, moving back a little but still sitting on his chest.

"The best," Peter answered. "Your friend sure knows how to give head."

Her smile grew wider. "So I hear."

She climbed down and laughed softly when Peter looked at the one still fondling his semi-erect penis.

"You do have a beautiful cock, Handsome," said a male voice. "And you do know how to come."

"What the hell!"

Peter jumped off the bed and grabbed the other one by the throat.

Someone jumped on his back. He felt soft breasts digging into his shoulder blades and an arm around his throat. The painted woman stepped into the space between him and the man.

"Please, let go," she pleaded. "He meant no harm."

"I told him I wasn't interested, the fucking fag," Peter yelled angrily.

"He gave you the best climax," the girl clinging to his back said. "You admitted it yourself."

"Knowing it was guy sucking on my dick makes me want to puke," Peter rasped. Releasing the throat he was choking, he glared at the other man.

"A mouth is a mouth," the guy sputtered, rubbing his throat.

"There is a difference, Mister." Peter pulled the arm of the girl in his back away from his own throat.

She came around to face him. "What if I gave you a nice blowjob, would you still be mad?" she asked.

Looking at her pleading face, Peter suddenly burst out laughing. "Tell your queer friend here to leave the room, and maybe I'll let you give it a try."

"Nice blowing you," the man giggled and left hurriedly when Peter lifted his fist.

Peter stared at the closing door, and then he turned around. "Lie on the bed," he ordered the smaller of the women.

She obeyed. "What now?" she asked.

Peter looked closer at her for the first time and found her quite pretty…and awfully young, but when you're forty-one anyone under thirty seems young.

He looked at the painted woman who had been quietly watching. "You lie beside her," he said.

The woman smiled and lay down beside the other one. Seeing them close together, Peter noted that she looked a little older. He also noticed the resemblance.

"Are you sisters?" he asked.

She nodded. "I am Stella," said the painted one. "And this is my little sister Mirabelle."

"Hi." Mirabelle's face reddened. "Are you just going to stare at us?" she asked.

Peter chuckled. "No, but I don't mind looking at you. It helps me to get horny."

Mirabelle giggled. "It seems to be working."

Peter looked down at his stiff member, and then he walked toward the bed.

"What are you going to do?" Stella asked.

Her eyes seemed large inside the black circles she had painted around them.

"Now I'm going to fuck you two girls until I drop." He grinned.

Mirabelle looked a little frightened when he opened her thighs. "Please, don't hurt us," she whispered.

He moved between her legs, grinning. "I didn't say hurt, I said fuck."

"Ohh…" She gasped when he entered her.

He was still angry, but also extremely turned on. He moved forcefully between the girl's widespread thighs, pushing his swollen organ deep into her sweet pussy. With every deep thrust, she let out a soft whimper that changed into ecstatic cries whenever an orgasm rocked her slim body.

"What is happening to me?" she sobbed, clutching her thighs against his hips. "I've never felt like this before."

"That's because you've never been fucked like this before," Peter said between clenched teeth. He pulled out of her and moved over to Stella, who had been watching.

At his touch, her legs flew open. She pulled up her knees until they pressed against her breasts. Watching Peter and her sister, had put her into a state of high excitement, and he entered her sex-canal with ease. Her position made it possible for him to penetrate her deeply.

Her breathing became ragged within moments, and he had to stifle her screams of pleasure with his kiss. After her third shattering climax, she wrapped her long legs around him, letting her heels rest on his buttocks. She writhed and bucked under him for a long time, whimpering like a sick child.

He went back to Mirabelle, who waited eagerly for his rampant prick. He had her kneel on the bed, and, standing on the floor, he hammered between her soft buttocks until she called for him to stop.

Then he did the same to Stella. Her painted, plump buttocks quivered every time he slammed into them.

When he was done with Stella, Mirabelle was ready for him again. Lying on her back, her legs wide open, she smiled at him. "Whoever you are," she whispered, "you are the best lover I ever had. I'd like to feel you come inside me." She touched his penis and held if for a moment, before she guided it toward her pussy. "It'll be alright. I'm on the pill."

He took her gently this time, moving with slow, deliberate strokes, savoring the feeling of her gentle hands stroking his back, her soft full breasts pressing against his chest as he lay on top of her.

The buildup was like a slow glowing ember that flared up to become a roaring fire inside him. The pressure became too great, and he exploded with the force of an erupting volcano that had been dormant for a long time.

"Now!" he called out, his voice harsh in the silence of the room. His penis seemed to gush forever. He crushed his mouth against the woman's searching lips, suppressing the roar that wanted to escape his own throat.

Mirabelle shook in his tight embrace as her own powerful orgasm washed through her.

It was over all too soon.

He held her for a long time, his semi-erect penis still inside her, trying to recall the pleasure he just experienced, but only the memory lingered on. Burying his face in her hair that had come undone, he inhaled the faint fragrance of her hairspray.

Sighing, he finally let her go.

"Wow!" Mirabelle breathed. "That was some orgasm!"

"I am jealous," her sister said. "Why not me?"

Peter grinned weakly. "She asked for it."

Stella threw up her hands. Her breasts jiggled deliciously. Peter looked at them, enjoying their beautiful shape. "Maybe later."

Chapter Seven

He must have dozed off. When he opened his eyes, the women were gone. Peter dressed and left the room.

Intrigued by laughter, music, and the clapping of hands, he walked into another room. He saw mostly men sitting around tables, smoking, and playing cards. In the center of the room moved two shapes. They looked like giant snakes, until he saw the breasts and black triangles between their legs.

Two women, either wearing black bodysuits or nothing but paint, like Stella.

He moved closer to watch.

Writhing and swaying around each other, their extremely slim bodies appearing boneless, they performed a sensuous and sexual dance. Their faces were covered with masks resembling striking cobras.

One of the dancers crooked a finger at one of the men clustered around them. He stepped forward into her embrace. Dressed like a Roman, he wore a kilt and soft leather armor.

The woman crouched in front of him. Putting her hands under his kilt, she pulled down a pair of black briefs. He stepped out of them and the girl displayed them triumphantly. Then she knelt down again, lifted up his kilt, and exposed his erect penis.

The watching men laughed and cheered.

Pulling him by his penis, the woman moved with him into the center. Then she put her hand on his chest and pushed him gently to the ground.

Lying on his back, the man's pole stood proudly. The woman swayed her snake body above him, her legs spread, her feet on either side of his hips. When her pubic area almost touched his straining

61

member, she began to jerk her lower body back and forth, grazing and teasing the swollen head with every forward movement.

A couple of times the rigid penis disappeared partially inside the black triangle. Peter heard the man on the floor moan noisily when that happened. His hands reached for the swaying hips, but she eluded him, hissing loudly as she did so.

She played her role quite well.

Meanwhile, the other snake dancer swayed her body above his head, her pubis almost touching his eyes. He lifted his head, his tongue sticking out, but the swaying pussy stayed out of his reach.

She sank down once, letting his tongue enter her briefly then she lifted up and moved toward the circle of men. Picking one, she pulled him with her, lowering her body to the ground.

Lying on her back, she opened her thighs wide, looking up at him. The man fumbled with his zipper, pulled out his stiff penis. He fell between her spread thighs and, with a triumphant yell, his hips pushed forward.

The other dancer had finally given the man below her what he craved. Taking his penis deep inside her every time she sank down, she writhed in the man's lap.

Neither of the men lasted long. They both came at almost the same instant. Their hoarse cries of pleasure were lost in the laughter of the watching men.

After that, the men were lining up to take their turns with the two snake dancers.

Peter walked out after a while, back to the crowded room below. He spotted a bar in the corner and headed for it. His body felt parched, and he needed a drink. Downing a double shot of Scotch, he enjoyed the strong roughness as it ran down his throat, and then he ordered a beer.

He turned when someone touched his shoulder.

When he saw a woman in a snake outfit he thought it was one of the two dancers, but then he noticed the difference. This woman was slim and tall, but not quite as thin as those other two.

A latex mask covered her head, only her eyes showed through. He noted the slit pupils; obviously contact lenses.

"Hi," she said.

"Hi, yourself," Peter said. "How are you?"

She giggled. "I am fine. Are you looking for some fun?" Her voice sounded strangely familiar.

"Do I know you?" he asked.

"Maybe." She tilted her head and looked at him.

He couldn't tell if she smiled underneath her snake mask. Her shapely body was covered with painted, delicate scales in all shades of iridescent green.

"Who does the artwork around here?" he asked.

"You like it?" She turned her body slowly in front of him. He admired her full breasts, fleshy round buttocks, and her flat belly. Her pubic area was hidden behind a thin piece of black, shimmering cloth, cleverly worked into the design.

"It's beautiful," he said. "You are beautiful."

"His name is Ramos," she said. "He is a great artist."

She had this weird, guttural accent he had never heard before, and yet...he couldn't lose the feeling he had met her before.

"What is your name?" he asked her.

She chuckled under her mask. Putting a hand on his cheek, she said, "Knowing a woman's name removes all the mystery of the encounter. Not knowing adds to the titillation." She looked into his face. "Do you want to get to know me better?"

Grinning, he pulled her to him. "I know a quiet place."

She pushed him away, gently. "There is another matter. I have a friend. She is part of the deal."

Peter shrugged. "Okay."

A second woman stood suddenly in front of him. Tall and slim, like her friend, her breasts a trifle larger, cone-shaped, her shapely body painted in blue iridescent scales.

Peter looked her over and gave a little wolf-whistle. "Any friend who is built like that is welcome to join us anytime," he said. He led them to the upstairs room he had been in before with Stella and Mirabelle. The bed was rumpled and gave evidence it had seen action not long ago.

"You seem to know your way around here," the first woman said. She flopped down on the bed, her legs slightly open.

"How about removing those masks?" Peter said. "I like to kiss when I fuck." He put his hand behind the other woman's head and pulled her close.

She shook her head.

"The mask stays on," the woman on the bed said. "It adds to the mystery."

The woman in his arms nodded.

"Doesn't she speak?" Peter asked.

She shook her head again.

"But she fucks." The one on the bed laughed.

Peter fondled the woman's breasts and bent to kiss them. Then he moved down and pulled away the cloth that covered her pubic hair. She didn't have much; only sparse copper-colored curls covered her Venus mound. Her labia were thick, and when his tongue entered her pink slit, he found it already moist.

She moaned and led him toward the bed. Falling backwards, she opened her legs and pulled him between them.

He was ready and pushed his rod into her welcoming sheath. She felt good and tight, as she moved under him in an almost familiar rhythm.

It felt like coming home.

He could tell, this woman possessed great passion, but she seemed to hold back. Peter looked into her snake eyes as he labored above her. "I wish I could see your face," he said. "I bet you're really beautiful."

She stared at him with those slit pupils but said nothing.

She took his full weight as he lay on her soft breasts. His hands moved under her body, grabbed her buttocks and then he began to push into her with greater speed and force.

She moaned and pushed up against him. Slowly, she seemed to lose her inhibition, and then she let out a loud gasp as she experienced her first orgasm.

Peter knew this would be a long session and slowed down to conserve energy. Soon the woman in his arms lost control and, bucking underneath him, she clawed at his back, raking her long fingernails across his skin.

She seemed like a tigress who had been disturbed in her sleep.

She surprised Peter with her strength, when she pulled close and rolled him over so she could be on top. Her firm breasts stood like two perfectly molded cones from her solid ribcage as she writhed above him.

Peter felt a little unnerved, looking into her cold snake eyes, but she was far from being cold. He had awakened the glowing embers inside her, and her fire burned brightly now.

This woman was hot. Her pussy was hot, and she used it with great skill on him.

Suddenly, she lifted off, leaving his rigid penis sticking into emptiness. She pointed to her friend.

Peter had completely forgotten about her. She lay on her belly beside them, watching through her expressionless mask. She turned away from him, but pushed her beautifully shaped ass into his lap.

Lying on his side, he moved into position beside her. His probing member slid between her fleshy buttocks, found the entrance to her vagina, and slid inside.

She didn't move much, just squeezed her inside muscles gently over his penis. Peter could move only slowly in this restricting position, but it felt good.

After a while the woman turned onto her stomach. Peter lay on top of her, her buttocks soft in his belly. He couldn't enter her deeply this way, but she felt wonderfully tight.

Putting his hands over her breasts, he spread her legs with one knee and pulled her up. Her buttocks lifted, and when she knelt in front of him, he pushed his rod deep into her.

On his knees now, he slammed gently into her fleshy cheeks, his hands clamped around her wide hips. She pushed back, lifted higher, arching her back. Then she cried out and doused his member with her warm discharge.

He turned her around then, took her from the front, and brought her to a number of powerful orgasms.

When he felt soft, demanding hands on his back, he pulled out and let the other woman pull him on top of her. She acted even more passionate than before. He almost lost it, when a hand cupped his scrotum and a finger pressed a certain spot.

He climaxed but didn't lose any fluid.

The woman underneath was like a wild fire out of control. Bucking and clawing at his back, he knew he would show welts, but he didn't care. The pleasure was so exquisite, and finally he couldn't hold it any longer.

He came inside her clutching pussy with a roar he was sure everyone in the building must have heard.

Then he collapsed into her cradling arms.

When he could breathe again, he pushed himself up and looked at the woman who had given him such pleasure. "I thought I had experienced orgasms, but this was incredible. I've never met a woman with such passion before. Who are you?"

She pulled him down and kissed him through her mask, and then she pushed him off, gently but firmly.

Peter looked at the other woman, who sat in lotus position on the bed. He reached over and cupped one of her breasts. "Such gorgeous bodies. Both of you." He smiled. "I am not an artist, but for me, there is nothing more beautiful than a shapely naked woman."

"Faces don't matter?"

"Of course they matter. Very much so. Beautiful bodies and faces go together." Peter studied her masked face.

She seemed to smile underneath her mask. "Maybe you'll change your mind when you see ours."

"Then show them to me."

She slid off the bed. "Take us to your place," she said. "Maybe we will."

"Leave this party now?" Peter asked.

The woman lifted her shapely shoulders. "Haven't you had enough yet?" She stood in front of him, hands on hips, legs slightly apart, very much the primitive snake goddess she symbolized.

Looking at her lovely body made him want her again. His gaze wandered to the other woman, who still lay beside him on the bed. She was slim and tall, maybe a little fleshier in places than her friend but just as beautiful and desirable.

He remembered her passionate lovemaking and made a decision. "Why not," he said. Kathleen and her friend Sue were gone for the week, so there'd be no problem.

He dressed slowly.

The women went to get their clothes. He met them in the vestibule. They were already waiting for him.

He chuckled when he saw the way they dressed. Black, long cloaks with hoods. He wondered what they wore underneath those cloaks.

Driving home didn't take long, only about forty minutes. The women, who had taken the backseats, were silent most of the way. When Peter looked in the rearview mirror he saw them slumped in their seats.

He parked the car inside the garage. He didn't need snoopy neighbors to see him bringing two women into his house in the middle of the night.

"Wake up, girls," he called softly, but they were already getting out of the car.

"Nice place," the one who did all the talking said.

Both women dropped their cloaks. As he had guessed, they were still naked underneath, except for their painted snakeskin and the thin loincloths.

"You must have lots of money to afford a house like this."

Peter laughed. "I do all right."

She walked over to look at one of the pictures on the wall. "You are married," she stated. "Your wife is very beautiful. Where is she?"

"She is not my wife. We live together," Peter murmured, feeling uncomfortable discussing his private life. "And don't worry. She isn't here."

"She left you?" She had a way of tilting her head when she looked at him, making him uneasy.

"I hope not," he answered, shrugged his shoulders. "What's the difference? She won't be back for days. I'm all alone."

"You love her?" she asked.

"If you must know," he almost shouted, angry with her and with himself. "I love her very much."

She stayed silent for a moment, just looked at him, and then she said with a quiet voice. "Then why do you screw around with other women?"

"I don't know," he said, just as quietly. "Maybe I'm just a horny guy. Anyway, it's none of your damn business." He looked at the other woman, the silent one. "Did you girls come here to argue with me, or do you want to fuck?"

The silent woman came up to him, put her arms around his neck and hugged him briefly then her hand dropped to his belt and began to undo it. Pulling down his zipper, she put a hand on his crotch. His penis reacted immediately under her soft touch. She pushed down his briefs and his pants. Then she knelt in front of him.

His penis was painfully stiff, and he moaned when she took it into her warm mouth. Grabbing her head, he held it and pushed his organ back and forth in her sucking mouth. Under her skullcap, he felt thick hair, and he wondered what color of hair she had and what she looked like under that serpent mask.

Soft breasts pressed against his back, and strong arms hugged him from behind. "Come inside her mouth," a voice whispered into his ear.

He was ready, but he held back. "No," he groaned. "I want some pussy first. Hers and yours."

The laughter in his ear sounded teasing. "Then do me first. I'm ready. Let her watch, she enjoys that, too. She'll be more passionate after. And I like to be watched."

He let go of the woman's head and pulled out of her mouth.

The other woman danced in front of him, her body undulating sinuously like the serpent she represented. Her belly rippled, her hips rotated, and her breasts jiggled deliciously. She turned to present her buttocks. Her body stopped moving, only her buttocks quivered.

He reached for her, but she eluded him, laughing.

"Bitch," he growled. "Don't tease."

She stood in front of him with open arms, her legs apart. She moved her upper body to make her breasts jump. This time she didn't slip away when he came close. He put his hands on her buttocks and buried his face in her jiggling, soft breasts.

She sank to the floor, her legs opened, and his hard penis entered sweet softness. Forgotten were her questions. Nothing seemed important now, only the soft pressure around his penis, the back-and-forth movement that produced such incredible pleasure.

They moved in unison for a long time. When they broke apart, she had experienced numerous orgasms. Peter hadn't come. He saved it for the quiet woman.

She had been observing silently, except for a few times when she ran her gentle hands over his back. Once she must have been crouching behind him, for she put her hands on his buttocks, moving with him as he moved in and out of the woman underneath him.

She motioned for him to lie down. Straddling him, she hovered motionless for a moment above his stiff penis. Then she sank down and, with a deep sigh, she took him deep into her.

She watched his face through her reptilian lenses as she rode him. The mask lent her a cold and impassive look, but her loud moans and deep sighs said something different.

Peter studied her lovely painted body and again he wondered what she looked like under the mask. He touched her large cone-shaped breasts. His thoughts drifted to Kathleen. She had breasts shaped like that. He had always liked them.

Funny, how every woman's breasts looked different.

He felt the pressure building up and knew he wouldn't be able to hold back much longer. Pulling the woman down to him, he swung himself on top of her. This position allowed him more control and let him achieve much higher climaxes.

"Get ready," he grunted. "I feel it coming."

He crushed her to him then, filling her receiving vessel with his gift. She accepted it with loud gasps of pleasure, her own fluid mixing with his.

Glued together, they lay in each other's arms for a long time, until their breathing became normal.

"Wow," he exclaimed, "you are some woman."

She touched his cheek and slid off the bed.

"Can we use your shower?" her friend asked.

"Of course," Peter said. He sighed as he watched them walk down the hallway.

Four painted lovely cheeks, almost too much to bear.

He lay on his stomach and watched the dancing flames of the gas fireplace. One of the women must have switched it on. Enjoying the warmth on his naked skin, he felt himself becoming drowsy.

What a weekend! He'd never fucked so much in such a short time before.

Suddenly, he felt drained and tired.

Chapter Eight

"Peter, get up."

Opening his eyes, he experienced a sense of disorientation. Two soft lips kissed him on the nose.

"Breakfast is ready," said a familiar voice.

Peter shook his head to clear away the cobwebs clinging to his mind and looked at the woman bending over him.

"Kathleen?" he croaked. "What are you doing here?"

Slapping his cheek playfully, she laughed. "I live here, or have you forgotten?"

"Of course not. It's just...are we alone?"

She gave him a questioning look. "Well...yeah, except for Sue. She's setting the breakfast table."

"When did you get back?" He sat up, holding his head. How much did I have to drink last night?

"A while ago. We found you lying naked on the floor. Couldn't wake you, so I covered you up." She looked back over her shoulder as she walked away. "What did you do here last night? Have an orgy?"

Peter got up and went to the bathroom. Looking around, he found no evidence that two strange women had been in there. Everything looked tidy.

After a quick shower, he felt better and joined Kathleen and Sue at the breakfast table.

"You look like you have a hangover," Sue Lin remarked, smiling sweetly.

"So how was your shopping trip?" Peter asked.

Kathleen shrugged. "Fine. We didn't really buy anything. But we had fun. How about you?"

"I had fun, too."

"Did you go see Connie?" Sue asked.

Peter stared at her innocent looking face. "Of course, I did. She's a very special lady."

Sue Lin nodded and smiled. "That she is. She thinks highly of you. She says you're quite a man, and that's some compliment coming from Connie."

Peter looked at Kathleen, but she said nothing, just smiled. He finished his coffee and looked at his watch. "I'd better phone the office and see what's up. What about you two? Any plans?"

"Not really," Kathleen said. "Sue has to get back to work, and I might give Evelyn a call. Maybe I can get together with her."

* * * *

"Peter, I was going to call you." Robert Palmer's deep voice boomed through the phone. "There is a new client I want you to see today. Big account. We want to make sure we get the contract."

"Fine, as long as I get the commission." Peter smiled into the phone.

His boss chuckled. "Straight down to the nitty gritty, huh. That's what I like about you, Peter. Now…you'll have to drive to the client's house, that's how he does business. He does nothing without his wife's approval. I hear she's one tough old bird, but I have confidence in your abilities. Just turn on the old charm and she'll come around."

"Do I have to take her to bed?" Peter grinned.

"Ha…ha…ha…" Robert laughed. "That's strictly up to you, my boy. Even though I don't know why you'd want to…with a girlfriend like Kathleen." His voice became serious. "I don't care if you screw her, just don't screw up this deal. This is big money. That's why I'm sending you. You're the best we have, Peter."

After giving Peter more details, he hung up.

Fifteen minutes later Peter was on his way…

Chapter Nine

The woman was naked.

She was also quite dead.

"The bullet entered the skull behind the right ear, destroying the brain tissue inside. Death was instantaneous. She didn't suffer." Inspector Burgess stared at the pallid corpse.

"Small caliber gun, 22, judging from the size of the entry hole." He looked up at the detective coming from an adjacent room. "How about the man?" he asked.

"Yeah…he's dead. Got it right between the eyes."

Inspector Burgess turned to the woman standing beside him. "Why are the Feds interested in this case, Agent Chandler?" he asked.

Special Agent Chandler shrugged. "These people are part of an investigation. I can't tell you any more."

"How did you hear of these murders so fast?"

"We have our sources," the woman said softly. "Let's leave it at that, Inspector."

The police inspector looked at her with narrowed eyes. "This case falls into our jurisdiction. You may have to divulge your sources."

Agent Chandler gave him a smile. "We'll see, Inspector. You'll have to take it up with my superior. So far, we have no official status. I'm here only out of curiosity."

"Curiosity killed the cat," murmured Burgess and made some notes in a little black book.

The FBI agent laughed. "I heard that, and for your information, I'm not a cat."

"No?" Burgess looked up from his notes. "You certainly hear like one, though."

"Training, that's all." The agent studied the pale nude form of the dead woman. "Why is this woman naked?" she mused. "Was she raped?"

The inspector shook his head. "There seems to be no outward sign of a struggle. We'll have to wait for the coroner's report to see if she was sexually assaulted."

The other detective chuckled. "You'd have to be pretty desperate to rape her. I mean…her being so fat and old."

"None of that, Ramsey!" Inspector Burgess spoke sharply. "She's dead. Give her the respect she deserves! Just because she is fat and not young doesn't mean she can't be desirable. My wife is…well…never mind."

"Sorry," Ramsey said. "I didn't mean to be disrespectful." He paused. "If you want my opinion, this looks like a professional hit." With a calculating look at the FBI agent, he added, "What do you think, Chandler? Maybe you and I can discuss that over a beer?"

Agent Chandler shook her head, smiled. I know a hit when I see one, and I see one right now. She was used to this. Being a beautiful woman in a male-dominated profession had its drawbacks, but she usually managed to use it to her advantage. Sometimes she got information a man would never get.

However, this was not one of those occasions.

"Maybe some other time," she said.

"Maybe," said the young detective, sounding disappointed.

The agent handed Burgess a card. "Please call me if something new comes up, Inspector. I'd like to be kept up-to-date." She looked at Ramsey and smiled then casually put one of her calling cards into his coat pocket.

She walked out of the house, knowing that Inspector Burgess wouldn't call, but it didn't matter. She knew who would call.

* * * *

Getting into her car, she glanced at the illuminated face of the car's digital clock.

1:17 AM

Shit! I hate these late-night murders. Can't they ever happen at a descent hour?

73

It took her over an hour to get home. She was too tired to take a shower, just brushed her teeth, and flopped onto her bed. She didn't even bother to take off her make-up.

When the alarm clock rang, it seemed she hadn't slept at all. After taking a shower and sipping her first cup of coffee, she felt better.

On her way out, she picked up the newspaper, which lay outside her apartment door. She usually dedicated the first thirty minutes in her office to reading the morning paper's headlines and the 'Classifieds'.

Traffic was heavy as she came closer to her downtown office. It looked like it was going to be another hot and humid day. She drove with her window open but closed it when the smog became too thick.

"Damn pollution," she muttered, "they should promote those electric cars more, but at the price they're selling, nobody buys them."

She slammed on her brakes when an impatient driver squeezed into the space between her car and the car in front. "Idiot!" she cursed loudly and honked her horn. When she saw the stiff middle finger shooting out of the passenger's window she honked again.

Suddenly, she relaxed and leaned back in her seat. Not enough sleep. She smiled as another thought entered her mind. Maybe the old adage is true. A good roll in the hay might just fix me up.

She hadn't taken the young detective's number, but it shouldn't be a problem to get it. When she arrived in her office, there was already a call on her answering service. "Hi, this is Detective Ramsey. Please call me back. Some new development might interest you. Here is my number..."

He must have given her his cell-number, because he answered the call immediately.

"I can't say much over the phone," he said, "but maybe we can meet?"

She smiled, had a good mind to tell him to forget it but changed her mind. "Okay," she said, "where?"

He told her, and she put down the phone. She knew exactly what he wanted; it was so damn obvious.

The problem was she wanted it too.

She found him sitting already at the bar. "A little early for a drink, isn't it?" she commented, shaking her head when the bartender approached.

"Sit down anyway," the young detective said. "You may be interested to know an arrest is being made right now."

"This soon?" she asked. "Who?"

He shrugged, downed his glass. "A nobody. Some salesman. Looks like he raped the woman, was surprised by the husband, shot him, then her...end of case."

"You sure have it figured out." Agent Chandler stared at him. "Who is arresting him?"

"Not us. The case was transferred to another precinct. Orders from higher up...way up!"

"That strikes me as very peculiar, especially if this guy is a 'nobody'."

She waved to the bartender. "Give me what he's drinking, and another one for him."

She took the glass, emptied it, and choked. "What the hell!" she sputtered. "What is this stuff?"

Detective Ramsey grinned. "Puts hair on your chest, doesn't it?" He looked at her ample bosom and winked. "Maybe we could go somewhere quiet and I could check?"

She shook her head in disbelief but smiled. "You certainly don't mince words, do you, Detective Ramsey?"

"Call me Jason. Now, let's get out of here."

He took her to a two-bit motel. "I busted a guy on some minor charges in one of the rooms," he explained. "I'll tell the attendant we'll have to check out something. No sense to pay for a room when you can get it free."

"Of course not," Chandler said. "I do it like that all the time."

She laughed when she saw his face. "Relax," she said in a low voice. "I don't make it a habit going to a motel room in the middle of the day to fuck a stranger I just met."

The man actually blushed. "And I thought I was being forward," he murmured. "You put me to shame."

She grabbed his arm when he hesitated outside the door. "Well, let's go in. We're two consenting adults, doing nothing against the law. No money will exchange hands, so you couldn't arrest me for prostitution." She gave him a sidelong glance. "Are you chickening out? After all, this is what you wanted, isn't it?"

"No, no, I'm not chickening out," he said hastily and pushed open the door. "It's just…I've never done this before."

"Are you married?" she asked, walking past him into the vestibule.

"No. I'm single and unattached."

"So am I. What's the problem?"

"No problem." He walked up to the desk and spoke to the old guy slumped in a chair behind it.

"Go right ahead," she heard the attendant's rasping voice. "Take all the time you want. You two can fuck in there as far as I'm concerned. I don't give a shit."

Ramsey came back, grinning, a key dangling from his finger.

She followed him upstairs, aware of the old geezer's eyes on her legs.

The room was shabby. A bed, a dresser, and an old wooden chair. There was no bathroom, no place to wash up…after.

As if reading her mind, Ramsey said, "Bathroom is down the hall. If you want to freshen up or something."

"I think I would," she said. "How about you?"

"Me too."

They walked down the hall together. She went into the room with the faded picture of a female shape on the door, heard him open the door to the bathroom beside it.

It sure wasn't fancy. A grimy toilet, a shower stall, and a filthy sink with a cloudy mirror. Someone had written on it with red lipstick For the best blowjob call 111-SUCK.

Any response to that message was questionable. How many guys would see it in the women's bathroom?

She used the facility, wiped herself with a wet tissue from a dispenser on the wall. She rubbed some of the dust off the mirror and looked at her image. The gray-blue eyes that stared back at her had an accusing look about them. What the hell are you doing here? You're twenty-seven years old. You have a good job with the FBI. You are beautiful and can have any man you want, and here you are in a shabby rundown motel, getting ready to fuck a man who means nothing to you. You're no better than the two-bit whores who walk the streets at night!

"I'm not charging for it," she whispered into the mirror. Her mirror image moved her full lips, mouthing the same words, as if mocking her.

She shook her short dark-blond hair, shrugged and stuck out a tongue at her double, who mocked her again by doing the same.

"I don't care what you think," she said. "I need a man."

Jason already waited for her when she returned to the room. He was sitting at the edge of the bed, naked. She smiled, began to slowly peel off her clothes.

Jason just watched, saying nothing.

When she was naked, his eyes traveled from her breasts down to her pubic area. "You shaved off your hair," he said.

She could see his penis rising between his legs. "I like it that way," she said, walked up to him and pressed his face between her breasts. "Suck them!" she commanded.

He groaned and licked her left breast. Moving to the other one, he took the rigid nipple between his teeth.

"Gently," she whispered, her fingers digging into his biceps. Then she straddled him, lifted her legs, and put her feet on the bed. He moaned, placed his hands under her buttocks, and raised her up. She was already sopping wet and, with a little cry, she slid onto his rigid member, felt him enter her deeply.

Snapping her pelvis back and forth, she rode him fiercely, until he pressed her to him in a tight embrace. Standing up, he turned around, fell with her onto the bed. He moved forcefully between her spread legs, his feet still on the floor.

She could feel a climax approaching, let it happen.

After a while, he pulled out, told her to move higher. She moved toward the head of the bed, lay there with legs spread wide. He took his time, licked her inner thighs, her vulva, her stomach, and her breasts.

Putting a finger into her, he gently stroked her clitoris. She moaned, doused his finger with her warm liquid.

"You're sure hot," he said hoarsely, falling between her open thighs.

Again, she cried out when his stiff mast slid into her. Keeping a steady rhythm, he brought her to another orgasm, then he suddenly stiffened, and just as she was ready for what she knew would be a tremendous climax, he pulled out, leaving her empty.

Grunting, he shook between her cradling thighs. She could feel his warm discharge flooding her belly.

Then he rolled onto his back, breathing harshly.

"That was terrific," he said after catching his breath. "Wasn't it?"

"Oh, sure," she said, trying to hide her disappointment. "It was wonderful." She turned, propped herself onto her elbows. "You could have come inside me," she said. "I'm on the pill, you know."

He shrugged. "I didn't know, but it doesn't really matter. I enjoy coming outside. I like to feel my prick jump in my fist."

"And I like to feel it throb inside my pussy," she said. "It's a great turn-on."

"Maybe next time." He gave her nipple a gentle twist. "Okay?"

"We'll see." She got up. "I'd better get going."

She wiped herself with a tissue she took out of her purse, and then she slipped into her panties.

He lay there on the bed watching her getting dressed. "You have a beautiful ass," he commented. "Nice and round."

"Aren't you coming?" she asked, reaching for her coat.

"In a minute," he answered.

She didn't wait for him. "See you around, Detective," she said as she walked out of the door. "And thanks for the tip."

She got into her car, angry with herself, angry with Jason Ramsey for being so damn selfish. Someday she'd find a man who would be able to satisfy her. Like that guy she had met at some party just a week before.

Now, there had been a real man…a stud.

Just thinking about him and that night made her thighs tingle.

There were no messages at the office, so she decided to take the rest of the day off and drive home.

After a long shower, she felt clean again and spent the rest of the day and evening reading a novel she had started over a month ago. The Virgin and the Monster from a distant star.

She had trouble falling asleep. When she finally did, her dreams were populated by bug-eyed monsters. They were chasing her down a dark alley, shooting sticky liquid at her out of giant penises. It was almost a relief when the alarm clock went off. She decided to have breakfast at the café, which was only five minutes away.

The morning paper lay as usual at her door the next morning. When she saw the headlines, she went back into her apartment.

"Damn it!" She reached for her phone and dialed Detective Ramsey's number. "What precinct is handling that murder-case?" she asked him.

He told her.

She hung up. Five minutes later, she sat in her car.

Chapter Ten

In the morning, the big detective came to Hartmann's cell. "You have a visitor," he said and took him into the visiting room. Peter looked at the woman who walked in moments later.

"Hi, Peter Hartmann," she said.

Her voice sounded familiar, but he didn't recognize her.

"Do I know you?" he asked, his eyes captured by her extremely beautiful face. She wore a black, long coat, open in the front, and he could see her large breasts straining against the thin material of her sweater.

"I am Stella." She smiled. "Remember me?" Turning to the big man beside her, she said, "Detective Slovik, would you please leave us alone?"

The big detective looked uncertain. "I dunno. That's against regulations, ma'am. He's considered extremely dangerous."

The woman smiled. "You want me to tell you what you can do with your regulations, Detective?" she purred.

"I'm leaving," Slovik rumbled. "But remember, I warned you." He shook his head and shot an angry look at Peter.

The woman removed her black coat and draped it over the back of a chair. Then she sank into the other one.

Peter managed to get a glimpse of a black, tight short skirt, and long, shapely legs, before she sat down. She reached up and pulled back her dark hair into a ponytail. "Remember me, Handsome?" she asked with a slightly different, sexier sounding voice. She smiled. "Maybe I should have had my body painted."

Peter stared. "Stella?" he exclaimed, images of a lovely naked body covered with a painted net-pattern flashing in front of his mind's eye.

"I see you remember." The woman chuckled. "You never told us your name, but I recognized you when I saw the pictures."

"Don't tell me you're a cop?" Peter said, still staring at her.

"Not a cop," she answered, her smile gone, her eyes studying him, "but I am working for the law."

"Lawyer?"

"No." She smiled again. "I work for the government. Mostly under cover."

Peter almost burst out laughing. "Another government agent…and again a beautiful woman. Let me guess…at that party, when you and your sister Mirabelle fucked me, that was part of a sting operation?"

She kept on smiling, but her eyes clouded over. "I was there on government business, yes, but what happened between us was strictly private. Nobody needs to know, okay? I am a woman, and I do have feelings and desires that need to be fulfilled sometimes." She reached over and touched his hand. "It was wonderful, and I kept thinking about you. So when I read your file, I felt obligated to talk to you."

"Interrogate me, you mean," Peter sneered, pulling away his hand.

"No, talk to you," she said softly. "To find out the truth."

"Why?"

"I like you, and I don't believe you're a murderer or a rapist. A guy like you doesn't have to rape old women when there are plenty of willing young, beautiful girls practically begging to be screwed by you." She looked into his eyes. "We suspect that Liebman was selling classified information to terrorists. He had government contracts, and he worked on top-secret projects. How did you get involved with him?"

"I never knew the man."

"Then what were you doing at his home?"

"Business," Peter explained. "I am a sales rep for Computer Regeneration Development. I was there to sign contracts. But you must know all that."

Stella stayed silent for a moment, her eyes never leaving his face. Suddenly, she said, "Do you trust your boss Robert Palmer?"

The question came unexpected. "What do you mean…trust?" Peter asked.

"How well do you know him? Are you socially involved with him?"

Peter chuckled. "With him? No. We have nothing in common."

"Except for his wife Linda." The woman's voice sounded businesslike, showing no emotion, but her face betrayed her, and her smile seemed forced. "I know a lot about you, Peter Hartmann. I know you've been living with a woman for five years. Her name is Kathleen. She's thirty-three, very beautiful. And yet...you cheat on her constantly. All the women love you. They think you're the greatest. Even after only one encounter."

She sighed, her gray-blue eyes large and shiny. "You're a bastard, Peter, a cheater and womanizer, but you're not a murderer." She reached out again and touched his hand. This time, he didn't pull away. "You're in deep shit," she said bluntly. "I'll try my best to help you. Do you have an attorney?"

Peter reached into his shirt pocket and pulled out Turner's calling card.

Stella took it and turned it over. Staring at the back of it, she said, "Fire him. He does not have your best interest at heart. This man is involved with very nasty people." She gave him a thoughtful look. "Don't trust anyone. Talk only to me. I'll get you a lawyer, a good one."

"How can I be sure you can be trusted?"

"I'm all you've got, Peter. Believe me." She paused. "Tell me about that mysterious government agent at the Liebman residence."

Peter shrugged. "Tall, slim, with a fabulous body for a woman in her early fifties. Black hair, not necessarily her real color. Hazel eyes, nice tits. Expert lover."

Stella smiled but didn't comment. "Anything else?"

"She had this regal air about her. You could tell this woman had class. She was very beautiful." Peter closed his eyes for a moment, trying to remember more details. "She had a tattoo around her navel. It looked like a coiled cobra, ready to strike."

"You're sure about the tattoo?"

Peter detected a sudden excitement in Stella's voice. "I'm sure," he said. "I remember admiring her smooth flat belly. I thought it unusual for her, a woman her age. Couldn't miss the tattoo."

"Princess Viper," Stella whispered. "Also know as Venom. She is an assassin, poisons her victims, and makes it look like a heart attack." Staring at Peter, she shook her head. "I can't believe it. You fucked Venom, and here you are...alive and well. That makes no sense."

82

"Why not?"

"She never leaves any loose ends. By the way, she's only about forty, and her hair color is never the same, right down to her pubic hair. She's a master of disguises, an expert in her field. The only thing that never changes is her tattoo, unless she covers it with plastic skin."

"You sound like you know her."

"She used to work for the CIA, doing the same work she's doing now. Except now, she is an independent contractor, hiring out to the highest bidder." Stella got up and began pacing back and forth in the room, a wrinkle between her brows.

Peter watched her, admiring her shapely figure. The tight sweater molded itself around her ample breasts. Her short skirt showed off her long, slim legs quite nicely.

She stopped pacing, noticing his look

"You are incurable," she said. "Can you ever look at a woman without mentally undressing her?"

"Is that what I'm doing?"

"It is so obvious you might as well shout it out loud." She smiled. "But I'm flattered. I like it when men admire my body. That way they won't notice my mind."

"I am admiring your mind, too." Peter grinned. "I hope it can help me out of the mess I'm in."

"I'll be honest with you, Peter," Stella said seriously. "The odds are not stacked in your favor. You've gotten involved with important and powerful people. They're out for blood. Ever hear of Jeremiah T. Liebman?"

"Can't say I have. Who's he?"

He's J. J. Liebman's brother. He's also Senator Liebman, one of the finest and most honest politicians you've ever met."

Peter laughed. "I've never met an honest politician yet. I believe I know his wife, Delta Liebman. Are you telling me this J. J. Liebman was selling government secrets? Wouldn't that make his brother suspect, too?"

"It would, wouldn't it?" Stella gave him a thoughtful look. "Now you are beginning to understand." She stood beside him. Putting a hand on his shoulder, she said, "I have to go." Then she bent down and kissed him on the cheek. "Remember, trust no one! Not even your girlfriend!"

She walked out of the door before he could ask her to explain.

Chapter Eleven

They took him to another room, one already occupied by a couple of other convicts…a big, ugly brute and a skinny runt with shifty eyes.

Peter noticed only two bunks.

"Where am I supposed to sleep?" he asked the guards.

They both laughed, and the big guard said, "I guess you'll have to work it out, tough guy."

After the guards left, Peter walked up to one of the bunks. "Mind if I sit on this one?" he asked the little guy. Before Peter could get an answer, the big brutish-looking guy stepped in front of him. "It's occupied. Sit on the floor," he growled.

Peter didn't feel like starting a fight, so he walked over to a corner and crouched down. Keeping his eyes half-open, he began to meditate, but the smaller of the convicts interrupted him.

"What you're in for, friend?"

Peter opened his eyes. "Murder," he said. "I'm supposed to have shot two people. I got framed."

"You claim to be innocent?" The little guy snickered and turned to the big fellow. "Did you hear that, Freddy? He's innocent. Just like us."

"Yeah, I heard," Freddy rumbled. "I guess that makes us brothers." He looked at Peter. "Who did you allegedly snuff out?"

"Some rich guy and his wife." Peter stared at the big man's ugly mug. "But I didn't do it. It's all a big mistake."

"Them cops are all a buncha assholes," the little man said. "Just stick to your story, buddy."

"Shut up, Jerry!" Freddy growled. "We weren't supposed to talk to this guy. Let's get it over with."

He got up from his bunk and advanced toward Peter. Something glinted in his hand. "Nothing personal," he said, "but we got a job to do."

He handed the object he carried to Jerry. It was a knife. "I'll hold him down, and you do it," he told the little guy.

Jerry took the knife and stroked it. "I dunno," he said. "It doesn't seem right." He looked at Peter. "Like Freddy says, it ain't nothin' personal, but you're our ticket outta this joint."

Peter was still sitting on the floor. "You're going to cut me up?" he asked.

Freddy grinned. It didn't improve his looks. He showed big yellow teeth. "Just your throat, that's all." He reached for Peter. "We'll make it quick."

From his sitting position, Peter kicked up with his foot, hitting the big man between the legs. Freddy howled, fell to his knees, holding his crotch.

As Peter rolled away, he kicked the knife out of Jerry's hand. Then he stood in a crouching position, facing his opponents. Jerry scrambled for the knife and picked it up again. Holding it high, he ran at Peter, who blocked the descending knife arm and punched the little man in the face. He felt cartilage give away, saw the blood flowing. A twist of his arm and the knife cluttered to the floor.

"You broke my nose," Jerry whined, pressing his good hand to his face. "And my wrist, too."

Peter had no time to feel sorry for the little guy. Freddy had recovered and lumbered toward him, his eyes yelling murder.

A sudden chill made Peter go cold. Forgotten and suppressed memories flashed through his mind. Dormant reflexes took over his body.

The big man never had a chance.

With a savage kick, Peter hit him in the solar lexis. When he lashed out a second time, he aimed for the head. As Freddy went down, Peter moved in and brought the edge of his hand down hard against the big man's fat neck.

Freddy's eyes rolled in their sockets. His big body hit the floor like a large sack of grain, and then he lay still.

The door to the cell was flung open, and a couple of guards rushed in. Behind them, Detective Slovik came slowly through the door.

"He's crazy!" Jerry screamed. "He attacked us, and now he's killed Freddy. Get me outta here!"

Peter had moved away from the big man on the floor. He stood with his arms hanging loosely, but his eyes were wary and watchful.

"Get your story straight, Jerry," Peter told the little guy, and then he looked at Slovik. "They were trying to kill me. They attacked me with a knife."

"A knife?" said the big detective. "Now, how would they get a knife?" He bent down and picked up the knife that had been lying on the floor in plain view. He slipped it into his pocket. "I don't see a knife. Anyone seen a knife?"

The two guards shook their heads.

"You see," Slovik said. "There never was a knife." He looked at Freddy, still on the ground, and then at Jerry's bloody face. "A fighting man," he commented, glancing at Peter. He kicked Freddy between the ribs. "Get up, you useless mountain of blubber."

Freddy opened his eyes and groaned. Shakily, he got to his feet. His little eyes focused on Detective Slovik. "Sorry," he whispered with a hoarse voice. "We tried. You never told us he was a trained killer." He gave Peter an accusing stare. "Did you have to kick me so hard? I think you broke something in my chest."

"You're lucky he didn't kill you, you idiot!" Detective Slovik said. "Now get the hell outta here."

Freddy and Jerry stumbled out of the cell. Slovik called in another guard. "You know what to do," he told him and left.

Peter was facing three grinning guards, their batons in their hands.

"I guess it takes professionals to do this job right," one of them sneered. "Let's do it, boys."

The coldness had not left Peter.

If faced with the choice to maim or to kill, go for the kill. But remember…there will be consequences. The voice of a ghost from long ago popped into his mind, unbidden. Never kill for the sake of killing alone.

He shook his head, forced back the memory.

There would be no killing here today.

His lips pulled back into a cold smile. They were so confident, these three. Poor suckers! Hiding behind their uniforms and their batons, they felt secure and invincible. They saw only one unarmed man.

One kick put the first one out of action. The second one didn't even have time to register his companion's fate, before he went down with a broken collarbone, which left his arm dangling and useless.

The last one backed off, swinging his baton in front of him.

Peter avoided the first swipe at him, dropped to the floor, and kicked his attacker's feet out from under him. A chop against the back of the head sent the guard sprawling to the cold floor, unconscious.

Amateurs! Peter looked at the three motionless bodies, cursing silently.

This wasn't going to help his cause, but they had left him no choice. Had he not defended himself, he'd probably be dead by now. He knew that it wasn't over yet. Whoever wanted him dead would not leave it at this.

He walked over to the locked door and began banging against it. When it finally opened, he yanked the guard into the room, pulled his arm behind his back and said fiercely, "Listen to me. I will not hurt you, but I want to talk to someone in authority. Now!"

"Easy, man." The guard struggled. "You're breaking my arm."

Peter eased up on the pressure, and then he pulled the gun out of the guard's holster. "Now, let's move slowly. We don't want any accidents." He opened the door again.

A group of uniformed cops stood around in the corridor. They looked at Peter and the guard as they came through the door.

"What's all the racket in there?" one of them asked. When he saw the gun Peter held against guard's head, his hand instinctively moved to his own gun, but Peter stopped him.

"Keep your hands away from your body. All of you!" he said sharply. "No one's going to get hurt if we all stay calm."

There were five cops. They all froze when he spoke, his voice sounding crisp and cold, like someone used to giving orders.

"You won't get far," one of them finally said.

"I'm not planning to go anywhere," Peter said. "I want a phone, and I want to talk to someone in authority. And I don't mean Detective Slovik."

The detective was just coming around the corner. He stopped, looked at Peter and the guard, saw the gun. At first, his hand moved toward his left side then he continued the upward movement and kept his hand in the air.

"You're full of surprises, Hartmann," he said. "I dug a little deeper into your past. It goes back only ten years, and then there is a blank of about five years. Those five years are stored away under 'Classified'. The FBI is not co-operating. What the fuck is going on?"

Peter smiled grimly. "Obviously more then your dumb brain can process. As I explained to these fine gentlemen, I want a phone, and I want it fast. I'm getting impatient."

"No need to phone anyone. Your lawyer is already in the station."

"If you're talking about Turner, forget it. He's not my lawyer. I fired him."

"I'm not talking about Turner." Slovik had come closer. "Who the hell are you, Hartmann? What did you do to my men?"

"Less then they deserve," Peter growled. "There was a time when I would not have been so kind. None of them would have lived...and neither would you, Slovik. I showed mercy because I know you acted under orders. And I'm aiming to find out whose."

Peter looked past the detective, at the man who came down the corridor. "Hello, Colonel," he said. "Long time no see."

"Hello, Peter," the gray-haired man said. "I see you have not lost your touch for getting into trouble."

Peter smiled grimly. "Can't seem to avoid it, sir. I'm surprised to see you, sir."

"Your face is plastered on the first page of all the major newspapers, son. You're famous." The colonel smiled. "A lot of people want your head."

"So what brings you here, Colonel?"

"It seems you need a good attorney."

"You, sir?"

The older man smiled. "Don't look so surprised. I used to be a damn good lawyer before I joined the Company. I've been practicing again for the last five years."

"You left the Company?" Peter asked.

The colonel had walked past the police officers and stood in front of Peter. "Nobody ever leaves the Company," he said in a low voice. "The only thing you're allowed is a leave-of-absence, Lieutenant. Put the gun down, and let's get out of here."

"Just like that?" Peter said dryly. He lowered the gun. Then he pushed it back into the guard's holster.

The guard stood uncertain for a moment, looked at the colonel, and then he hurried away to join the group of watching cops. Seeing him freed, they all reached for their guns, including Detective Slovik.

The colonel turned around and faced the police officers. "You seem to be in charge," he addressed the big detective. "I want to talk to you."

"Move aside, and let me have the prisoner," Slovik barked, advancing slowly, his gun leveled at the colonel.

The older man sighed. "I'm going to reach into my inside pocket, and I want you to look very carefully at what I'm going to show you, Detective." His lips smiled, but he didn't seem amused. "And, please, take that gun out of my face. It makes me nervous."

Slovik watched the colonel open his coat, but he kept his gun aimed. The colonel pulled something out of his pocket and flipped it open.

Peter knew what it was and suppressed a chuckle.

The badge was a fake.

"FBI?" Slovik shouted. It sounded almost like the challenging roar of some primeval predator. "First this woman. Now you! Who the hell is this guy? Some kind of foreign spy or terrorist?"

The colonel pocketed the badge and pulled out a piece of official looking paper. He waved it in front of the detective's eyes. "This man has immunity. The rest is classified information." Lowering his voice, he said confidentially, "It would be in your best interest if you forgot what happened here, Detective."

Turning to Peter, he said, "Come, we have work to do."

Peter followed him down the corridor. When he passed the big detective, he winked and said, "Tell your employer to watch for me. I'll be looking for him."

They picked up Peter's stuff at the front desk and walked out of the door. The colonel's car, a big shiny black Cadillac, was parked in front of the building. In a no-parking zone.

Peter smiled. The colonel hadn't changed in the last ten years. He sank into the passenger's seat and sighed.

He had tried, but it seemed, he couldn't outrun his past. It had finally caught up with him.

Gunning the powerful engine, Colonel Abraham Bender chuckled. "Well, Lieutenant McDiarmid, I told you a long time ago that your weakness for women would be your downfall some day."

Peter didn't say anything. He was watching the big sedan that had pulled out of the parking spot behind them.

There were two men inside. Two men with hats and dark glasses.

"We have a tail," he said.

The colonel nodded and smiled. "The old habits are coming back, aren't they?" he said. "Don't worry, that's one of ours."

They drove in silence for a while, moving in and out of traffic. The colonel seemed relaxed, but Peter wasn't. A sense of danger kept him alert. Like the colonel said, old habits never die. He remembered Stella's parting words. Trust no one.

"By the way, I am Peter Hartmann now. Lieutenant McDiarmid is dead, remember," he said.

Colonel Bender gave him a sidelong glance. "It doesn't matter now, you know. They will find out who you really are."

"Who's they?"

"The people you pissed off."

Peter laughed harshly. "There's only one party who has a right to be pissed off, and that's me."

"Obviously, many people don't see it that way." The older man shook a cigarette from a case and pushed it between his lips. Lighting it with the car's lighter, he took a couple of deep drags and offered the cigarette to Peter. When Peter shook his head, he crumpled it into the ashtray. "My doctor tells me to give it up. Tells me to chew gum instead. It's not easy." He chuckled. "I still have my own teeth. No telling what chewing gum will do to them. Maybe his son is a dentist. I don't trust doctors."

A few drops of rain spattered against the windshield. He turned on the wipers and cursed when streaks of wet dust obscured his vision. He slowed down and pulled over to the curb. The car behind them followed suit.

The colonel looked at Peter. "The police will be looking for you again. That detective may be slow, but he isn't stupid. By now, he's probably found out that there are no release papers for you. He'll be furious and looking for blood. You'll have to disappear for a while."

Peter studied the colonel's face. "Why are you doing this, sir?"

"I owe you, son. You saved my life back then. I am still alive because of you."

"I did my duty, sir, that's all. I may have saved you, but I couldn't save my partner, my best friend," Peter said bitterly. "Sometimes I wish it were me who had stayed behind."

"McAllister was as good as dead, Lieutenant." The colonel's voice had an edge to it. "You can't blame yourself for his death. Let it go."

"Someone blamed me. That's why I am who I'm now. A man stripped of his identity, honor, and now accused of murder. I have managed to build a good life for myself, and now you tell me I must give it up...again?" Peter never raised his voice, but he was filled with anger and bitterness.

"If you want to get out of this alive, you will follow my advice." Colonel Bender spoke gently. "This is my gift to you, Peter. I am doing this on my own. The Company has nothing to do with it."

"You are not a practicing attorney, right?" Peter stated. "You're still with the Company."

The older man smiled. "Like I said, nobody ever leaves, unless they die. As far as the Company is concerned, you are dead and buried. So stay buried." He sighed. "That business with the newspapers is bad, and someone is bound to start digging. We don't want that. The faster you disappear, the better for everyone concerned."

"We must save the government the embarrassment. Nobody must find out what we were involved in ten years ago," Peter said, his voice dripping sarcasm. "Don't worry, Colonel, I'm still a good patriot. I have no interest in digging up the past."

"Good." The colonel held out his hand. "Goodbye, Peter. Operative Lamber will take you to a safe place. Trust him, he's a good man."

Lamber wore a dark suit, dark hat, and dark shades. He couldn't have looked more obvious. Peter smiled as he followed him to his car. Heavy rain fell now, and Peter slid into the backseat, shaking water from his eyes.

The guy in the passenger seat could have been Lamber's twin. He nodded when Peter said, "Hi."

They took off, following the traffic for a while.

"This is Adam, my new partner," Lamber said. "He's okay."

After that, nobody spoke. The only sound was the swish…swish of the windshield wipers and the drumming of the raindrops.

Peter didn't feel relaxed. His uneasiness had increased. He noticed the lightness of traffic.

Suddenly, Adam broke the silence. "Make a right turn into the next back lane," he said to Lamber.

"Why?" Lamber asked.

"Just do it!" Adam spoke sharply.

Lamber made the turn. "What's going on?" he demanded.

The back lane was narrow, with tall dark buildings rising on either side.

Peter saw the gun in Adam's hand, aimed at Lamber's head.

"Stop the car, slowly," Adam ordered. Before the car even stopped moving, he added, "Sorry."

Peter heard the muffled sound of a gunshot, and old reflexes took over. His left hand shot out, clamped around the gun-hand, two stiff fingers jabbed into Adam's throat, opening up an artery. He hit once more with the edge of his right hand across the bridge of Adam's nose, hearing cartilage break with grim satisfaction.

He knew Adam was dead.

And so was Lamber. His head was a bloody mess.

"Shit!" Peter cursed. He didn't take Adam's gun with the silencer but took Lamber's instead. Then he checked Adam's inside pockets. He found a wallet and a thick envelope. Shoving the wallet into his pocket, he opened the envelope and wasn't surprised when he saw a wad of hundred-dollar-bills and a picture.

His face was on the picture..

A paid assassin!

Who wanted him dead? If not the Company…who then? Obviously, there was a security leak somewhere. How else would Agent Adam know his whereabouts?

That brought up another question. Who was Adam's real employer?

Peter rifled Lamber's pockets and found a couple of full clips for the gun.

Time to leave!

Outside, the rain had changed to a steady drizzle. It was wet and cold. Peter pulled up his collar and walked away from the car. He didn't see anyone else in the dark back lane and hoped nobody would remember seeing him.

Looking back once more, he rounded the corner to enter a busy street. There were a few pedestrians about, most of them young people. He stopped in front of a display window and looked at his reflection. He looked terrible, unshaven, his suit wet and crumpled. A homeless person presented a more favorable image.

He chuckled. Actually, that's what he was now…homeless person.

They were probably watching his house. He couldn't go back there. Neither could he go to his office.

Again, he looked at his reflection in the glass. He needed a place to clean up and a change of clothes.

Walking slowly down the sidewalk, he began looking for a motel, and found one not too far away. It looked like a fleabag, but it would have to do. The best place to hide out for a while.

Just as he was about to enter the place, he heard a car pull up. When he looked at the car, he saw a young, dark-haired woman in the driver's seat. She waved to him and opened the passenger door from the inside.

"Are you looking for a place to stay?" she asked. "Why not come with me." She spoke with a thick Hispanic accent.

Peter hesitated and looked at the car. An older model showing signs of rust. Then he shrugged. Why not? He slipped into the passenger seat and closed the door.

"How much is this going to cost me?" he asked, studying the woman.

She had smooth brown skin, thick black hair that spilled around her shoulders, and a pretty face. "Can you afford a hundred for the night?" she asked, smiling, "and twenty-five for a bath," she added.

"Good enough for me." Peter grinned.

She laughed and pulled away from the curb. "It's not far," she said. "Just down the block."

Her place was not fancy, but it was clean.

"You look like you could use something to eat," the woman said. "I'll fix you a sandwich while you take a shower."

"All right." Peter closed the bathroom door but didn't lock it. He stripped and stepped into the shower. The warm water felt good on his skin and slowly eased the tension out of his muscles.

What the hell had gone wrong?

A few days ago, he had a good job, a nice place, an expensive car, not to mention a woman he loved. Now it was all gone. Here he was…a fugitive, accused of murder, an uncertain future, and no place to run.

Life certainly was not sweet at the moment.

He dried off, looked for a razor, found one in a drawer. It even worked. After brushing his teeth, he felt much better. He hung his shirt and pants over the curtain rod to dry. Then he put on his briefs, draped his jacket over his arm, and walked out of the bathroom.

The woman turned to look at him and smiled. "Wow!" she exclaimed. "Talk about an improvement. I knew I'd find a prince underneath that stubble and those wet rumpled clothes." She looked him up and down. "I think I'll skip the food and go straight for the dessert."

Peter grinned. "Isn't that usually the guy's line?"

She came up to him and stroked his chest. "I'm not your usual-kind-of girl."

"Well, then let's find out," Peter said, threw his jacket onto the sofa and pulled her to him.

She came easily into his arms. Her mouth opened, and he kissed her. She felt warm and alive, and it was good to embrace another human being. She had slipped into a thin dress. When he lifted it up, he touched naked buttocks. With one hand, she pushed the straps over her shoulders. The dress slid down, pooled at her feet.

She was naked underneath.

Peter stepped back a little to look at her voluptuous figure, her full breasts, the flat stomach, and her round and firm buttocks.

Smiling, she put a hand on his briefs and pulled them down. "Oh, my," she murmured, getting down onto her knees.

Soft fingers encircled his already hard penis. Peter moaned as her lips closed over the swollen head, almost cried out when she began sucking. After a few moments, she set him free and pulled him toward the bedroom. "Come," she whispered.

In the semi-darkness, she gently pushed him onto the bed and straddled him. Her moist vagina closed over his aching member and took him deep inside.

He closed his eyes, enjoying her gentle fucking. She didn't seem in any hurry and neither was he. When she cried out, he grabbed her soft hips and pulled her down hard, feeling her warm discharge as she experienced her orgasm.

After her third climax, they changed positions. She lay with widespread legs, looking up at him. A mass of black hair covered her mound, and he could barely see her cleft. Taking his time, he probed her labia with his penis. He just pushed deep enough for his slippery head to be engulfed, moving it leisurely in and out.

She moaned and lifted up. He snapped his hips forward and slid deep into her. Their lovemaking became more furious, and when Peter finally exploded inside her, both of them were sweating profusely.

His hoarse shouts blended with her loud cries of pleasure. She dug her heels into his quivering buttocks as he lay between her soft thighs, pumping his liquid into her.

When it was over they didn't separate, just lay there gasping, embracing each other.

"Puta Madre," she finally whispered. "You sure needed a woman badly. Almost as much as I needed a man."

Chapter Twelve

Her name was Carmen Juanita Gonzales. She had just lost her job at the garment factory where she'd been working for seven years.

"The owner, Mr. Benito, he is the Diablo himself," Carmen said fiercely, her dark eyes blazing passionately. "Seven years I've been slaving there. Seven hard years, and now a computer replaces me. Mr. Benito doesn't care about people, only money."

Peter smiled and reached across the table to touch her hand. "That is the world we live in, Carmen. Money is all that seems to matter. Do you need money?"

"Of course I need money. Why do you think I picked you up? I said to myself: Carmen, what are you good at besides sewing clothes. Fucking, that's what I'm good at. And men pay a lot of money for a good fuck." She chuckled. "Not to mention that I like it."

She looked at him with her dark eyes. "You may not believe it, but you are actually the first customer. I mean you're not the first guy I screwed, but you're the first guy I did it with for money." She shrugged. "Let's face it, to be good at something you have to practice a lot. Right, muchacho?"

"I agree." Peter grinned. "You want to practice some more?"

Carmen laughed. "A little later. I am hungry." She took a bite from a sandwich. "You are very good at it. With your good looks…you make love to a lot of women, no?"

"I like to practice as much as possible. I love women, especially beautiful women like you." Peter said, smiling. "I don't usually pay for sex, but with you, I'll make an exception. I need more than sex."

He became serious. "I don't know anything about you, Carmen, but I don't think you're cut out for this type of business. First rule: Never bring a customer up to the place where you live. Do it in the car, in a motel room or at his place. Also, sooner or later, you'll pick up a customer who may want to harm you. You need someone to protect you. Usually that's a pimp, and that is not a good idea, either. You'll be a slave. He'll make all the money while you end up fucking for crumbs. For the rest of your life…that probably won't be very long."

Carmen lowered her eyes for a moment, and then she looked at him defiantly. "You don't think I don't know that? Tell me, what else can I do?"

"I am in a bit of a predicament myself," Peter said thoughtfully. "Maybe you can help me. I'll pay for your services."

"As long as it's nothing illegal."

"That's why you won't ask me any questions. The less you know, the safer you'll be."

Carmen looked suddenly scared and uncertain. "That doesn't sound too good to me. Are you in trouble with the law?"

Peter held up a hand. "No questions, remember? I'll pay you one thousand dollars on top of what we agreed upon. Okay?"

"A thousand bucks?" Carmen's eyes lit up. "Muchacho, for that kind of money, I'll make love to you all night…to you and your five brothers."

Peter laughed. "I don't even have one brother. Sorry. But I'm available for the night. Tomorrow we'll go shopping for some things, and tomorrow night I'll need your assistance. Don't worry. It's not dangerous. Do you have a telephone?"

"Right over there." Carmen pointed to a small table.

Peter got up to get his jacket from the sofa. When he lifted it, the gun clattered to the floor. Carmen looked at it but said nothing. Neither did Peter.

He found the card Stella had given him.

Stella answered after the second ring.

"Stella, this is Peter."

"Where the hell are you?" Stella's voice sounded upset. "They found Lamber and Adam. Both dead. What happened? Did you kill…?"

Peter cut her off. "I didn't kill Lamber. Listen, I don't have much time. Your line may be monitored. Be at the 'Half-Moon Disco' tomorrow night at around eight. Wait by the bar. Alone. See you."

He put down the receiver, saw Carmen watching him.

"You're meeting a woman?" she asked.

He nodded. "A woman who can possibly help me."

"What do you need me for? I'm not into kinky sex."

"No sex. You will meet her for me. She may be watched." Peter studied the woman, looking at her short dark hair. "We'll need that wig of beautiful long hair you wore when you picked me up. That and some other stuff."

"That's an expensive wig. I only wear it to special occasions."

"I'll pay you twice the money you paid for it."

"You must be very rich to throw around your money like that…or in deep shit."

"Very perceptive," Peter said. "I'm not rich."

Carmen chuckled. "In deep shit, then. Very deep." She opened her arms and walked up to him. "Looks like you and I are cousins under the skin. Come, let's make love until we drop."

They sat on the floor, facing each other. Peter stroked her breasts, while she gently rubbed his back. Looking into each other's eyes, they seemed like two lovers with not a problem in the world.

Her hand went down to touch his penis, milking it gently. Holding his hard member, she edged closer, guided it slowly into her. The position they were in didn't leave much room for movement. She contracted her inner muscles gently and relaxed them again in a slow, steady rhythm. Her vagina felt like a warm, tight fitting sheath around his penis.

He played with her brown thick nipples, cupped her full breasts, while studying her features. She had wide cheekbones, beautiful dark eyes, and full sensuous lips. When she smiled, she displayed white even teeth. Her brown skin felt smooth and flawless.

"You are beautiful," he said. "You deserve better."

She laughed. It made her breasts bob gently up and down. "Next you tell me I should be a movie star. I've heard that before. From Pedro Gomez. He makes porn-films."

"No, I mean it. If you really want to stay in the sex-business, I could get you in touch with a lady who runs an escort service. The women who work for her seem quite happy. There is also the potential for good money."

"Are you her agent?"

"No, just a satisfied customer."

"Customer?" Carmen stopped her slow movements. "You told me you never paid for sex."

"I don't. I was there only once. It was a freebee."

Carmen resumed squeezing him. "A freebee, huh?" Her breath caught in her throat as she experienced a small orgasm. She relaxed a little and smiled. "I can almost understand why. If I could afford it, I would pay you. You make me feel so good."

Peter grabbed her buttocks, lifted her a little higher, and then he rolled her onto her back, stretching out his legs. Her thighs opened wide as he began to move energetically between them.

She climaxed again a few moments later, this time much more intense. Her little cries of pleasure spurned him to greater efforts. As he rammed his rigid penis deep into her, Carmen began to rotate her body underneath him, lifting up every time he pushed down.

He pulled out, turned her around. She knelt on the carpet, her fleshy, round buttocks sticking up. Peter cupped her from behind, shoved his hard organ back into her creamy pussy. Grabbing her wide hips to steady himself, he knelt behind her and fucked her in that position for a long time. Once in a while he would let his hands wander to hold her swinging breasts, and then he took hold of her shoulders and watched her arching back as he made her whimper with delight.

After a while they moved back into the bedroom, and he let her ride him until he finally came inside her with tremendous force.

Her eyes were closed and her mouth wide open, emitting little mewling sounds, as she doused him with her own fluid. He lunged up one more time, held her hips to press her deep into his lap. Then it was over.

She collapsed on top of him and lay in his arms until her breathing came back to normal. They both got up to take a shower together. In the shower, they explored each other's bodies, but neither had any strength left for another session.

* * * *

...They were young and lovely, swaying with sinuous movements and dancing around the three young soldiers. Images of snakes and scaly dragons were painted in iridescent colors on their slender, graceful bodies, covering them completely.

Their slanted black eyes glittered, their undulating lower bodies teasing the watching men.

"Isn't this great, Peter?" One of the young men whispered and slapped his friend's thigh. "I think I'll fuck each one of them. Aren't they just beautiful?"

Peter laughed. "They are beautiful. But you won't fuck them, Donald McAllister. I will." He reached for one of the dancing girls. She eluded his grasp, swayed away into the third soldier's arms. She landed in his lap.

The girl sat facing him, straddling his legs. In the dim light of the flickering oil lamps, Peter could only guess what her hands were doing, but when he saw her naked buttocks lift up and slowly sink down again, he knew.

A deep moan from the soldier confirmed it. The girl was fucking him.

Peter took another drink from the small porcelain cup. Rice-wine. He didn't really care for it, but that's all they offered.

A soft warm body pressed against him from the back. He twisted around and put his arms around the slim waist. His tongue licked the flat belly, traveled lower.

She let it happen. Then she pulled him into another room toward a cot and fell onto it, her slim legs open, inviting.

He didn't need any encouragement. His hard pole slid easily into her. She gave a little cry, moving beneath him.

He fucked her for a long time, until she finally put her small hands on his chest to push him off. Disappointed, he pulled out, still erect.

She slipped away, but another girl replaced her. The girl smiled, her painted arms reaching up. Crouching on top of her, he touched her small breasts and kneaded them gently. She moaned, touched his penis, and began massaging the swollen glans with two fingers.

Almost exploding, he rolled between her widespread thighs, found her moist opening, and entered warm softness. Climaxing inside her undulating belly, he never stopped moving. She came with a series of little shrieks.

There were three or four more girls after her. He didn't count. As he lay on his back, the girls took turns riding him. All of them were beautiful, young, and slender. Like many Asian girls, they had small breasts, but he didn't care. Their pussies were hot and tight, and they all used them expertly.

As one girl moved above him, the others danced and swayed around them, their painted bodies gleaming in the flickering light. They were chanting, but he didn't understand their language…

* * * *

Hearing a sudden noise, Peter sat up and opened his eyes. The room lay in semi-darkness, silent, except for the gentle snoring of a woman beside him. Momentarily disoriented, he realized where he was.

In a strange bed with a strange woman.

Carmen.

He lay silent for a while, staring at the ceiling.

That recurring dream again, but he knew it wasn't really a dream, more like reliving something that happened a long time ago. Twenty-one years, to be exact.

He had been twenty, on special assignment in Saigon. The place he dreamed of…a brothel.

He went back to sleep.

Back to his dream…

* * * *

…Her face was covered with a dark, silky cloth. Only her eyes were visible, black, and shiny. She stood there like a vision, the moon large and bright behind her, silhouetting her slender lovely form.

She came to him, slowly, hesitating, as a blushing bride comes to her lover for the first time.

"She's a virgin," the woman who ran the brothel told him. "We've kept her for you. You are the one they call Cobra. Your friends told me. Her name is Serpa. She is my daughter. You are the Chosen One. It has been foretold."

The other girls were hiding in the shadows of the tall shrubs, which grew profusely in the garden, watching with eager eyes. Waiting for him to fulfill the prophecy.

They were members of a secret cult. The Sisterhood of the Cobra.

The prophecy told of a man from a far country, a man of great sexual prowess with the mark of the Cobra on his body.

He didn't believe in that mumbo-jumbo. He only saw a beautiful young woman. A virgin. Ready and eager to be fucked by him, So he went along with them, played their game. The fact that they'd be watching didn't bother him.

Had he not screwed them all before?

They gave him a ceremonial drink. A cup of rice wine, but he suspected that cup contained more than just wine. His head felt light; his skin tingled. His loins seemed to be on fire, and between his legs, his penis stood like a rod of iron.

Grinning, he opened his arms. "Come here, my little snake, let The Cobra embrace you," he said, laughing.

The young woman stood in front of him now. She was quite tall, the top of her head even with his eyes. She looked at him, black eyes glittering, but only for a moment, and then, demurely, she lowered her long lashes. Her hands touched his muscular chest, traveled down his belly. Her fingers curled around his erection.

Groaning, he lifted her silken mask, wanting to kiss her, but she shook her head, moved her face away from him. Then she let go of him, stepped back and knelt down. Her hands touched him again.

He watched as she moved her head closer. Her long black hair spilled forward, obscuring his view, but he felt her soft lips encircle his swollen glans. Her mouth opened, and then her teeth grazed the head of his penis.

He slid in deeper, ready to explode.

She may be a virgin, but she sure knows how to give head.

After a while, she released him and looked up at him. Then she stood up, took his hand, and led him toward a narrow bench. She lay down on it, her legs spread wide.

In the bright light of the moon, her body sparkled with shimmering colors. The paintings of serpents and flying dragons seemed to be alive, as the shadows of tree branches played across them.

She was a goddess and he was a god.

Even though he was bursting with desire, he stood there, drinking in her unearthly beauty.

Time stood still for a moment.

Then the moment was gone.

Grunting, he moved on top of her, between her open, inviting thighs. His hand touched her swollen mons, his finger found the slit, rubbed her clitoris. With a sudden forceful thrust he entered her, encountered a moment of resistance, and then he slid inside.

He heard her cry out softly as he took her virginity, hesitated, then began to move inside her. She was extremely tight and it took all of his willpower not to come immediately, but he was an experienced lover, knew how to prolong the act.

It didn't take long until she cried out again, but he knew he didn't cause her any pain.

He heard chanting. When he looked up, he saw writhing painted bodies swaying all around them, just like the night before.

However, this time there was a difference.

None interfered with him and the woman underneath him. She was the only one he made love to. How long he plunged between her soft thighs, he didn't know. It seemed like an eternity.

When his climax finally came, he reached a high he had never experienced before. The fire spread from his loins through his entire body, and the force of his eruption seemed like the spewing of a volcano. It left him empty and spent.

Collapsing into the woman's arms, he lay there panting for a long time. When he stirred again, he was alone with her. She pushed him off with gentle hands. He watched her walk away, into the shrubbery.

He sat staring into emptiness and never saw the three men approaching stealthily from the trees. Only when the faint shadow of one of them fell across his feet, did he look up.

"You will die, American pig!" said a harsh voice.

Only instinct and fast reflexes saved Peter from certain death. The thud of a machete biting into wood brought him back to his senses.

Swift and angry, he struck back, like the cobra he was supposed to represent, but his stiff fingers encountered emptiness. He dropped, rolled away from the shadow following him. Kicking out with one leg, he made contact, but not hard enough.

His opponent moved back, stood bathed by pale moonlight.

He was tall and wiry, his upper torso naked. Peter noted the bulging muscles of chest and biceps.

The rays from the moon glinted like fire in the black slanted eyes. "She was promised to me," the man hissed, pointing an accusing finger at Peter. "And you spoiled her!"

Peter looked for the man's accomplices, but they stood aside, merely watching. He shrugged. "Sorry, man. I didn't know. What's so special about her anyway? She's only another whore."

"She is now!" roared his accuser. The moonlight fell across his mask of a face, contorted with rage.

Peter tried to judge the man's age and figured him to be close to his own.

"She is Serpa, the Virgin-goddess of the Cobra," the man said. "And I am Scorpion."

Only then did Peter see the tattoo of a scorpion on the man's chest. "Is that supposed to mean something?" he asked, still watching the other two, but they didn't move. He had subconsciously fallen into the stance of the striking cobra.

They called him Cobra for a reason.

Suddenly, the whole situation struck him as quite comical. The Cobra and the Scorpion. Fighting over some girl. The Virgin-goddess. He felt like an actor in a Grade-B-movie. "I am the Cobra," he said, grinning.

The man who called himself Scorpion hissed and attacked.

Peter was ready, moved before his attacker could reach him. He was confident in his abilities but soon realized that he had met a worthy and dangerous opponent.

They circled each other like two graceful dancers, attacked and counter-attacked, each using a deadly form of martial arts.

Any other time Peter would have had no problem defeating his foe, but he was tired from the sexual encounter and the drug in the wine began to take its toll.

A strike to the left of his head made him dizzy for a moment, a foot in the chest sent him staggering backward. His reflexes were slowing; he felt the strength leave his body. Another blow and he found himself on his back, staring into a pair of black, deadly eyes, waited for the clawed hand to rip open his jugular.

Then he blacked out.

When he came to, he lay on a hard cot, felt gentle fingers massaging his chest. He tried to sit up, but a soft hand pushed him back down.

"Relax, you've been injured. You're lucky, it's not serious, just ugly bruises."

He recognized the soothing voice as that of the older woman. Serpa's mother.

"What happened?" Peter croaked, wishing for a drink.

"Your friends came," she said. "Without them, you may be dead. I'm sorry this happened to you."

"Where is that other guy? He called himself Scorpion. Who is he?"

"He belongs to the Order of the Scorpion. They are criminals. They extort money from us for protection. His father is the big boss. He thinks we belong to him."

"Why do you pay them?"

"These people are ruthless. They'd kill me." The woman sighed. "That is just the way it is."

"Can't you go to the police?"

"The police?" She laughed. "This is Saigon, not America, my young innocent friend. I'm a whore, not a businesswoman. Who cares about whores?"

Peter stayed silent, studying the woman's face. The single light bulb hanging from the ceiling threw enough light for him to see her exquisite features. He lifted a hand, touched her face, and traced the outlines of her full lips with his finger.

"I never saw your daughter's face," he said, "but if she is only half as beautiful as you then I was indeed lucky to have been the one to take her virginity."

The woman smiled.

"She was the lucky one. You may scoff at our beliefs, but your coming here has been foretold. You have the Mark of the Cobra on your arm. I knew you were the one when I saw it, and your sexual powers proved it."

Peter looked at the tattoo on his right arm. A coiled cobra wrapped around his arm with the head resting on his wrist. "I had this done after I began studying martial arts. I use the movements of the cobra in my disciplines. There is nothing mystical about it."

"You may not think so," she said, stroking his arm.

He reached up with his other hand and touched her breast. Then he slid a hand into her kimono.

She was naked underneath. Gently, he began massaging her breast.

She sighed and moaned. A quiet, almost lonely sound. "You want to make love to me?" she asked with a low voice. "I could be your mother."

He chuckled. "I've had women probably older than you."

"Really?" She smiled. "I am thirty-five years old."

"Old enough," he said, grinning, and put his hand behind her neck to pull her down.

"Let me take this off first," she whispered, slipping out of her kimono.

Peter stared at her slim beautiful body, the narrow waist, the flaring hips. Below her flat belly, dense black hair covered her mons. Then he stared at the tattoo of a coiled cobra on her full left breast. It was almost identical in style to the one Peter had on his arm.

She smiled when she saw him looking at it. "Now you do believe?" She lay down beside him, laughed when his penis rose to her touch. Then she was on top of him, her soft breasts pressing against his chest.

Her legs parted and he slid into warm, soft moistness. When he pushed against her, she brushed his lips with hers.

"Don't move." she whispered. "Let me."

She began to fuck with an expertise Peter had never encountered before. She moved her body in ways he didn't know existed. Her vagina seemed alive, a living entity between her legs. It vibrated and rippled the length of his penis, constricting gently until he thought his penis would be strangled in the gentle vice, and then the pressure was gone.

Twisting and undulating above him with sinuous grace, like a giant snake, she should have been called Queen Cobra. What he used in his martial arts, she used in her lovemaking.

The movements of the cobra.

As they moved in perfect unison, Peter cried out, "If there was a chosen one it was you, not your daughter. You and I are one."

When he thought he would climax, she did something to the root of his penis, keeping him from coming, but letting him experience a powerful climax.

She swayed above him, her black slanted eyes boring into his, her face contorted, but more beautiful than ever. Suddenly, she laughed and increased the speed of her rotating bottom.

"Come now!" she cried suddenly.

The pressure had been building inside him, and he didn't need any encouragement. He let go and roared as the heat spread from his loins through his entire body.

Her vagina squeezed and sucked to the rhythm of his spurts.

When he finally stopped ejaculating, his skin tingled and he could still feel the gentle pulsing of her vagina, like a hot satin glove around his semi-erect penis.

Smiling, she stretched out on top of him, her lips parted, pressed against his. He opened his mouth; let her tongue enter. Still inside her living vagina, he felt his penis go rigid. Putting his arms around her, he rolled her onto her back. She pulled up her knees and opened her thighs wider. He began to move between them, pushing deep into her with every thrust.

She moved against him, her warm body writhing underneath him.

They stayed like that for an eternity. Again, he felt the pressure rising, and when he came inside her, it happened with great explosive force.

Breaking apart, they lay gasping for air. She cradled him in her warm arms and soft thighs, his face nestled between her breasts.

"I've made love to a lot of women," he said after a while. "Some of them quite experienced, but never have I met anyone like you."

She chuckled softly. "I come from a long line of courtesans. My mother taught me everything I know."

"Maybe I should make love to your mother." Peter grinned. "She must be quite a lady."

"She was." The woman sighed. "She's dead. She was killed two years ago in a plane crash."

"I'm sorry to hear that." Peter lifted up and rolled onto his back to lie beside her. "Where did you learn such good English?"

"I grew up in America, in Washington. My father was a diplomat. My mother and I moved to Saigon after my father died. I was seventeen years old."

He turned to look at her…

* * * *

…One moment he looked into a face with black, slanted eyes, the next it was the face of a Hispanic woman. Still beautiful, but different.

Her eyes were closed.

He closed his own eyes again, tried to bring back the dream, but it faded away, like fog into a dense forest.

Chapter Thirteen

He went to the bathroom and when he came back, he saw Carmen sitting up, rubbing her eyes. She looked at him and smiled. "I'm exhausted," she said, "but I feel good. No man has ever made me feel that way, and I thank you for it. Now I guess I had better make you some breakfast. You said you had a busy day ahead."

She slipped from the bed and padded toward the bathroom. Peter watched the sensuous play of her nude brown buttocks and sighed, admiring her graceful beauty…the proud way she moved, the way she held up her head, her narrow waist, her flaring hips, and her round, solid buttocks. He drank her beauty the way a thirsty man would pour down a delicious drink.

He could never get enough. It wasn't just the sex. It was the warm soft body pressing against him, the smell, the passion, the pressure of warm thighs against his hips, the tight, moist softness when he slid into a welcoming vagina. It was the hot breath, the moans and cries of pleasure, the ecstatic moment of a woman's orgasm. His own release and the love he felt for her at that moment.

He needed that and loved it more than life itself.

That was his vice.

Peter waited for Carmen to come out of the bathroom. She was still naked when she did. Again, he feasted his eyes on her beautiful face, the firmness of her breasts, her taut, flat belly, and the black triangle covering her feminine mound. Her legs were long and shapely and she walked with the grace of a ballet dancer.

"Do you work out?" he asked, watching her wiggle into a pair of lacey panties.

She seemed somewhat startled by his question, but then she laughed. "Work out? No, why do you ask?"

He shrugged. "You have such a shapely body. I'm just wondering."

"You're sweet. I used to do ballroom dancing. You know...rumba, samba, tango...all those Latin-American dances. They give you a good workout." She forced herself into a pair of tight-fitting jeans and looked up. "Aren't you going to get dressed? You make me feel uncomfortable looking at me like that."

"I'm sorry," Peter apologized, "but you look so delicious."

Carmen laughed. "Don't get any ideas. I'm finished for the day. You'll wear me out. To be honest, I am a little sore." She pulled a sweater over her head.

Peter watched sadly as her breasts disappeared inside the loose-fitting folds and sighed. "Well, I guess, that's it then. I think I'll take a shower."

"Make it a cold one." Carmen laughed and looked at his semi-erect penis.

When he came out of the shower, Carmen had fried up some eggs and bacon. "You need a hearty breakfast," she said, chuckling.

After breakfast, Peter explained his plan to Carmen. Then they went shopping.

When Peter gave Carmen the money he promised her, she put it under her mattress.

"Aren't you afraid someone might break in and steal it?" Peter asked.

Carmen laughed. "In this neighborhood? I feel quite safe. Nobody around here has enough money to make it worthwhile breaking into a place."

Peter shrugged. "You can never be too careful."

* * * *

After driving for over half an hour to the Half-Moon Disco, they parked Carmen's car a block away from it. Carmen gave Peter a long hug and a kiss. Before she released him, she whispered, "Adios, amigo. Good luck."

They walked into the disco together, into the blaring noise from over-sized speakers and the flashing lights washing over the throng of dancing men and women. Pushing through the crowd, Peter searched for a table close to the bar and managed to find a couple of empty seats. Looking around, he spotted Stella immediately sitting on a barstool. He pointed her out to Carmen.

Carmen gave him a curt nod, got up and headed for the ladies' room. Peter's eyes followed her as she walked away, gorgeous in her long black wig, tight red short dress and her black high leather boots. The purse she carried looked a bit bulky and large, but it wasn't too obvious.

When she was out of sight, Peter waved over a waitress. "You want to make a quick twenty bucks?" he asked, chuckled when she gave him a startled, almost angry look, but then she smiled. "With your looks, you can get just about any girl for free."

"Maybe I don't want just any girl," Peter teased, handing her an envelope and a folded twenty-dollar bill. "Give this note to that lady at the bar over there. But please, be discreet. Okay?"

The girl gave him another inquiring look, and then she headed for the bar. Peter got up and left, his destination the hotel across the street. He booked a room under the name of Jerry Smith. "My wife will be arriving in a few minutes," he told the attendant. "She'll be asking for me. Anyone else, tell them you've never heard of me, all right?"

The attendant looked at him with a knowing smile. "Sure, Mr. Smith."

Peter slipped him ten bucks and went up to his room.

The expected knock on his door came about fifteen minutes later. He opened up, and Stella walked in.

She looked just as delicious in the tight red dress and long black hair as Carmen. She took off the dark glasses, threw them on the table, and flopped onto the bed. "Take these damn boots off my feet," she said. "They're killing me. How can any girl have such small feet?"

Peter chuckled and began pulling at the boots. "They are tight," he said, laughing. "Maybe you just have large feet. Ever think of that?"

"Oh, you!" Stella pouted. She had pulled up the already short dress to reveal the whole length of her thighs. Now she spread them slightly.

Peter stared at the dark, fuzzy triangle.

"You're not wearing any panties," he stated the obvious.

"They would have shown in this tight dress," Stella said tersely. "Your new girlfriend never wore any either." Then she smiled and pulled up her legs.

Peter pushed down his pants, freed his straining member, and moved between those inviting spread thighs. Stella lay back, lifted up, and let him enter her. "Hello to you, too," she gasped. "I was worried about you, you big lug. What happened?"

"Later," he grunted. "Let's finish saying hello first."

She must have needed it badly, because it didn't take long for her to have her first orgasm. Peter let her down from her high, and then he pulled out and stripped off his clothes.

Stella slipped out of her dress.

Naked, they looked at each other, Stella enjoying Peter's muscular physique and Peter delighting in Stella's soft, sensuous body. She lifted her arms, making her breasts jiggle. Peter moaned and moved into her embrace, kissing her gently at first, and then he returned her demanding kisses fiercely. Her hand moved between them, took his searching hard penis and guided it back into her creamy, hungry love channel.

He moved with steady, strong strokes between her soft thighs. She pulled them higher until her legs were almost draped over his shoulders. This position allowed Peter to enter her more deeply and, grunting, he pushed his massive organ as far as possible into her sucking, deliciously soft love box.

His climax came with tremendous force and mind numbing pleasure. Shouting hoarsely, he emptied his gift into her receiving vessel, only vaguely aware that Stella also experienced her own earth shattering orgasm.

She relaxed her legs and let them fall open. "Wow!" she exclaimed after her breathing returned to normal. "You certainly know how to carry a girl to new heights."

Peter grinned weakly. "And you know how to make a guy reach those heights. You can't fly without an airplane."

Stella laughed. "I suppose I'm the airplane. Thanks, Mister."

Peter kissed her. "One of the best airplanes I've ever flown."

"Of which there are many." Stella smiled and stroked his cheek. "I guess there is a compliment in there somewhere."

"I guess." Peter rolled away from her, sat up and looked at the door. "You weren't followed, I hope," he said, staring at Stella's spread legs.

She's very supple, he thought, fleeting glimpses of different possible positions with her flashing through his mind.

Stella saw him staring, frowned and, suddenly self-conscious, brought her knees together.

He put his hand between her legs and touched the swollen mound of her femininity. She smiled. "Haven't you had enough?" she asked.

He shook his head. "I never have enough. I'm always horny, and you look so delicious." He bent to take one of her nipples into his mouth, teased it with his teeth. With one hand, he stroked her clitoris and with the other, he gently squeezed her breast.

"You're an oversexed bastard," she whispered, her breath catching in her throat. She pushed him away. He rolled onto his back. Stella followed and straddled him. Then she turned around.

Peter stared at her white buttocks as she mounted him, saw and felt his hard penis slip into her moist pussy. She moved slowly up and down, impaling herself again and again on his shaft. Her buttocks clenched tightly together every time she lifted up, spread again as she flattened them against his taut belly.

Peter watched in fascination. She still wore the wig, the long black hair spilling down past her shoulder blades. He reached up to take her breasts into his hands, squeezed them gently. Stella moaned and began to move faster. Then she stopped moving and sat quivering in his lap. He felt her strong, warm discharge.

She lifted up, grabbed a pillow and lay on top of it, face down. The pillow elevated her hips, making her buttocks stick up.

Peter lay on top of her, entered her from behind. Another position that allowed him to enter her deeply. He moved slowly in and out of her, supporting his weight on his elbows. He liked the feel of her soft buttocks digging into his groin.

They made love like this slowly for a long time. Then he put her on her back again and together they reached another mind-blowing climax.

"I can't anymore," Stella finally gasped. "I hope you are satisfied. Had I known this I would have brought along my sister."

Peter chuckled. "Ah, Mirabelle. I remember her. Quite a little dish. She was really your sister?"

"She really was and still is." Stella smiled. "And quite a nympho, I might add."

Peter laughed. "Just like her big sister, and don't you deny it. You love sex as much as I do."

Stella pushed against him. "I don't deny it, but you are getting heavy, lover."

Peter rested the weight of his upper body on his elbows, but his lower half was still cradled between Stella's soft, strong thighs. She squeezed them together, pressing them into his hips, and then she opened them.

"Come on," she said, "be a good boy and pull out."

Peter sighed and pulled his semi-erect penis out of her. Then he rolled over onto this back.

Stella looked at his member. "You're incredible," she said, shaking her head. "I should have brought Mirabelle." She lay silent for a while, her gaze on Peter's face. "I'm supposed to bring you in," she said finally.

"Who ordered you?" Peter asked.

"Orders came from the top." Her gray-blue eyes searched his. "You told me that you didn't kill Lamber. How about Adam?"

"Somebody put a price on my head. He killed Lamber in cold blood. Adam deserved to die."

"You're cold, too, Peter McDiarmid. Do you also deserve to die?" Stella's voice was level, without emotion.

Peter didn't blink. "So you dug around in my past. What else did you find aside from my real name?"

"Not much but enough. Information about you is deeply buried and hard to find. I know that you worked for The Company, Special Ops. What exactly you did I don't know, but I can guess."

"Guess."

"There is always some dirty work the government needs done, stuff the general public never hears about."

"Like what?" His voice sounded flat, bored.

Stella shrugged. "Getting rid of political trouble makers, for instance, here at home or maybe in a foreign country. Or supply weapons to rebels, perhaps a missile or two. Need I say more?"

"You think that is what I did?" Peter asked.

"I didn't say that at all. I'm only guessing. By the way, you look quite alive for a person who is supposed to be dead."

"You're walking on dangerous ground," Peter said softly, his hand suddenly around her throat, his fingers and thumb digging into tender flesh. "I could kill you just like that."

Her eyes grew large. "I know but you won't," she whispered, her body trembling slightly.

"No," he said. "I won't. Ten years ago I would have, but not now."

"Why not now?" Stella rubbed her throat.

"Because now I am Peter Hartmann, not Peter McDiarmid. McDiarmid died ten years ago. By the way, what made you decide to dig up my past?" He looked thoughtful. "You couldn't have found out all this in a couple of days. Did you check up on me after our encounter at that party? Somehow I can't believe I made that much of an impression on you."

Stella smiled. "Your sexual prowess did impress me, but I already knew about you long before that."

"How?"

"I am a Special Investigator. A few months ago, Rhonda Liebman came to us. She suspected that her husband was engaged in illegal activities. She confronted him with her suspicions, and ever since then she was afraid for her life. There were a couple of other companies involved, Beta Research Inc. and Computer Regeneration Development. Your company."

"Interesting," Peter remarked. "How does that involve me?"

"It was just part of the process to have you investigated. After all, you are one of the top reps. When I discovered Peter Hartmann didn't exist ten years ago, I became interested. I took your fingerprints, don't ask me how I got them, and ran them through our computer base. I discovered an identical set belonging to a Peter McDiarmid. Nobody special, actually. College, army, the usual, but then suddenly the information was classified.

"When I reported my findings I was told to leave it alone. I did. When I met you at that party, I didn't know you were the Peter Hartmann I had been investigating. You never told me your name."

She smiled. "I didn't really care who you were. I only wanted to get laid." She became serious. "Then I saw your picture in the paper and I became intrigued. A friend of mine, who is somewhat of a hacker, managed to get into your file…and what a file it is. I wasn't guessing about your activities with the Company, as you probably suspected."

"Who else knows?" Peter asked, looking at the ceiling. He acted distant, almost uninterested, but the muscles of his jaws tightened.

"Except for the people who knew you from before, just me," she answered.

"As far as you know." Peter turned his head. "Obviously, someone wants me dead. I don't know why, or who, but I will find out. And you will help me."

Stella sat up and looked down at him. "How can I help you? I'm supposed to bring you in. If I fail to do that, they'll be watching me."

"Who?"

"Whoever is after you, damn it! I don't know." Stella got out of bed. Peter watched her open the large bag Carmen had given her. She pulled out a pair of panties, a bra, jeans, and a thin sweater. She dressed under Peter's watchful eyes.

"You're beautiful," he said in a soft voice.

Stella stared at him, startled. "What?"

"I said you're beautiful…and very sexy."

"And you're impossible," she said, throwing up her hands. "Is that all you see in me? A beautiful, sexy woman?"

"It is the truth, but as I told you before, I also admire your mind." Peter smiled. "You're an investigator, right?"

"You bet!" Stella glared at him. "I'm very good at my job."

"Even though you're a little oversexed."

"Touché." Stella threw a pillow at him and then sat down at the edge of the bed. "What do you want me to do?"

"I'll have to get to a computer terminal, and I'll need your access code."

"You got it. We can go to a library." She looked at Peter's wristwatch. "What time is it?"

"Ten forty-five, in the evening," Peter answered.

"Ten forty-five?" Stella repeated. "Why did I bother to get dressed?"

Peter shrugged and grinned. "I asked myself that same question. But I enjoyed the action."

Chapter Fourteen

Peter rifled through the wallet he had taken from the dead agent. "Roy Adam," he said. "According to this license, he worked for the Sanitation Department. Special Investigations. It figures, considering the dirty work he was involved in." He glanced at Stella, who sat beside him. "Twenty-five thousand bucks, that's what they paid him. I thought I was worth more than that. Can you get me into the City's personnel files?"

Stella nodded, working the keyboard. She was fast. Peter nodded with approval.

"I'm in," she said. "Adam's name is the second one. There are numbers and letters beside his name.'"

"Code," Peter said. "I recognize it. He was on the Agency's payroll."

It didn't take Stella long to bring up the screen and find Adam's file.

Peter looked at her with admiration. "That hacker friend of yours…is you, right?"

Stella didn't comment, just smiled faintly. "It seems he's been with the Company for six years. Look at this…he was put on special assignment three days ago. He transferred from another department."

"The Company," Peter said. "Lamber introduced Adam as his new partner. Who signed the transfer?"

"Edward Shaw, Colonel Edward Shaw."

"That son-of-a-bitch!" Peter hissed. "He used to be DEA. Never liked him."

"I suppose he hates you," Stella stated.

"You bet your cute little ass, and the feeling is mutual. So, now he's a colonel and works for the Agency." Peter kept his voice low and calm, but his eyes showed his suppressed anger. "That man is dangerous. He is cunning, smart, without scruples, and carries grudges forever. You don't want to cross him."

Stella closed the screen. "We'd better move. By now, they know someone's been snooping. They won't know who, I've covered my tracks well, but they'll still able to trace it to this location."

She drove him back to the hotel. "I have to check in at the office."

"What will you report?"

She shrugged. "You never showed."

He gave her a quick kiss. "Be careful."

* * * *

Back in the hotel room, Peter phoned his residence. Kathleen wasn't there. Retrieving his messages from his answering machine, he heard a disturbing message but didn't recognize the voice.

Peter Hartmann, this message is for you. We have your girlfriend. Meet us at Connie's and bring the item you took at the Liebman residence. You better be there, Hartmann. We mean business. You have forty-eight hours.

The message was nearly twenty-four hours old.

He phoned Connie.

"I have a message to meet some people at your place," he said, without introducing himself.

"Hi, Peter. How are you?"

"Do you really care how I am? Let's cut the bullshit. Who are these people, and how are you involved?"

"Whoa, Peter, what language," Connie said. "Doesn't sound like you at all. I have nothing to do with this whole thing, except as a mediator. I will let them know you called. Can you make it about seven o'clock tonight?"

"I'll be there." Peter hung up. He was disappointed. Somehow, he had not expected Connie to be part of this. How much of a part, he didn't know. Her sister Sue Lin was also suspect.

How about Kathleen? He shook his head. No, she wouldn't be involved, somehow he would have known. She wasn't the type.

He looked at his watch. Almost noon. He had the whole afternoon to do…what? Nothing. There was nothing to do but wait until evening. Hiding like a scared rabbit from the hunters.

This was not like him. He wasn't a rabbit. He was a hunter.

There had to be something he could do, facts he needed to sort out.

Stella. Did he trust her? Not completely, but he didn't have much choice.

Colonel Bender? Maybe. He was a Company-man, and he would always put the Company above everything else. If that meant sacrificing someone, he wouldn't hesitate. But then again, Peter had been his protégé. Back in the Service, Peter had trusted him with his life.

Shaking his head, Peter dismissed the Colonel as a suspect. He might even be his strongest ally. Going through his pockets, he found the Colonel's number.

A woman answered.

"Is Colonel Bender there?" Peter asked.

"May I ask who's calling?"

"Peter McDiarmid," he said on an impulse.

"Just a moment, Mr. McDiarmid, I'll see if he can take your call." The woman's voice sounded pleasant, business-like.

"Peter." The Colonel didn't sound surprised. "You're alive. I expected your call sooner."

"I was occupied with other business, sir," Peter said, "like trying to find out who wants to kill me. You should screen your men more carefully, sir."

"I'm sorry about that." Colonel Bender seemed sincere. "Lamber was a good man. I didn't know about Adam, he had just been transferred to us."

"From the Agency. I know." Peter smiled when there was a pause on the other end.

"I won't ask you how you know," the Colonel said, "but I can guess. I'll find out who's responsible."

"You mean who transferred him?" Peter hesitated, but decided he had nothing to loose. "Ask Colonel Edward Shaw. He can tell you."

Another pause, then, "I'm not surprised. But I can't discuss this over the phone. Where are you?"

Peter chuckled. "By now I've probably been made, but I won't be here. I'll be in touch." He put down the receiver. Looking around the room, he became aware of the silence. The room was furnished with a small table, a dresser, and a double bed. The maid had made the bed while he was out. Even though he had paid for another night, the time had come to move out.

Checking the gun he had taken from Lamber, he shoved it back into his belt. The clip was full, and he had a couple more clips in his pocket. Buttoning up his jacket, he threw the key onto the table and closed the door without locking it.

Nodding to the desk clerk, he walked out the door. He walked slowly, looking for a place to eat. Spotting a small diner in a side street, he decided it would do.

The place looked clean, and when he opened the door, the smell of homemade soup and freshly brewed coffee tantalized his taste buds. Out of habit, he chose a table in a corner, where he could observe the entrance.

Not that he expected anyone to come barging in. Nobody really knew where he was, but he had left the relaxed and peaceful world of the ordinary man and entered once again the ugly and violent environment he left behind so many years ago.

He watched a young couple at one of the tables. So happy and carefree. Envisioning them making out in the backseat of a car, Peter smiled, remembering his own youth before he joined the Service. Just like these two, he didn't have any idea how ugly this world could get at any moment. They were ignorant of what went on around them, what certain levels of government did at home and abroad. Not many people knew, not those two, not the older couple or the young woman at one of the other tables, not the old man next to them, nor the waitress who brought his order.

He sighed and downed his beer.

Fuck it all!

He was almost finished with his meal, when the door opened, and three men entered the diner. One of them was older, dressed casually in a gray business suit, the other two younger, a little grubby looking. Both wore long, black coats.

Peter casually moved his hand under the table, pulled out his gun and removed the safety. His left hand held the empty glass.

One of the young men began closing the blinds on the windows. The other one locked the door and put up the Closed sign. Then he turned around and, grinning widely, pulled out a submachine gun from the folds of his coat. Peter recognized it. A Micro UZI, made in Israel, capable of firing twelve-hundred-fifty rounds per minute. Luckily, the magazine only held twenty. Enough to kill everyone in this room. He also saw the silencer.

"Ladies and gentlemen, may I have your attention, please." The young man laughed and turned to the older man. "I always wanted to say that."

The other man smiled thinly. "Get on with it!" He spoke with a strong, southern accent. "And point that thing away from me, you moron."

"Right, boss. Whatever you say." The younger man turned his attention back to the people in the room. "This is a stick-up, but I guess you figured that out by now. My buddy Vic is going to come to your table. You will give him your wallets and any other valuables you may be carrying."

The one called Vic finished closing all the blinds. Grinning like his friend, he approached the table with the older couple and the young woman. "You heard my good buddy Marc," he said with a somewhat nasal voice. He rifled through the wallet the man handed him, pulled out some bills, the rest he threw on the floor. "That's all you've got, old man?" he cursed. "A lousy sixty-five bucks?"

"That's all I have," the older man said, a slight tremor in his voice. "Take it or leave it, you filthy bandit!"

Vic backhanded the old man, leaving an angry red mark on the man's cheek. "Shut up, you old fool!" Then he laughed. "I'll take it." He grabbed the older woman's purse, emptied its contents. Lipstick, some pillboxes, and a few coins clattered onto the tabletop. "Fucking shit!" he cursed. "There's not even enough money here for a fucking hamburger."

"Get her ring, you idiot!" Marc called to him. "I can see those diamonds from here."

The old woman cried out when Vic reached for her hand. "Please, not my ring," she whined. "It's an old heirloom from my grandmother."

"Must be worth a few bucks then," Vic said. He began pulling on the ring. The woman screamed when the ring wouldn't come off.

"Take your grimy hands off my wife!" the old man said hoarsely in a show of bravado.

Vic cuffed him against the side of the head. "I told you to shut up, you old fucker," he cursed. He picked up one of the knives on the table. "I'll get if off."

The old woman screamed again. "Please, no," she whimpered. "Don't hurt me. Just give me some time."

"You've got five minutes." Vic turned to the younger woman, who sat petrified in her chair. "How about you, young lady?" he said with mocking politeness. "May I ask for your purse and ring, please?"

The young woman began to pull frantically on one of her fingers. "It's worth nothing," she whispered, "Just a cheep keepsake."

"Let me be the judge of that," Vic said harshly. The ring came off; he took it and put it into his pocket. "Now the purse!"

Again, he emptied the contents on the table. Except for a few bills and some loose change, he found nothing of value. The old woman's ring had finally come off, and Vic pocketed it. Then he walked over to the table with the old man. He didn't meet any resistance there. The old man had only a few bucks in his pocket. He didn't even have a wallet.

The next table was the one with the young couple. Vic looked at the girl and grinned. "Hi, Blondie, what's your name?"

"Veronica," the girl said huskily, staring into Vic's face. "I can't get my ring off, either. My fingers are a little swollen."

Vic looked her up and down. "I have an idea," he said, "let's go into the ladies' room and put some cold water and soap on your finger. That always works."

The girl sighed audibly. "Okay. Thank you." She got up.

When she began to walk toward the ladies' room, Vic followed her. He looked back at his two accomplices and winked. "It may take a while. Why don't you finish up?"

"Don't take too long," his older companion grumbled. Then he turned toward Marc. "Go ahead, and do what you gotta do. I can wait."

Marc grinned. His teeth gleamed white in his black face. He took off his long coat, hung it over a chair. Then he walked over to the table with the older couple. "It's your turn, honey," he said to the young woman with them.

"What do you mean?" she stammered.

"I'm going to fuck you, but first your mother here will have to give me a blowjob to get me into the mood."

"I'm not her mother. I'm her aunt," the old woman blurted out.

"Who the fuck cares," Marc laughed, unzipping his pants. "Take it out, and start sucking!"

"Now hold it just a minute." The older man started to get up. Marc knocked the butt of his UZI into his stomach. "Sit down, you old mother-fucker, and watch."

Moaning in pain, the older man sank back into his chair and watched with helpless rage as Marc grabbed his wife by the hair and pulled her toward his exposed penis. "Take it into your mouth, you old bitch!"

"I can't" the woman wailed. "I've never done anything like this before."

"Then it's about time." Marc laughed hoarsely. "Just open your mouth."

"Leave her alone," the girl spoke up. "I'll do it."

"You...I wanna fuck," Marc grunted. "Let your aunt have the pleasure."

Peter felt sorry for the old couple, but there wasn't anything he could do. Not yet. Marc still held the submachine gun in his hand, aimed at the woman's head.

The man in the gray suit just watched with amusement.

Until now, none of the three had even thrown a look in Peter's direction. As if noticing him for the first time, the man in the suit looked at him, and then he began to walk slowly toward his table.

He stopped in front of Peter. He held a gun in his hand, casually aiming it at Peter's head.

"Good day, Mr. Hartmann, or do you prefer McDiarmid?"

Peter smiled. "Does it matter? Either way you're going to shoot me. Me and everyone else in this room."

"What makes you think that?"

"Isn't it obvious? Everybody in this room will be able to identify you and those two assholes, Vic and Marc, even if those are not their real names. But as stupid as they are, they're probably using their own names."

"They're no Nobel Prize winners, I agree," chuckled the gray-clad man, "but they're good at their job."

"Which is what?" It was Peter's turn to chuckle. "Robbing people and fucking young helpless girls in the toilet?"

"Ah, that." The other man shook his head slightly. "It disgusts me, also, but they're a couple of good boys and I have to let them blow off some steam sometimes. Good for their moral."

"Some steam it is," Peter snorted.

From the ladies' room came muffled screams and loud moaning sounds, quite audible in the suddenly silent room.

"What is he doing to Veronica?" the young man cried out. He scrambled to his feet and stumbled toward the backrooms.

When he passed the table where Marc was getting his blowjob, Marc pointed his weapon at the young man's head. "Take one more step and I'll blow your head right off," he grunted, letting out a moan. "I don't like to be disturbed when I'm busy."

"But my girlfriend…" cried the young man.

"Don't worry about her. She's having the time of her life. Vic's a great stud. The ladies love his big fat cock." He returned his attention back to the young woman. "Take off your panties and lean over the table."

She complied. Her silky black panties lay on the floor. She bent over the table. Marc lifted up her dress to expose her white buttocks. Then he stepped behind her.

"You swine!" The anguished cry came from the old woman's lips. She threw herself at Marc, clawed at his face.

The gray-clad man took his attention away from Peter for a second. The gun wavered.

Peter had waited for a moment like this. The bullet from his gun entered the gray-clad man's throat, just below the chin, leaving a small hole. The back of his head exploded in a mess of gray and bloody matter.

Someone screamed.

Marc stared at the toppling body of his boss, locked eyes with Peter. He swung his submachine gun in Peter's direction, his left hand on the older woman's throat.

Peter registered all this with clinical detachment. Everything seemed to happen in slow motion.

His bullet took Marc between the eyes. Slowly, like a discarded doll, the black man's body crumpled, pulling the older woman with him. As his body hit the floor, the girl at the table sobbed loudly and slid off the table.

Sitting on the floor, shaking, she stared at Marc's lifeless body. At one of the other tables, a couple of patrons looked in horror at the pool of blood forming on the floor.

Peter shifted his attention to the back, where Vic appeared in the doorway of the ladies' room, without his black coat, just a short vest, and no pants.

"Why did you guys start without me? I wanted to…" He stopped when he saw Marc on the floor. "What the hell!" he cursed and reached into his vest pocket.

Peter fired a warning shot into the doorframe beside his head. "The next one spatters your brain all over the place," he said sharply. "Put your hands behind your head, and walk slowly toward me."

Fixing his gaze on Peter, Vic lifted his arms. "Are you going to shoot me?"

"That's entirely up to you." Peter watched him come closer. "I don't care either way. Give me the right answers, and I might just let you go."

"What are the right answers?" A sudden calculating look appeared in Vic's eyes.

"The girl? Is she unharmed?"

"I didn't hurt her."

"You raped her."

Vic grinned. "Hardly. She almost begged me to fill up her tight hot pussy."

"You're lying!" The anguished shout came from Veronica's boyfriend.

"It's the truth. When did you fuck her the last time?"

"She's not that kind of a girl." The young man blushed. "We've only kissed…so far."

Vic laughed. "I rest my case. Man you're stupid, you don't know what you're missing. Veronica loves to fuck, just ask her last boyfriend."

"I don't believe you!" the young man shouted angrily. "If I had a gun I would shoot you myself."

"Go, fuck yourself!" Vic turned his attention back to Peter. "Can I put on my pants? This is kinda embarrassing."

"Later." Peter smiled grimly. "Who sent you?"

Vic shrugged. "Mr. Barkin here arranged everything. He told us we could have some fun with the women first. After that…" He looked around the room and shrugged again. "We were supposed to leave no witnesses."

"What did Mr. Barkin really want?"

"I dunno. He told us to leave you alone. He'd deal with you himself. You had something he wanted.'

"Like what?"

Vic shook his head. "He never said. I didn't ask."

Peter stared at Vic. "How did you find me?"

"We followed you from the hotel."

"How did you know I was there?"

"That FBI broad you're screwing..." Vic smiled. "We've been watching her car."

Peter nodded. "I see. Who are you working for?" he asked, his eyes boring into Vic's.

"For Mr. Barkin." Vic looked at the dead man on the floor and added, "I guess I'm unemployed at the moment."

"One might think so, but I have a feeling you won't have to worry about how you'll be spending your time from now on." Peter's gaze was thoughtful. "You haven't given me much. And there is still this thing with you raping the girl."

"I told you, I didn't have to rape her. She was willing. Ask her."

"I think I might be able to clear that up."

Peter turned his head to look at the man who had come out of the kitchen. "Who are you?"

"I am the cook. Also the owner of this establishment."

"Okay. How can you help us, Mister…?"

"Toni Benito." The man seemed uneasy. Hesitating, he said, "I hope this won't get me into trouble. We've had some problems with our washrooms. You know…gay guys making out…you know what I mean. Well, anyway, I've had a camera installed to see what's going on in there."

"So you saw the whole thing?" Peter asked.

"No…I got it on video. The camera starts taping when someone enters the room. We could watch it."

"Now?"

"Yes, now. It's all set up. Just give me a second." He seemed eager to please.

The big screen in the corner flickered to life. Toni fast-forwarded the first couple of scenes, just some women coming and going.

Then Vic and Veronica entered.

"Please, don't hurt me." Veronica's voice came clearly over the speakers.

"If you're nice you'll have nothing to worry about," Vic said. "Take off your clothes. I like my women naked."

"Okay." Veronica began to strip. When she was nude, she looked expectantly at Vic. "You know," she said, "my boyfriend, he's never made love to me and I'm really horny sometimes. Before Daniel, I had this boyfriend. His name was Vic, just like yours. We used to make love almost every night. He was a real stud. I miss him and his...you know."

"Where is he now, this stud of yours?"

"He moved away. That's when I began dating Daniel. He is real nice and everything, but he's kinda old-fashioned. He thinks we should at least be engaged." Her eyes grew large as her gaze dropped.

Vic had taken off his pants, but his back faced the camera.

"Wow!" Veronica exclaimed. "You sure are big."

Vic chuckled. "He's all yours, honey. Just sit over there on the counter."

The girl obeyed.

Vic moved between her spread legs.

"Let's kiss a little first," the girl whispered. "I think it might hurt if you push it in already."

"Okay," Vic said hoarsely, "but we don't have all day."

"I'll be hot in no time, I promise," the girl said, her voice husky, breathless.

They kissed. It didn't take long before Veronica's hands clasped Vic's clenching buttocks. "Now!" she gasped. "I'm ready."

Vic's hips snapped forward.

"Oh...oh..." the girl sobbed. "This feels wonderful. You fill me up so. I've missed this."

Vic began rocking between her clenching thighs.

"I think I'm coming," the girl cried out. "I'm going to scream."

Vic put his hand over her mouth. Only a muffled scream escaped Veronica's lips. "We don't want them thinking I'm killing you." He chuckled and put his hands under her buttocks.

Picking her up and carrying her, without uncoupling, Vic walked to the middle of the room. Sinking to his knees, he put her on her back. Then he moved forcefully on top of her. His long coat covered his thrusting naked buttocks.

"But you are killing me," she sobbed. "…killing me with pleasure. Ohh…this feels so good."

Again, he put his hand over the girl's mouth to stifle her scream. "You are some horny bitch," he moaned. "I never had a hot cunt like yours."

"I want you to take me from the back," Veronica gasped.

Vic thrust one more time into her, and then he pulled out and watched her get onto her knees.

"The floor is hard," she complained. "Give me your coat to kneel on."

Vic hesitated, but then he shrugged and removed his coat. He spread it on the floor; Veronica moved over, arched her back and pushed up her rump.

"Nice ass," Vic grunted and got into position behind her.

The angle was perfect. Peter could easily see the girl's thick pussy-lips below her white cheeks. She reached between her legs to take hold of Vic's stiff searching penis. Guiding it toward her pussy, she arched her back even more to take the big pole deep into her. "Ah…" she moaned and began milking, "I've needed this for a long time."

Vic's hairy buttocks clenched and unclenched as he pumped behind the girl, his hips smacking into Veronica's fleshy buttocks with each deep thrust. His hands grabbed her moving hips for support.

A dull popping sound and then a second one made him stop in the middle of his thrust. "What the hell," he cursed, pulled out and ran toward the camera.

Then the screen went blank as Toni shut off the player.

The diner was strangely silent.

"I told you." Vic's sneering voice broke the silence. "She was fucking hot for it."

"Shut up!" Peter told him. "Appearances can be deceiving. She may have acted under duress." He didn't believe it. The video didn't leave much room for doubt. Neither did he believe that the girl was such a good actress, but she deserved a chance to tell her story.

"That's right," a sobbing voice came from the direction of the washroom. "I did act under duress."

Everybody looked at the girl standing in the open doorway, still naked, in her hand a gun. "That tape is a lie!" she screamed. "That son-of-a-bitch raped me and I'm going to kill him."

"Now hold it, Veronica." Vic spoke up, a touch of panic in his nasal voice. "Nobody raped you. That tape proves it."

"It was all an act. I thought if I appeared willing he would not kill me." She sounded hysterical. "You have to believe me. I would never do anything like that with a stranger." Her eyes searched her boyfriend's. "Daniel, you believe me, don't you?" she said with a small, pleading voice.

"I don't know," Daniel said. "That was quite some act you put on. Pretty convincing, if you ask me."

"That's all it was…an act, Daniel, an act. I was crazy with fear. Fear makes people do things." Tears were streaming down her face. "Please, Danny, please, believe me."

"He believes you," Peter said gently. "Now, put down that gun before someone gets hurt."

The gun dropped from her fingers, cluttered to the floor. Slowly, she walked toward her boyfriend, a shy smile playing around her lips. "Hold me." She put her arms around him.

Daniel held her awkwardly. When one of his hands accidentally touched her naked buttock, he jerked it away, as if he had touched something hot.

The girl whispered something into his ear.

"No," he almost shouted. "I told you, not until we're engaged."

He pushed her away and stared at Vic. "You spoiled everything." His voice was barely a whisper. "I'd like to kill you myself."

"Nobody gets killed anymore today." Peter looked at Toni Benito. "You've got some rope or tape? Tie him up, and then call the cops."

He bent down and rifled through the pockets of the dead man at his feet. Taking only the driver's license, he put everything else back. Then he noticed the ring on the little finger of the dead man's right hand. Pulling it off, he dropped it into his pocket. He would study everything later. Now it was time to depart.

Throwing a twenty on the counter, he said, "Keep the change," and walked out of the door. He hailed a cab and told the driver to take him to the bus depot.

Sitting comfortably in the cab, he pulled out the ring and studied the intricate design. A scorpion with its stinger raised, ready to strike.

The same design he had seen on the back of Thomas B. Turner's calling card.

Stella had warned him to stay away from Turner because of his association with some nasty people.

Peter chuckled. He had probably just eliminated one of those nasty people. This scorpion had missed its intended victim. He slipped the ring on his finger. It fit. Maybe it would prove to be of use.

Then he studied the driver's license he had taken from the dead man.

Theodore Ronald Barkin.

All the way from Dallas, Texas.

I guess his accent wasn't as phony as it sounded. Peter smiled grimly. Why would they bring in somebody from another state just to get him? Who were these people? What did they want from him?

He needed to talk to Stella again.

"Wake me when we get there," he instructed the driver and closed his eyes. He had the feeling it might be a long night ahead.

"Okay, boss," he heard the cabbie say, but he was already drifting away.

It seemed only moments later when the cabbie woke him.

Peter rented a deposit box, took some money out of the envelope, and stashed away the rest. On an impulse, he took out his wallet and put it into the box. For today, he'd be Theodore Donald Barkin. He had the man's driver's license.

Then he called Stella from one of the payphones. He told her to park her car a couple of blocks away from the depot and meet him in the little park across from there.

She was there forty-five minutes later.

Chapter Fifteen

"Tell me about these people." Peter showed her the ring.

Stella stared at it. "Where did you get that?" she asked, a slight tremble going through her body.

Peter looked into her gray-blue eyes and smiled. "You're beautiful and extremely sexy when you get like this," he said. "And I feel like making love to you right now."

She smiled faintly. "You're just horny," she told him, "but this is serious business, Peter. How did you get this ring?"

"From its owner, a Mr. Theodore Ronald Barkin. At least that's what his driver's license said."

"Never heard of him."

"He's from Dallas, Texas."

"Shit!" Stella exclaimed. "Senator Liebman is from Dallas. I wonder if there is a connection."

"Who are these people, Stella?"

"I told you before. They are very dangerous. Drugs, kidnappings, extortion, rape, porn, murder…you name it."

"I've dealt with the Mob before."

Stella gave him a long look. "This is not the Mob. They call themselves The Order of the Scorpion. We don't know who their leader is. All we know is that they are ruthless and clever, with no honor. We do know who some of the members are, but we've never been able to prove anything. Like you friend, attorney Mr. Turner."

"He's not my friend."

"Just a figure of speech." Stella looked thoughtful. "I assume the previous owner of this ring is not among the living anymore?"

"Your assumption is correct." Peter chuckled. "That scorpion missed its mark."

"How did he find you in the first place?"

"By watching and following you."

When Stella looked around, startled, Peter touched her hand. "I don't believe there is any danger of someone following you right now. Not until word gets back that Mr. Barkin was unsuccessful."

"How did it happen?" Stella asked, curious.

Peter filled her in, leaving nothing out.

"They were right about you," Stella commented. "You are a dangerous man. I told you once I didn't believe you are a murderer. I still believe that. You kill easily, yet you let one of them live."

"He was a smalltime hood. Barkin probably recruited him and his buddy for this job. It seems he wanted to make it look like a robbery gone wrong. I would have been just one of the victims."

Stella nodded. "You're probably right. I'll see what I can find out about this Barkin, if that is his real name. What are you going to do now?"

"I have to meet some people." Peter sighed. "They've got Kathleen."

"Your girlfriend? Who are they?"

"I'll find out tonight. There is this woman, Connie Lin-Carter. She runs an escort service, among other things. She is involved. How...I don't know. She says she is only a mediator."

"I could run a check on her, too, but I may not be able to get any information until tomorrow. By that time, it may be too late." She bent over to kiss him. "Be careful," she whispered, stroking his cheek.

They were sitting on the grass, under a tall oak tree. Peter became aware of the rustling leaves, as a slight wind moved them against each other. A squirrel chattered noisily in the upper branches. He looked up into the sky and took a deep breath, filling his lungs with fresh, clean air.

"It is a beautiful day and so peaceful. Hard to believe there is such ugliness out there. I've killed three people in as many days, and I may have to kill again. I thought I left all this violence behind. I was determined never to live that life again, and now I find nothing has changed. How quickly and easily I was dragged right back into the ugly world of intrigue, violence, and murder."

Stella looked into his eyes. Touching his lips, she traced the outlines with her finger.

"I think I love you, Peter," she said quietly. "I know you're living with another woman, and you probably love her, even if you cheat on her. Because of that, I'm not afraid to tell you how I feel. Maybe after this is over, you and I can still see each other."

Peter smiled and stroked her hair. Then he kissed her lips. "You're a beautiful, caring woman," he said. "You deserve better."

"Who would want an overworked, underpaid, oversexed secret agent like me?"

"I would."

"You've got me." Stella smiled gently. "Be careful tonight. You're not invincible, even if you seem to think so."

"I'll be careful." Peter reached into his pocket, handed Stella the key from the deposit box. "I want you to keep this for me," he said. "There is something else…find the mole in your department."

They got up, brushed the grass from their clothing. Peter walked her to the car. Stella lifted up on her toes, touched her lips to his. "See you tomorrow."

He watched her drive away. "See you," he murmured. Then he waved down a passing taxi.

He had one hour.

* * * *

Julie received him at the door. She smiled sweetly when she saw him. Her black eyes sparkled mischievously. "Hi, Peter, will you let me make love to you again today?"

"I don't think so," he said gruffly, but when he looked into her beautiful face, he smiled. She looked so innocent in her tight jeans and overly large T-shirt. Just a young girl, forced to grow up fast and do things a girl her age shouldn't be doing. Even though she was eighteen, she sure didn't look that old. He couldn't believe she was involved in any of the other stuff, not sweet little Julie.

He put a finger under her chin, and then he bent to give her a quick kiss. "Is your mother in?" he asked.

"She is busy, but she instructed me to take you to the party that's waiting for you."

She took him down a flight of stairs and led him to a closed door. "In there," she said and stood, hesitating for a moment. "Oh, you're supposed to give me your gun." She held out her hand. "Nobody else is allowed one, either."

Peter shrugged and handed her the gun. "Don't hurt yourself with it." He watched her walk away. Then he opened the door and entered the room.

Three people waited inside.

Robert Palmer was one of them.

"Hello, Peter," his employer said. "How are things with you today?"

"Go to hell!" Peter cursed and stared at him. "All these years of deceit. All that talk about being loyal to the country and the flag, Mr. Patriot. I trusted you, and now I find you're involved in this ugly business."

Palmer smiled. "That's all it is…business."

"You know, I always gave my best to your company," Peter said. "Many times I went out of my way to secure an account, and this is how you thank me?"

"I never worried about thanking you, Peter. My wife Linda took care of that." Palmer was still smiling, but it was not a friendly smile.

"I don't have the faintest idea what you're talking about," Peter said, trying to bluff.

Palmer rose from his leather chair and pointed a finger at Peter. "You son-of-a-bitch!" he shouted. "You've been fucking my wife, and you have the nerve to still look me in the eye and deny it?"

Peter shrugged. "Maybe if you had paid more attention to her instead of fucking Helga, your wife's private secretary, Linda might not have come to me for consolation. By the way, how did you find out? Did Linda tell you?"

"No, she didn't. There are cameras in my office. I have it all on video," Palmer snapped.

"Well…now that pleasantries have been exchanged, maybe we can get to the business at hand." The man who had spoken was short and squat, with a bald head and a big bushy beard.

Peter shifted his gaze from Palmer to him. "And who are you?" he asked belligerently.

The man bowed his head slightly. "I am Yussof Robowich, Director of Beta Research."

"Well, I am pleased to meet you, Mr. Robowich," Peter said with sarcasm. "What can I do for you?"

"You can give us the material you stole from the Liebman residence, and all will be forgotten," Robowich said with a pleasant voice.

"Where is Kathleen?" Peter asked.

"She is doing fine." Robowich smiled jovially. "First, hand over the stuff!"

"You get nothing until I know Kathleen is safe." Peter spoke sharply. "If she has been harmed, you will all pay dearly."

"She has not been harmed," said the third man, who had been sitting quietly until now. He spoke with a high, nasal voice and a slight lisp.

"I don't believe we've been introduced," Peter said. "How do you fit into the picture?"

The man chuckled. "My name is not important. Call me Justin. I am in the entertainment business. I make adult movies."

"Pornography," Peter sneered.

Justin spread his hands. "I just fill a niche that needs to be filled. If I don't do it, someone else will. We are all businessmen here." He leaned forward. "By the way, Mr. Hartmann, you are in no position to demand anything. We hold all the cards. Let me show you something. Come, have a seat and watch."

He pointed to a large TV screen in the corner. Suddenly it came to life in vivid color.

Heavy breathing suddenly filled the room.

The screen showed a close-up of a pair of naked white buttocks moving up and down. It became soon obvious that they belonged to a female. When they lifted up, a thick, rigid penis became visible between them.

The angle of the camera shifted, the picture changed. The face of a young girl filled the screen. It held an expression of either great ecstasy or pain. The girl was beautiful and appeared to be quite young.

Peter recognized Julie. They must have done something to her face with makeup, because she looked even younger than in real life.

Her face faded out, her whole body became visible, as she moved it expertly up and down, impaling herself on the rigid mast of the man underneath her.

"I will make you come again, and this time will be even better," Julie's voice came over the speakers, but its pitch had changed to the voice of a much younger girl.

Again, the angle changed. A man's face appeared.

"You are a bunch of perverts!" Peter exploded when he recognized himself.

Robowich laughed. "We are not the perverts, Mr. Hartmann. You are the one fucking the little girl. Can you imagine what the authorities will do to you if this tape should fall into the wrong hands?"

"Shut if off!" Peter yelled. "I've seen enough."

"Not yet," Justin's nasal voice cut in.

Peter was forced to watch the next scene. Julie was on her knees, her rump sticking up. The camera moved to her rear and zoomed in on her slightly spread legs and on her hairless pussy.

Then a man entered the scene, only the lower part of his body was visible. He displayed an erect penis. Approaching Julie from the rear, he dropped to his knees behind her. With one finger, he stroked her pussy, slowly pushed his finger into her. Julie sighed, arched her back to push up her buttocks. The man grabbed his penis and guided the swollen head toward her vagina.

The camera zoomed in for a close-up then moved back, showed the man's buttocks moving back and forth, concentrated on the rigid shaft being pushed in and out of the girl's pussy. A shot of her face. Her eyes were closed, her mouth slightly open. Moans of pleasure echoed through the room.

Then a close-up of the man's face. Peter wasn't surprised to see his own face again.

"Hey," Peter called out. "That never happened."

"It did in my movie," Justin said, chuckling. "With a little bit of editing. But wait, there is more."

The picture faded, showed a new scene. The camera must have been in the ceiling. The broad back of a man lying of top of a female, his naked buttocks clenching and unclenching, as he moved between two slim widespread thighs.

Small hands were digging into his back.

A different angle. A close-up of his stiff rod moving in and out of a hairless vagina. Suddenly he pulled out, erupted over the girl's smooth belly.

Again a close-up of Peter's face and then Julie's.

"You have a big cock," she said. "I will make you come again."

"You squeezed every last drop out of me," came Peter's voice over the speakers.

Peter began to laugh. This was just too comical. "I must admit, you are an artist," he said. "You make Julie look like a little girl. She isn't. As small and young as she might appear, she is of legal age. Also, let me tell you again, that incident never happened. For one thing, I always come inside. I'm curious to see what else you dreamed up."

"You are right, my friend, there is much more to see," Justin said.

The scene on the screen changed. On a wide bed three naked figures moved.

One man and two women. The women wore masks. Their bodies were covered with beautiful, colorful scales. They looked like giant snakes.

"Does this bring back memories?" Justin asked.

"The snakes look familiar," Peter admitted.

The next scene showed the man kneeling behind one of the snake women and smacking his hips forcefully into her soft painted buttocks. The man faced the camera. Again, Peter saw himself.

"One camera behind the mirror," Justin explained, "and a couple more in the corners of the room. This new technology is fantastic, isn't it? These cameras are so tiny; you never see them, unless you know where to look. Everything is automatic. As long as there is movement the cameras roll."

He looked away from the screen. "So what is the point of all this?" he asked.

"The point?" Justin laughed. "Be patient, just a couple more scenes."

Suddenly, there were two men in the picture. He was not in the scene. He watched the action with disgust but little interest.

However, the next scene made him sit up.

It showed a naked man lying casually on a wide bed. Two more people entered the picture, another man, and a naked woman. She had a beautiful body, luxurious auburn hair that spilled over her shoulders, but Peter couldn't see her face.

The man, who brought her in, pushed her toward the bed. She stumbled and fell to her knees.

Looking at the woman, the man on the bed smiled and said, "I can see we'll get along well. Come closer."

Still on her knees, the woman edged toward the bed.

"Make me hard," the man said.

The woman shook her head.

"Do as I say or you'll be sorry," the man said.

The camera zoomed in on the woman's shapely round buttocks and on her large cone-shaped breasts. Then it showed the man kneeling behind her, his erect pole between her fleshy cheeks, touching her swollen labia.

The camera cut and showed the woman's face.

"You sons-of-bitches!" Peter shouted as he stared into Kathleen's green eyes.

The picture faded away.

Peter looked at the three men, his eyes cold. "You harm her in any way, and you're all dead!" he said between clenched teeth.

"She's fine," Justin assured him. "Not everything you see on a screen is real."

"That looked pretty real to me." Peter growled. He was beginning to hate that man's nasal, lisping voice. "What is it you want?"

"You know what we want," Robobich said.

"I have absolutely no idea," Peter said. "Why don't you fill me in?"

Palmer sighed. "Peter, Peter, don't be difficult."

"Fuck you, Robert," Peter told him. "I'm not talking to you."

"Gentlemen," Robowich said. "Let's all calm down. Mr. Hartmann, if you co-operate, we might even cut you in. We've sold four computer chips to one of our trading partners. Each chip is worth ten million dollars. One chip is missing, the most important one. Without it, the other three are worthless. We believe you have the fourth chip. In addition, a certain disk is missing. It holds important information that could be damaging to a lot of people if it fell into the wrong hands. We want that also."

"I don't know what you're talking about. I never killed the Liebmans, and I took nothing of value."

"If you don't play ball, Mr. Hartmann, we might just have to make another movie, a snuff-movie. With your girlfriend as the star. And it will be real." Yussof's voice was cold and hard. "Maybe we can persuade you." Suddenly, he had a gun in his hand. Before Peter could react, he felt a sting in his cheek.

Then the room began to turn.

Chapter Sixteen

Aware, but unable to command his body, he knew they had drugged him, probably with some kind of truth serum.

He lay on a flat surface. Somebody was talking, but he didn't recognize the voice. He answered questions but couldn't remember what he said.

Then he was alone for a long time, drifting in and out of sleep. When he was finally able to think clearly again, he felt extremely horny.

He heard the opening of the door, discovered he had limited head movement, and watched Connie walk into the room.

"You're alive and well, I trust," she said, smiling down at him. She wore a thin, semi-transparent gown. The light coming through the open door outlined the graceful curves of her body.

She stretched out on top of him and kissed him. "I have no control of this situation," she whispered into his ear. "I am just another pawn, that's all. Give them what they want and walk away."

"What about Kathleen?" he murmured.

"Don't worry about her. She'll be all right, I promise."

"How do you fit into this, Connie?" he asked.

"I provide a service, and I'm trying to keep things from getting out of control. That is all I can tell you. It's business."

She got up. He watched her walk through the partially open door. Closing his eyes, he waited for her to return. It didn't take long before he heard the soft pattern of bare feet on the floor.

He didn't open his eyes when she began unzipping his pants and pushed them down, freeing his erection. He moaned when the sweet warm softness closed around him and grabbed for her thrusting hips.

Her hips seemed wider and fleshier than he remembered. When he opened his eyes, he found it quite dark in the room. He couldn't see the woman above him.

"Hello, Peter Hartmann."

"You're not Connie," Peter said, "but you sound familiar."

"I am known as Princess Viper," she said.

"You!" Peter said sharply. "Are you going to kill me now? Finish the job?"

She laughed and tightened her pussy-walls. "With this?" she asked.

Peter moaned. "You'll manage. I hear you poison your victims. Maybe you've got a poisoned cunt."

"Poison is just one of my weapons," she said softly, "but I have to admit, it's my favorite. It is fast, painless and clean. Not like some of your work."

"I am not in that business," Peter said, watching her shadowy form writhe above him.

"But you were once," Viper said. "I know much about you and the things you did, Peter McDiarmid."

Peter inhaled sharply. "What do you know?" he asked.

"Everything. Tell me about Donald Mc.Allistor!"

"He was my friend."

"Yet you left him to die in Colombia."

"I don't know what happened to Donald. He wasn't with us when he got hit. Shaw told us he was dead. There was nothing I could do for him, and it was my duty to get Colonel Bender out of the country. He had been wounded in a shootout with a bunch of drug dealers."

"Why didn't you wait for Donald?"

"I wanted to, but they assured me Donald was dead." Peter wanted to stop, but she kept on milking him.

"You never saw him dead, did you?" she asked. "You never went back to look for him."

"After I got the Colonel home, I planned to go back, search for him, just in case there was a chance he might still be alive, but I received orders to leave it alone. All records were erased from the files. We never were in Colombia. It never happened. Then they hung me out to dry. They retired me, gave me a new name, a new identity. Officially, Peter

McDiarmid died on assignment, location unknown." Peter's voice sounded harsh and bitter in his own ears.

He grabbed the woman on top of him, pulled her down, and then he turned with her in his arms, thrust deep into her, letting his frustration and anger guide his actions.

She was strong and met his thrusts with equal force. "Do you swear what you just told me is true?"

"I swear. Not that it matters anymore."

"It matters to me." Gasping, she pushed up. "You're angry and I don't blame you." She panted beneath him. "You got a rotten deal."

Then they were both silent. Only their bodies spoke. When his climax approached, he crushed her to him, shuddering as he exploded inside her. She quivered in his arms as her own orgasm reached its peak.

After that, they lay in each other's arms, gasping for breath. Then she kissed him gently. "I believe you," she said softly.

"Did you kill the Liebmans?" he asked.

"It was a job," she said. "Nothing more."

"What about me? How do I fit in?"

"You were supposed to be the fall-guy. I guess you pissed off somebody badly." She stroked his back. "I didn't know anything about you until later. I'm sorry."

"Why?"

She shrugged. "Maybe I'll tell you someday. By the way, I am not involved with the people who are after you. I did my job, and I'm done with it. Just give them what they want, but don't trust them."

"I didn't take that stuff," Peter said. "I thought you did."

"No, I didn't. I finished my assignment and got the hell out of there. I was told a cleanup crew would take care of the rest. You know the procedure."

"Then where the hell is that computer chip and that disk?" Peter asked.

"I can't help you there, but I suggest you either find them or convince those people you don't have them."

Peter looked up when he heard someone enter the room and saw Connie standing by the doorway.

"Sorry, to interrupt," she said, smiling, "but I think you should leave. I don't know what you told those guys, Peter, when you were drugged, but they must have gotten something out of you. They may be coming for you."

"I have no place to go and no transportation. I'm a fugitive, remember?"

Princess Viper sat up. "You can come with me. You'll be safe."

Peter dressed hurriedly, while Viper disappeared, presumably to get her clothes. Connie led him out of the room to a backdoor, where Viper met them a few minutes later.

"Good luck," Connie said quietly. Then she kissed him on the cheek.

"Thank you," he grumbled, not certain if he should be angry with her or be grateful for her help.

Viper's small sports car was parked in the back lane. Peter still felt a little sluggish as he followed her to the car.

She drove down the darkened lane, and then she hit the street. They didn't encounter much traffic in the dark of night.

They sat silent for a while. Peter closed his eyes and listened to the steady hum of the engine. He worried about Kathleen, wondered if she was okay. He didn't have the missing computer chip or the disk. Viper claimed she didn't either.

Who did have them?

Was there someone else involved?

Viper had mentioned the cleanup crew.

The Agency!

Somebody in the Agency wanted him dead, and he could guess who. Colonel Edward Shaw, the man who had signed Adam's transfer.

But why?

Shaw knew of Peter's past. Peter suspected Shaw had betrayed him, was almost certain of it, but he couldn't prove anything.

The Agency had hired Viper to assassinate the Liebmans. How was the Agency involved?

Another government cover-up?

Peter sighed and looked at Viper. The interior of the car was not dark. Enough light came in from the city lights outside to give him a clear view of her. She looked younger than the last time he'd seen her. Her long black hair hung loose, softly curling around her shoulders, framing a smooth face with full lips.

When she turned her head to glance at him, he noted her deep green eyes.

Last time her eyes had been brown.

Contact lenses, either then or now. Probably then.

She smiled when she saw him studying her. "Like what you see?"

"I see a beautiful woman," Peter answered. "A woman I've had sex with. A woman I know nothing about, except for the rumors I've heard. A woman who fucked me in more ways than one and wants to help me now. Can I trust that woman?"

"You can, and you should, Peter," she said. "Right now, you need every friend you can find."

"Why that sudden compassion for a man you don't know? A man you helped frame for murder?"

"Things have changed." She looked at him, smiling faintly. "You are wrong about one thing. I do know you, Peter McDiarmid. I've made an intense study of your file."

"How could you?" Peter asked. "My file was buried deep."

Viper chuckled. "I've been at this for a long time and managed to learn a few things along the way. You'd be surprised what can be found if you know where to look and how easy it really is. Everybody can be found."

"You looked older the last time I saw you," Peter said, changing the subject.

"It didn't seem to inhibit your sexual performance." Viper laughed. "I've never met a man like you. Such sexual power, such stamina. It would be a shame to lose that talent because of your early demise." She gave him a sidelong glance. "Do you have any children? Sons, maybe?"

"None." Peter sighed. "And I'm afraid there is not much chance I ever will have any. Something to do with my sperm count."

"Well, that's nature for you." Viper shrugged. "You get shortchanged in one department, but you get compensated for it in another. It would be nice to pass this sexual prowess on, though. Who knows, if you tried hard and often enough, you'll succeed one day."

Peter grinned. "I'm trying."

"I know." Viper smiled. "Maybe the right woman hasn't come along yet."

"Maybe."

Viper slowed the car and pulled into a side road. They came to a gate; it opened when she pushed a button on her dashboard.

Dim lights framed a long winding driveway. The house at the end loomed large in the dark. A floodlight sprang to life as they approached a triple garage. One of the doors lifted, and Viper eased her car inside.

"Nice place," Peter commented.

"It's not mine," Viper said, "but I know the owner."

She took him up some carpeted stairs, led him to a closed door. "This will be your room for tonight," she said in a hushed voice. "Someone will call you for breakfast in the morning. Good night."

She turned to walk away. Peter touched her arm. "Where will you be?"

"Not in your bed. But don't worry, I'll be around."

Chapter Seventeen

Peter slept soundly without waking up once, but morning came much too soon.

A knock on the door brought him to full awareness. "Come in," he called, getting out of bed.

The door opened, a girl in a maid's uniform walked in. Her eyes widened slightly when she saw him standing beside the bed, completely naked. "Good morning, sir," she said, trying unsuccessfully not to look at his half-erect penis. "Breakfast will be served in fifteen minutes."

"Thank you," Peter said, not bothering to cover up. "May I ask where?"

"In the dinette."

"Let me take a quick shower. I'll be ready in a jiffy," Peter said.

"I'll wait until you're ready." She blushed a little, noticing his smile. "Dressed and ready to go, I mean."

Peter chuckled and walked into the bathroom. Leaving the door open, he stepped into the shower. He was in good spirits, feeling almost playful. Under different circumstances, he would have probably made another conquest with that girl. She was pretty enough to arouse his interest.

Then he checked himself. What the hell was he thinking?

Here he was, in a stranger's home, with no idea whose place it was. He had only Viper's word that he was in a safe place. The word of a woman who was partially responsible for his current predicament. For all he knew, he had walked into the lion's den.

He dried off, brushed his teeth with the toothbrush and toothpaste he found, ran his fingers through his hair, and walked back into the bedroom.

The maid still waited for him.

147

"Sorry, I don't have any formal wear." He grinned.

She smiled. "I'm sure your attire will be just fine, sir." He noticed her eyes flickering admiringly over his physique. She blushed again, this time even deeper.

He dressed and looked at his watch. "Twelve minutes," he said. "I think we'll be okay."

The girl said nothing, opened the door and walked out. He followed her, admiring her long slim legs. She wore a typical maid's outfit. Short skirt, meshed stockings, high heels.

She knew he was looking at her. He smiled when he detected a bit more of a sway in her hips than was normal. Little vixen. She's quite aware of her sexuality and her impact on me.

By the time they'd walked down some stairs and arrived at their destination, his mind was filled with all kinds of sexual fantasies.

Viper sat at one end of a small table in the middle of the room and opposite her sat a male figure. He had his back to Peter.

"Sleep well?" Viper asked and smiled.

"Quite well, thank you," Peter said, stopping at the entrance to the room.

"Come, join us." Viper pointed to the chair beside her.

Peter walked closer, pulled the indicated chair away from the table, and then he froze.

"Hi, Peter McDiarmid," the man at the table said. "Glad to see you're well and healthy. Word was you are dead."

"That's what I was told about you." Peter looked at Viper. "What the hell is going on?"

"Sit down, McDiarmid. We have a lot to talk about." The man looked up at him, held out his hand. "Good to see you, old friend."

Peter grabbed the man's hand and held it tight. "Donald McAllister. I can't believe it. How can you be so casual about this? All these years I thought you were dead, blamed myself for letting them bully me into not going back for you." Peter sat down, looked again at Viper who sat there, smiling. "How do you fit into this?" he asked.

"She's my sister," Donald said, chuckling. "Maureen McAllister."

"Your sister? That's why all the questions last night. Why?"

The woman shrugged. "I wanted to find out the truth…from you. It seems you've been made the fall guy once before. You were blamed for my brother's disappearance in Colombia and for the mission's failure."

"I was? That explains why they wanted me out of the Company." He turned to Donald. "What exactly happened back there?"

"It's a long story, Peter. Maybe we should have breakfast first."

Peter nodded, leaning back in his chair. Looking at his former friend, he shook his head. "I still can't believe it. You haven't changed much, a little older, a little heavier, but otherwise the same."

Donald smiled and poured a glass of orange juice. "Appearances are deceiving. I'm not the same man I was ten years ago, Peter. Time changes a man. I've seen too much, heard too much and done things you may not approve of. I've become cynical."

"I also have changed," Peter said, letting Donald fill his glass. "We all have."

"Some more than others," Donald said. "I see you still keep in shape. That hasn't changed."

Viper laughed. "He is in good shape. I can vouch for that."

"My sister…the Love Goddess. That hasn't changed either."

"She's a beautiful, passionate woman." Peter smiled. "She can put to shame many a twenty year old. She's not only beautiful; she also has a lot of experience."

"Thank you for the compliment, Peter." Maureen gave him a big smile. She seemed happy about something. "My brother doesn't approve of my sexual escapades as he calls them. But he is no saint either, as you may find out." She bit into a piece of toast, wrinkled her nose as some of the crumbs fell onto the tabletop.

The maid put a plate of scrambled eggs and bacon in front of Peter. He looked up and said, "Thank you."

The girl's cheeks seemed flushed. "More coffee, sir?" she asked.

Peter nodded and let her fill his cup. Her other hand brushed his cheek, seemingly by accident.

Maureen watched her walk away and laughed. "I think Michelle has a crush on you, Peter."

Peter chuckled. "I seem to have that effect on women, especially after they've seen me naked."

Donald threw up his hands. "That hasn't changed either."

149

When they were finished with breakfast, Donald invited Peter into the library. The room was richly furnished. Leather-bound books filled a wall-to-wall bookcase. Expensive oil paintings almost completely covered one wall. A gun cabinet stood in one corner, stocked with a couple of rifles, a shotgun, and some handguns.

Peter sank into a huge leather chair. "You've done well for yourself," he commented, studying the three-foot statue of a beautiful naked woman. "Your taste in art has to be commended."

Donald walked over to a liqueur cabinet, pulled out a bottle and a couple of glasses. "Brandy?" he asked.

"Sure," Peter said, lifting his shoulders. "I usually don't drink this early in the morning, but I have a feeling I might need a stiff one."

Donald filled the glasses, handed one to Peter. Setting the bottle on top of the hammered copper plate of a small antique table, he took a chair opposite Peter's. "Yeah, I've done well, but I paid a heavy price for my wealth."

He sipped on his brandy. Then he pulled out a cigar. "Cuban," he said. "You want one?"

"No, thanks," Peter declined. "That's a habit I never acquired."

"You should try it," Donald said around the cigar, lighting it with an antique looking lighter. "It relaxes you. Like meditating. You do that, don't you? I spent six months in a Colombian prison and over a year living in the jungle. Had plenty of time to think."

"So what happened?" Peter interrupted him.

"You remember the mission?" Donald stared into a thick blue smoke ring. "We were supposed to take out Señor Fernando Gomez, one of the drug lords, right?"

"That's how I remember it," Peter said.

"Wrong! It was doomed to failure from the beginning. You see, I knew what was going to happen, or at least I thought I knew. That son-of-a-bitch Edward Shaw, who was with the DEA at the time and heading the mission, double-crossed me."

"How?"

"You and I, Peter, we were good friends, but you didn't know me as well as you thought. You didn't even know I had a sister. I was sick of the Company. I wanted out. When Shaw made me an offer, I took it. While you and Colonel Bender were going after Gomez, two other DEA agents and I were supposed to intercept a deal that was going down between Gomez's gang and a dealer from the States. Shaw and I would split the take. The deal would have netted me five million dollars." McAllister smirked. "Well, it didn't work out. Shaw had another, more lucrative deal, with Gomez. We were ambushed, the two agents died. I was left for dead. I took a shot to the head that left me unconscious, but it wasn't life threatening."

"How did you survive?" Peter interrupted him.

"Like I said, they thought I was dead. They took our papers so we couldn't be identified. A group of local farmers found me and took me to the nearest town. I had no identification, and they found me among a couple of dead guys, gun in hand. As it happens, I speak Spanish fluently and," he grinned, "with my dark handsome looks, I can pass for Hispanic. For my own safety, I thought it best not to tell them I was an American. They threw me in jail. After six months, I managed to escape, joined a bunch of rebels with no cause, just to survive. Lived in the jungle most of the time for a year."

He emptied his brandy, poured another one. "I got tired of that, joined another bunch of losers. After that, I moved north, with a dead man's papers, through Panama, finally ending up in Mexico. I entered the States as an illegal immigrant. I had money. Don't ask me how I got it. Once back home, it was no big deal to get a new identity. By the way, my name now is Alexander Buchanan."

Peter chuckled. "So I wasn't the only one who changed his name. Why did you?"

"I contacted my sister Maureen, who told me that according to official records our mission never took place. Unofficially, she heard that I had been betrayed and possibly killed by my good friend and partner Peter McDiarmid, also listed as missing. When I heard that a certain Edward Shaw was now with the Company and he was a colonel, I decided to stay dead."

He gave Peter a thoughtful look. "I never believed what they said about you. Until just a few days ago, I actually thought you were dead. Maureen and I usually never talk about her assignments. I know what she does, but that is her life. This time she broke tradition and told me about her encounter with you."

They sat silent for a while. Donald puffed on his cigar, while Peter poured another brandy. He sniffed it, his eyes on his former friend. "What exactly do you do, Donald?"

McAllister gave him a long stare. "I deal in merchandise. Antiques, art, drugs, pornography."

"You make porno-movies?"

Donald leaned back in his chair, blew a couple of smoke rings. "I don't make them. I distribute them. I leave the making to my partner Justin Hamilton."

"Justin!" Peter exclaimed. "I've met that sick son-of-a-bitch. He's your partner? That means you're involved in my girlfriend's kidnapping!"

"Justin and I have a loose partnership. I am not aware of everything he does, but I don't believe he's kidnapped your girlfriend."

"He put her into one of his porn-flicks. They threatened to star her in a snuff-movie. You know what that is, don't you?"

Donald smiled. "Justin would never do that. He's a weasel, loves pornography, and is quite artistic, but he is not a murderer. A lot can be done with computer-generated special effects these days."

"Then explain to me, Donald, how Kathleen ended up in one of his flicks?"

Donald shrugged. "I can't explain it." He gave Peter a curious look. "How well do you know your girlfriend, Peter? Maybe she's involved."

"Somehow I can't believe that. What would she get out of it? We've been together for five years now. I think I know her well enough. She wouldn't do that to me, not freely." He looked thoughtful. "What is your partner doing with Yussof Robowich and my former employer Robert Palmer?"

"They probably hired him. I hope he didn't get in over his head. I'd hate to lose him. He's made me a lot of money."

"Drugs, pornography, and probably prostitution, too." Peter shook his head. "You have changed, Donald!"

"It's business, Peter. It allows me to live the way I do. I don't have to like it. For the record, I'm not into prostitution." Donald's eyes became hard. "I don't owe anyone an explanation. People who I trusted stabbed me in the back. I put my life on the line for this country, and the government, which represents this country that I love so much, betrayed me.

"As long as people like Edward Shaw hold high government positions of trust, I have absolutely no respect for the laws they are supposed to uphold. In Colombia, they threw me in jail without a trial. Back here in the States, nobody bothered to find out what really happened. Nobody cared. They would have left me to rot.

"If it were known I was back, they would probably put me in prison. Shaw would see to that. Actually, he most likely would have me murdered."

Donald crushed his cigar into an ashtray, anger plain in his face. He stared at Peter. "How about you, my old friend? You are running from the law, even though you are innocent. You and I, we're both trying to survive in our own way."

Both men turned to look at the door when they heard the sound of clapping. Maureen stood there, dressed in tight jeans and a small halter. "Quite a speech, brother," she said. "I haven't heard you talk this much for a long time."

"How long have you been standing there?" Donald asked.

"Long enough to say As usual you speak the truth." She sat down beside him. "How about one of those cigars?"

Peter watched her wet it with her tongue and then light it. "It's not good for you," he said but smiled.

She pushed it slowly back and forth into her mouth, a little at a time, as if she were sucking on something. Her green eyes were bright as she looked at him. "As long as it feels good, it is good," she said, blowing smoke out of the side of her mouth. "I'd like you to accompany me tonight. There is something I want to show you, something that may be quite important for you to find out."

"What about Kathleen?"

"She is quite safe, I'm sure of that. Like my brother said, Justin is not going to harm her."

"I'm not worried about Justin. It's Yussof Robowich who worries me."

Maureen stood up. "I don't know this Robowich, but I wouldn't worry so much about Kathleen. See you at six."

Donald watched Peter and chuckled. "She seems so ordinary, doesn't she? A beautiful, sexy woman. A little cocky sometimes, but otherwise quite harmless. Many men are fooled by that. She is quite an actress, you know. Today she looks like this, tomorrow she may decide to look and act like a successful businesswoman, or a ballet dancer, or some female warrior from the Amazon. Do you know that she speaks five languages fluently and a dozen different accents? She has black belts in kung fu, tai-kwon-do, and karate. She's also a fairly good boxer and an expert marksman."

"And a killer," Peter said thoughtfully. "Can I trust her?"

"Absolutely."

Peter looked at Donald. "Can I trust you, old friend?"

"That is up to you. I would have given my life for you back then. Nothing has changed." He got out of his chair. "I have to go to a business meeting. Make yourself at home. Michelle will serve you lunch at noon or whenever. Just call her on the intercom. If there is anything else you need, call her. I'll be back late tonight, so I won't probably see you till tomorrow." He held out a hand.

Peter stood up and took it.

"It's good to see you, old friend," Donald said. He let go of Peter's hand and turned to leave. Then on an impulse, he reached for Peter's shoulder and pulled him close for a quick moment.

Surprised by the show of affection, Peter watched him walk away. "Good to see you, too, my, possibly, one and only true friend," he murmured.

Even before they joined the Company, they had been through a lot together. Four months in the desert of Kuwait during Operation Desert Storm, depending on each other daily for survival. They had been more than friends. They had been brothers.

If there was one thing he could be sure of, it was Donald McAllister's trust and friendship.

He looked around to check out some of the books on the shelves, when he heard the soft footsteps of someone approaching.

Michelle.

She stood hesitating in the doorway. "Would you like to use the sauna, sir?" she asked, her face coloring a lovely shade of rose, as she said that.

Peter smiled. "Will you join me?"

"If that is your wish," she said.

"It is my wish but only if you want to," Peter answered. "I'm not telling you to do it."

"I think I would like to." She blushed even more.

"Well, let's do it then," Peter said, enjoying the girl's shyness. He found it a great turn-on.

The sauna was just down the hall.

Michelle looked at Peter and began to disrobe. Peter stripped also, watching the girl's clothes come off. She was quite slim. Naked, she looked even younger, with her small firm breasts.

"How old are you?" he asked on an impulse.

"I'm nineteen, sir." She looked at his erection and giggled. "Is that for me?" she asked with sudden boldness.

Peter pulled her to him. "Just for you, honey, unless you don't want it."

"Oh, yes." She sighed, put her arms around his neck and covered his face with kisses. He kissed her lips, probing her mouth with his tongue. She tasted of mint.

Moaning, she moved one of her hands down to touch his penis.

He put his hands under her round buttocks and lifted her up. Her legs circled his hips. His searching penis touched the entrance to her vagina and he found her moist and ready. She moaned loudly and kissed him fiercely when he slid easily into her.

Peter had his back against the wall. Michelle planted her feet against it and began pushing herself up and down on his shaft, swinging back and forth on his arms. He had strong, muscular legs, but he soon felt them give away. He walked with her to a padded bench and sat down. She clung to him, her small breasts warm and soft against his chest.

Her tight sheath moved rapidly over his rigid shaft, tantalizing his engorged glans with its velvety softness. He experienced a series of orgasms but never went to a full climax. Knowing that this girl needed more than just a hurried piece of tail, he prolonged it as long as possible.

It took all of his concentration not to come. After losing her initial shyness, Michelle became a demanding, passionate lover. Peter stretched out on the bench. Watching the slim body of the eager girl undulating above him, he enjoyed the way she gyrated her curvy hips.

She had fair skin, slightly freckled, and her hair showed a hint of copper. She looked extremely beautiful with her red lips parted and her eyes closed. His gaze traveled to the spot where they were joined. Her light pubic hair was sparse and her swollen labia were clearly outlined as his mast disappeared between them with a steady rhythm.

Pulling her down, he got up and, still connected to her, he put her onto her back on the bench. Her legs flew wide open as he began to fuck her with deep, powerful strokes.

She opened her eyes and looked at him. "Please, don't get me pregnant," she whispered, moaned as her body began shaking from a powerful orgasm washing through her.

Peter felt her discharge but never stopped moving. When her body relaxed again, he said, "Don't worry, you won't get pregnant. I am quite sterile."

She smiled and looked into his eyes. "No man ever made me feel the way you do," she gasped and tightened her vaginal muscles around his moving shaft. "What is this liquid coming out of me? Is it blood?"

Peter chuckled. "No, honey, it's your g-spot. Consider yourself lucky. Not every woman experiences what you are."

"Oh...oh...here I go again," she cried out. "What are you doing to me, sir?"

"Making you very happy, I hope." Peter groaned and gave a suppressed shout of pleasure as his own climax came rushing up. Grabbing her buttocks, he thrust deep into her and filled her to the brim.

Together they rode the wave of their passion until Peter finally collapsed inside her arms. Both of them were breathing hard, their bodies slick with perspiration.

"You are an extraordinary man, sir," Michelle said. "I didn't know pleasure like this existed."

"Call me Peter, Michelle. No need to call me sir, not after this."

"Hi, Peter." Michelle smiled. "Pleased to make you acquaintance." Then she giggled like a schoolgirl. "I feel so naughty. I've never done it the way we did it. The boys I've been with just know one way, man on top. And before I really got into it, they were finished. Not like you, sir, I mean...Peter."

He kissed her gently. "Have you ever done it doggy-style?"

"Doggy-style?" she asked. "No."

"Well, then let me show you. Kneel down on the bench." When Peter pulled out of her, Michelle looked at his erect penis.

"You're still stiff," she said, her eyes large.

"I'm not like other men," Peter said, "I can do it for a long time."

She knelt on the bench. He moved behind her, grabbed her hips, and put his penis between her white cheeks. When his penis touched her anus, she turned her head and asked, "Like that?"

"No, not like that," he said, moving lower.

She arched her back instinctively. He felt himself sliding into her well-lubricated love-channel and groaned, relishing the sweet feeling of her soft pussy-walls enveloping his hard shaft.

Holding onto her hips to steady himself, he began to rock back and forth between her white round cheeks, slowly at first and then with ever increasing tempo. He thrust hard and furious, making her cry out every time he slid deep into her.

"This is almost too much," the girl cried out. "I think I'm going to die."

"I think you're just coming alive," Peter grunted, watching her rotating hips. Slamming into her soft buttocks, he began to slow down. His hands moved to her taut breasts, cupped them. Then he grabbed her shoulders, held on for support.

Her bottom revolved around his shaft with incredible speed. He stopped moving, just stayed inside her.

Michelle clawed at the bench top and emitted a series of high sounds, announcing her orgasm. Milking him, she tightened her inner muscles so much, Peter found it almost impossible not to come, but he managed to hold back.

The day was young.

When he pulled out, Michelle looked over her shoulder back at him. "Anything wrong?" she asked.

"Oh no, nothing is wrong, sweet." He sat down on the bench. "Come, sit in my lap."

She climbed down from the bench and stood, facing him.

"Turn around," he told her.

She turned, presenting her deliciously round buttocks. He touched them, grabbed her slim hips, and pulled her into his lap. His erect penis slid between her descending thighs. She obviously knew what he wanted.

Her hand went down and guided his mast into her pussy. He felt her soft lips touch the head, and then he slid back into her creamy love-channel.

"This feels nice, too," Michelle gasped. She sank into his lap, taking his penis deep into her.

"It sure does." Peter groaned and put his hands over her small breasts, cupping them tightly, and pressed his cheek against her back.

Michelle's feet touched the ground, giving her support to move up and down. He didn't move, just let her do all the work. Her pussy was soft and creamy and slid easily over his shaft.

Feeling the beginning of another climax, he let it build up slowly. Usually the second one was stronger than the first one and he knew this one would not disappoint him. Faster and faster the peak approached and then it hit with the force of a sledgehammer.

"Now!" he called out hoarsely, his fingers digging into the girl's breasts. "Now…!"

Michelle's sweet bottom ground into his lap, taking his pulsing member deep into her gushing inflamed vagina. She lifted her head high and dug her fingers like sharp claws into his thighs. With every throb of his exploding organ, she cried out, "Oh…oh…ohh…!"

Then her head fell forward and her movements stopped. He held her in his arms, his hands gently massaging her breasts, suddenly aware of the only sound in the room.

Their ragged breathing.

"Wow," the girl exclaimed after a while. "And I thought that last one was good."

Peter smiled into her slick back, tasting her salty sweat. "Who knows, the next one might even be better."

Michelle laughed. "Don't tell me, you're not finished. I'm exhausted."

"So am I. Let's forget about the Sauna. I'm ready for a cool, long shower."

Michelle left his lap, reluctantly, it seemed. They both stepped into one of the shower stalls. Giggling, Michelle rubbed Peter down, her hands lingering between his legs.

She knelt in front of him, playfully took his penis into her mouth and sucked lightly on it. She looked up at him, the spray of water showering her face. Her coppery hair was plastered against her head and her green-flecked eyes were large.

Peter could see the mischief in them. Chuckling, he closed his eyes and let her suck him until he was fully erect. Easing out of her mouth, he pulled her up and whispered into her ear, "It would be a shame to waste an orgasm just on myself. Bend forward."

She turned, bent her upper torso, touching the tiled floor lightly with the tips of her fingers. Her legs were slightly spread, her bottom up.

The warm water sprayed over her round buttocks. Peter moved behind her, got into position and put the tip of his penis between her thick labia. Then he slid into her, sighing deeply as he felt her soft, warm sheath closing around his stiff member.

Holding her hips, he moved slowly behind her. There seemed to be a steady pulse in the spray of water that flowed from the showerhead. He adjusted his rhythmic movements to that pulsing.

In and out...in and out...

Staring at her slim back and her rotating buttocks, he carried them both to another climax, not as earth-shattering as the last one but still quite satisfying.

After that they finished showering, both of them too exhausted to even talk.

Michelle dressed quietly and gave him a shy kiss on the lips. "Thank you, Peter, for this wonderful experience. I will never forget it...or you," she whispered. Then she slipped away.

Peter watched her thoughtfully and went back to his room.

Chapter Eighteen

Maureen woke him at six o'clock. "Well," she said, "what did you do? Sleep all day?"

"Not all day," he said, rubbing the sleep from his eyes. "But maybe I should have."

"Go, wash up, and meet me in thirty minutes in the parlor." She walked out of the room, tall and sexy, her body sheathed in a tight leather outfit.

Peter stared at the closing door. "Wonder what she's planning for me tonight, dressed like that," he murmured.

Thirty minutes later, they drove away together in her little sports car. It only took twenty minutes to get to their destination, clearly an industrial area. Maureen parked her car in front of a large warehouse.

They took the elevator up to the fourth floor. The place looked like a gym. Peter saw exercise equipment everywhere and a large workout area with thick mats on the floor. He counted fifteen people. All of them female. All of them nude.

Two of the girls were sparring on one of the mats. Their movements were graceful and perfectly controlled. It looked almost like a dance, but Peter knew better. He watched them with great interest.

"They are good," he said to Maureen. "What discipline are they studying? I don't recognize it."

She smiled. "Mine," she said. "It's a mix of karate, kung fu, tae kwon do, t'ai chi chuan, and something else."

"This is your school?"

She nodded. "These are the best of the best. But you will never see them taking part in any tournaments."

Peter looked at her, his interest aroused. "Are you training an army?" he asked.

"Sort of." Maureen chuckled, but her eyes were cool. "My own private fighting force. Some day I'll be too old to do my jobs. These girls will do my work for me."

"You're training assassins?" Peter looked around the room. All the girls were tall, beautiful, their bodies in top condition.

Beautiful and deadly.

"Come, I'll introduce you to my two star pupils."

They walked over to the two sparring girls. The girls relaxed and watched them come closer.

Both girls had oriental features; they looked very much alike. Only one seemed pureblooded, her cheekbones high, her eyes slanted and dark, while the other one possessed gray eyes. Peter guessed their ages to be around nineteen or twenty.

"Meet Nancy and Petra," Maureen said. "They're cousins."

"Not really," the one with the gray eyes said. "Nancy is my niece. I'm her aunt."

Nancy laughed. "Petra is also a week older than me. That's why she is so slow."

Peter smiled. "I'm Peter Hartmann. Pleased to meet you, ladies."

They giggled. "We're no ladies," Nancy said. "What I mean…"

"What she means is that we are girls," Petra interrupted, "but not actual ladies. Though we could be…" She blushed a little. "We are also quite naked in front of a strange man."

"I don't mind," Peter laughed, trying not to stare too much.

They were young, but their bodies were fully developed. Slim, beautifully formed, with nice, good-sized breasts. The small black triangle below their flat bellies was hardly visible on their suntanned skin.

"Are you into martial arts?" Petra asked.

"I practice it," Peter said.

"Maybe you'd like to show us some of your moves," Nancy said, her dark eyes sparkling.

Peter grinned. "In the nude, I suppose?"

Nancy blushed. "Well, of course."

Maureen had been listening to their friendly bantering. Now she smiled and grabbed Peter's arm. "Maybe another time, girls. By the way,

Nancy, it's almost time for you to get ready for tonight. You haven't forgotten, have you?"

"Oh, no, I haven't." The girl was suddenly serious. "I'll be ready."

"Come on." Maureen pulled on Peter's arm. "We still have things to do."

They left the warehouse, stopped for a quick bite to eat at a fast food restaurant, and then they drove to another location, a large mansion, nestled among giant maple trees. Maureen parked her car with the other half dozen or so already there.

The house was old, but Peter could tell it had undergone extensive renovations.

A lot of stone and stucco.

Two high, Greek-style pillars flanked wide concrete steps leading to a large entrance door. Maureen walked in boldly, without announcing herself. Peter looked up at the huge chandelier hanging from the high ceiling, its crystals sparkling with all the colors of the rainbow.

They walked down a flight of stairs and through a wide corridor until they came to a door at the far end. It stood ajar, and Maureen pushed it open.

"Hello, René," she called. "I've brought you a canvas."

The room was obviously a studio. All sizes of paintings hung on the walls or stood on the floor, some finished, some partially done. In the center stood an easel with an empty canvas. Peter saw tubes and jars full of paint and an array of paintbrushes on a counter.

At the end of the room another door, slightly open.

"I'm coming." The voice sounded high and cracking.

The door opened and a stooped-over figure shuffled into the room. Arms like sticks stuck out of sleeves too large. White hair hung loose from a balding head, spilling over skinny shoulders.

Had the man stood up, he would have towered over Peter. He smiled when he saw Maureen then he looked at Peter with clear, bright blue eyes.

"Him?" he asked.

Maureen nodded. "I want snakes crawling all over his body," she said.

"Snakes!" The old man threw up his thin arms. "Always snakes! But what the hell…" Still looking at Peter, he said, "Strip."

Peter shrugged and started to take off his clothing. When he stood in his underwear, Maureen laughed. "That too. I want every part of your body covered."

Peter removed the last bit of his clothing.

René rubbed his hands gleefully. "Now this should be fun," he said in his cracking voice. "At last, a body worthy of my talent."

"What about mine?" Maureen pouted.

"You, my dear, are a woman and very beautiful indeed. I've done lots of beautiful women, but this is a fine specimen of a male. Maybe some day he will model for me. I'd like to paint him."

"You can talk to him. He talks, you know, and he even understands what you say. He's not just a handsome body. He is actually quite intelligent." Maureen chuckled and touched Peter's cheek.

Peter smiled. "Thanks for the compliment, Maureen. Mind telling me what's going on?"

"Just be patient. All in good time. For now, let René do what he does best. I'll be back in an hour."

She walked out the door, closing it softly behind her.

Peter watched the old man, as he bustled around selecting paints and brushes from the counter.

"Come over here, young man," René said. "I want you to stand on this mat, under the light."

The old man began to paint. His brush moved with deft strokes over Peter's body, covering his skin with a multitude of shiny colors. Occasionally he would step back, inspect his work, and then he would chuckle, pick a different color, and keep on painting.

Finally, he seemed to be finished.

"There is a mirror over there, young man, if you want to look at yourself and my work of art." The old man sighed. "Too bad it will all be washed away in the morning."

"You could always take a picture," Maureen said from the open door. She had a loose black cloak covering her body. Walking up to Peter, she looked him over.

"You've outdone yourself this time, René," she said. "Sometimes I think you can read my mind." She pulled Peter toward a full-sized mirror.

Peter stared at his image. His whole body was covered with crawling snakes. Large ones, small ones.

One seemed to dominate all others. The head of a striking cobra was painted in the center of his chest and the rest of the snake's body circled around his lower torso, with the tail running down the front of his thigh.

"Isn't it beautiful?" Maureen asked, obviously delighted.

Peter grunted. "It does look impressive. I hope it's not permanent."

Maureen laughed. "We have a special spray that removes it completely. After a shower, it will all be gone." She touched his forearm, trailed the tattoo. "Except for this."

"I hope so," Peter said. "I've had it for a long time."

Maureen pulled something out of a bag she had brought with her. "Here, put this on."

Peter took it from her. It looked like a mask. The head of a snake, a cobra. He slipped it over his head. Holes for his eyes only slightly obscured his vision.

He watched Maureen put on a similar mask. She pulled out something else. A cloak. She threw it over his wide shoulders. Then he followed her out of the room, down the stairs, to another part of the house. They entered a room that lay in semi-darkness.

As his eyes adjusted, he saw people wearing long, black robes, their heads covered by large hoods.

Maureen took Peter to a slightly raised dais. On it stood two throne-like chairs. "Sit," she told him.

Peter obeyed. Maureen took the second chair.

Suddenly, the room vibrated with the dull sound of a gong. The people in the room moved toward the dais and looked at Peter and Maureen.

Peter couldn't make out the faces hidden in the darkness of theirs hoods. He sensed Maureen standing up. When he turned his head, he saw her raise her arms above her head.

"My sisters," her voice rang through the room. "I have called you to take part in an important event. Tonight a prophecy will be fulfilled. As has been foretold, He has come to deliver us from the sting of the Scorpion. King Cobra!"

"King Cobra. King Cobra!" Their voices echoed in the room. Female voices. They undid their robes and let them slide to the floor.

Peter stared at their naked bodies, their breasts, their exposed pubic mounds, their covered heads and faces.

A naked girl stood in front of Peter and handed him a goblet.

"Drink from the offering," Maureen said beside him.

Amused, Peter took the goblet and put it against his lips. He managed to empty it, even though the hole in his mask was just a small slit. The liquid tasted like sweet wine, but moments later he realized there had been something else in that offering, something that began to confuse his thoughts and started a raging fire burning in his loins.

The naked females parted and formed a line on each side of the room.

Through a skylight fell the rays of the full moon, bathing the beautiful nude body of a young woman with its pale light. She moved slowly, her hips swaying to the rhythm of the chanting watchers. Her full round breasts stood in contrast to the rest of her body, which seemed covered with large, shimmering scales.

He moaned.

Suddenly, he found himself back in Saigon, in a moonlit garden.

"Serpa," he whispered. Without conscious thought, he rose from his chair and started walking toward the girl. His cloak slipped from his shoulders.

They met in the center of the room. Peter looked into her black eyes. He couldn't see the rest of her face, hidden behind a thin cloth of silk.

She touched his chest, let her hand slide down across the hard muscles of his stomach, down to his groin. Slim fingers curled around his tremendous erection.

She lowered herself to the floor, pulled him down with her. Her legs opened, he fell between them and, with a loud groan, he sank his hard member into her welcoming soft sheath. She cried out softly and pushed up against him.

His head swam. Delirious, he moved between her strong satiny thighs.

"Take it easy," the girl whispered into his ear.

"Serpa, Serpa," he whispered. "It's been so long."

"My name isn't Serpa," she said fiercely. "I don't know what they gave you but snap out of it!"

Her sharp voice seemed to bring him back to reality. "What's happening?" he asked, listening to the chanting female voices. He shook his head to clear it.

"I'm Nancy," the girl whispered as she writhed beneath him, milking his throbbing penis. "You're the guy Maureen brought to the gym, aren't you?"

Peter grunted, kept pushing deep into her.

"I'm supposed to be a virgin," she gasped. "I guess you've noticed I wasn't. Don't tell them, okay?"

"I won't," he said hoarsely. "I don't care if you are a virgin or not. I don't care about anything. All I want is to stay inside you forever… Why do I feel like this?"

"You've been drugged, you big idiot," Nancy whispered, and then she cried out as her body was gripped by a powerful orgasm.

The effects of the drug seemed to wear off, his thoughts began to clear, and he became aware of his surroundings.

The women were still chanting. They had moved closer, he could reach out and touch the nearest. Gentle hands pulled him off the girl and pushed him onto his back.

They began straddling him, one after the other.

He watched a woman hover momentarily above him, watched her descending. Then he slid into another creamy sheath.

The woman bent forward, her large breasts grazing his chest. She lifted her mask and then his and kissed him. Her tongue forced open his mouth. Kissing her hungrily, he hardly noticed the capsule she dropped down his throat.

"Sorry," she murmured, "but this is necessary. You won't remember much in the morning."

She kissed him gently then she left him.

His vision began to blur; he found it almost impossible to formulate clear thoughts.

In a moment of clarity, he became aware of Nancy, the painted girl, mounting him.

"I am the last one," she said with a low, gasping voice. "You have to come inside me. Can you do it?"

He nodded, grabbing her hips. Then he pulled her into his lap, roared, as his throbbing penis erupted. She moaned, lifting her head high.

A soft cry escaped her open lips, but the collective triumphant cry of the watching women drowned it out. Then she collapsed on top of him, lay gasping in his arms.

"You are truly King Cobra," she gasped, her eyes wide in admiration. "What they said about you is true. No normal man can last this long."

Suddenly extreme fatigue seemed to absorb what little energy he had left.

Nancy rose. A pair of women led her away.

Someone took his hand and pulled him up. "Come," a soft voice said.

He followed the woman out of the room. They walked in semi-darkness. He was barely aware when he fell onto a bed, asleep before his head hit the pillow.

When he awoke with a slight headache he remembered little of the previous night.

Chapter Nineteen

"Well," said a woman's voice. "How do you feel?"

He looked up at the woman standing beside his bed, immediately smitten by her extreme beauty.

"I feel fine," he said, conscious of being naked under the thin sheet covering his body. Studying her face, he asked, "Have we met? You look familiar."

She smiled. Without a word, she began to unbutton her blouse, opened it. She didn't wear a bra. Staring first at the swell of her full breasts and then at the tattoo on the left one, he moaned. "You!" he said. "But how can that be?"

She sat down beside him, took his hand and put it on her breast. Warm and soft in his hand, he became aware of the steady beat of her heart behind it.

"I've never forgotten you," she whispered. "You were so young then." She stroked his cheek. "We thought you were dead."

"I saw you in my dreams," he said. "You made love to me."

She smiled again, her hand warm on his cheek.

"In my dreams I remembered you, those nights in Saigon, your daughter Serpa." He sat up and put his hands to his head. "Serpa," he said. "Last night. What happened? She was there. I can still see her body swaying in the moonlight. She was as beautiful and young as back then."

He stared at the woman. "How is that possible? How could she still look so young? And all the others, all those beautiful faceless women giving themselves to me. It must have been one of my dreams."

"No dream, Peter," she said gently. "It happened."

"But Serpa? How?"

"It wasn't Serpa. It was her daughter."

Peter stared. "Her daughter? How old is the daughter?"

168

"She's twenty."

Peter shook his head. "It happened twenty-one years ago. But I can't get a woman pregnant."

Her smile was as gentle as her touch. "Oh, yes, you can. You did."

"Are you telling me that the girl I had sex with last night is my daughter?" Peter looked horrified.

"Nancy?" She chuckled, obviously enjoying his discomfort. "No, Nancy is not your daughter."

"Then who is?"

"Her name is Petra. I named her after you."

"I don't understand," Peter said, confused. "If Nancy is Serpa's daughter, who is Petra's mother?"

The woman's black eyes sparkled. "I am," she said. "You were right when you told me that I was the Chosen One. Our union produced a beautiful girl. You'd be proud of her."

Peter sat silent for a moment, and then he said, "I've met her. She is beautiful, just like her mother."

"Thank you." The woman smiled. "By the way, she doesn't know you're her father. I told her that her father is dead." She sighed. "You know, Petra should have been the Virgin-Goddess last night, because she is still a virgin…and my daughter. But I couldn't do that to you. So we chose Nancy. She is a wild one, and no virgin, but you probably noticed that."

"You said Nancy is Serpa's daughter. Who is her father?"

A dark cloud crossed the woman's features. "When you took Serpa's virginity, you angered a young man who wanted her for himself. You fought him."

"Scorpion?" Peter said, memory rushing up like bitter bile.

"That's right. He wanted his vengeance, so he raped Serpa. He got her pregnant."

"That son-of-a-bitch!" Peter cursed. "I should have killed him."

"He almost killed you, Peter. He is a dangerous man. He might have killed us, given the chance."

"When did you move to the States?"

"Your friend Maureen helped us. Even then she already belonged to the Sisterhood."

"She was in Saigon?" Peter asked.

The woman nodded. "She was trained there. I assume you know what business she's in, or don't you?"

"I know. I used to do similar work." Peter shivered underneath the thin covering, remembering the things he had done.

"Are you cold?" the woman asked. With a little smile, she shed her clothes. Peter had a brief glimpse of her nude voluptuous body before she joined him under the covers. Her body felt warm and yielding as she pressed herself against him.

"You haven't changed much," he said.

"Not much." She laughed. "You're being kind. "I am fifty-six years old, my breasts are sagging, I've gained weight; I need glasses…"

Peter kissed her on the lips. She opened her mouth to let his tongue touch hers. He rolled on top of her, between her opening thighs and slid deep into her welcoming softness. She moaned, biting his lips. They didn't talk.

She cried out when a strong orgasm gripped her body. "You truly are extraordinary," she gasped.

As much as Peter enjoyed coupling with this woman, he didn't make it last as long as he would have liked. He was still tired from the night before, but he finally let his own climax build. Conscious and in control, he came with a mighty burst and suppressed the urge to shout triumphantly. Instead, he just moaned deeply and crushed his mouth to hers.

After getting back his breath, he asked, "Where you there last night?"

"Only as a watcher."

"How about my daughter…our daughter?"

"No." She shook her head. "She wasn't there."

His hand stroked her breast, trailed the tattoo of the cobra. "What happened to Serpa?"

With a mystic smile she said, "Her name is Connie now."

"Connie," he repeated. "That's why she looked so familiar. She reminded me of you."

"She is a lot like me. Not like my other daughter, Sue, who has a mischievous streak in her. Nancy should have been Sue's daughter." She looked at Peter, a strange look on her face. "You know," she said, "you can boast quite a record. How many men can say they've had sex with a girl, her mother, her grandmother, and her aunt?"

"Not many, I suppose," he mused. "Does Connie know who I am?"

"She didn't when you first came to her establishment, but she knows now."

"You said you were at my house that night. Does that mean my girlfriend Kathleen is involved? How does she fit into this?"

She didn't answer. He lay still on top of her. With a sudden twist, she turned them both and put him onto his back. Then she began to rotate her bottom. She had her eyes closed. A strand of her black hair covered half her face. "This is Nirvana," she whispered. "Everything is perfect. You and I are one."

Their bodies seemed to meld together, moved in perfect unison.

"Kathleen," she said suddenly. "She is one of us."

"Kathleen? An assassin?" he blurted out, still gasping for breath.

"Not all of us are assassins. There are many facets to our organization." She freed him, slipped off the bed. "I can't tell you anything about Kathleen. She has to do that herself." Naked, she padded out of the door. "I'm going to take a shower."

The image of her voluptuous body still in his mind, Peter put his hands behind his head and lay there, staring at the ceiling. These last two weeks had certainly been eventful and his whole life turned upside down.

Five years he'd been living together with a woman he knew nothing about.

She was thirty-three years old. Born in Seattle to Suzan and Bernhard McGuinness. No siblings. Left home at age seventeen, moved to L.A. Became a model.

Presently doing part-time modeling for Global Crown Agency.

He had never bothered to accompany her to any shoots, never been to any of the shows where she modeled, had never shown an interest in her work. He had only one excuse, she had never asked him to come.

How neglected she must have felt all these years! No wonder she got bored with him and joined the Sisterhood.

When she brought home Sue Lin that night he should have suspected that there was another side to Kathleen.

Kathleen…the demure devoted beautiful girlfriend.

Quite an actress!

What else did she hide? What exactly, besides modeling, did she do for the Sisterhood?

Someone entering the room interrupted his thoughts. Maureen. "I see you have company," she said, looking at the little heap of discarded clothing on the floor.

Peter grimaced. "An old acquaintance, but I think you know who I'm talking about."

"Mai Lin Cheng, now Mai Lin-Carson," Maureen said. "Yes, I know who she is. She's a good friend. I saved her from death at the hands of one of the most dangerous men I've ever met. Guess who was responsible for the danger she was exposed to?"

"I was twenty, and she the madam of a brothel," Peter defended himself. "I meant her no harm."

"No, you didn't, except you fathered a child with her."

Peter rolled his eyes. "So you know, too. I thought it was a secret. Until today even I didn't know."

Maureen sat down at the edge of the bed. "Only I know. She didn't even tell Serpa, her daughter. You know her now as Connie."

"Connie," he said thoughtfully. "She was so young and innocent then…a virgin. Do you know she was the only virgin I ever made love to? Hard to believe, but it's the honest truth."

Maureen looked up as Mai walked in, naked and sparkling clean. "Hi, Mai. Are you done with him?"

The older woman laughed. "For now, but you can't get enough of a man like Peter."

"I know." Maureen sighed. "He's a rare specimen. One woman could never claim him for herself."

Both women laughed.

Peter shook his head. "I'm not a piece of meat, ladies. I have feelings, you know." He chuckled. "You're right, I've never been faithful to any woman, not even to the woman I call my girlfriend." Speaking of her sobered him up. "Kathleen. Where is she?"

"She is safe," Maureen said. "Don't worry about her."

"I thought my former employer Palmer and his accomplices had her."

"She was never in any danger. She was a willing participant, but we'll let Kathleen explain that to you." Maureen touched his shoulder. "Don't be hard on her. She didn't have much choice."

"I'd better leave," Mai said. Fully dressed now, she bent down to kiss him on the cheek. "Goodbye, Peter." She touched a finger to his lips. Then she walked out of the door.

Maureen got up, too. "See you later," she said, following the other woman.

Peter was ready to get up when another person walked through the door.

Her auburn hair fell softly around her creamy shoulders. She smiled, but there was no sparkle in her green eyes. "Hello, Peter," she said, standing uncertain beside his bed.

He sat up, pulled her down, and kissed her. When they broke apart, he could see the tears in her eyes.

"I love you, Peter," she said. "Whatever happened, it doesn't change that."

"I love you, too," Peter told her, "but we have a lot to talk about."

Kathleen looked around the room. "Connie told me I would find you here. This house belongs to Maureen. How do you know her?"

"I've only known her for a short time. Her brother and I used to be good friends."

"I didn't know she had a brother, but then again, I don't know much about Maureen. Nobody really does."

"How did you get involved with the Sisterhood?" Peter asked.

Kathleen looked startled. "You know? I'm a member only through Sue Lin. We work together. She introduced me, but I'm not really a full-fledged member, just an associate. I don't take part in the secret ceremonies."

"I see," Peter said, letting out a sigh of relief. Obviously, she didn't know about his part in one of those ceremonies. He stroked her silky hair and looked into her green eyes. "I thought you were in grave danger. Robert Palmer, that son-of-a-bitch, and his partner told me they were holding you for ransom. Unless I gave them what they wanted, they'd use you in a snuff-movie. They showed me some videos."

She blinked back a few tears. When she looked at him, her eyes shone wet. "I'm sorry I put you through this, but Robert showed me a video of you and Linda. Then he told me you had something they wanted and if I helped him to get it, he would see to it you would not be blamed for the murder of that couple. In the meantime, he said, you should sweat it out in jail for a while to teach you a lesson."

"That bastard!" Peter cursed.

Kathleen nodded, gave a deep sigh. "Things changed when someone got you out of jail. He became nasty and blackmailed me to make that video he showed you."

"I don't understand. Why did you agree? What does he have on you?"

She lowered her eyelids. Peter noticed wetness on her cheeks. "Years back I've made some soft-porn movies. Somehow, Robert got hold of them. He threatened to show them to you." She looked into Peter's eyes. "I didn't want you to see them."

Peter stroked her cheek. "It wouldn't have bothered me, honey. I've done some things I'm not proud of, but that is all in the past."

Kathleen smiled bravely, and Peter realized how beautiful she was. How could I have ever cheated on her? He vowed to never do so again.

"Nobody ever threatened me physically. I don't believe they would have hurt me." Kathleen shrugged. "But then…who knows?"

"So you were free to leave anytime?" Peter asked. "Where did you stay?"

"I stayed with Sue Lin most of the time." She hesitated. "The only one I didn't really trust was Yussof Robowich."

"But in the end, they let you go. I wonder why, because I never gave them anything."

Kathleen smiled. "I think they are afraid of you, Peter. I don't know why. You've never harmed anyone. I know you're into that kung fu stuff, but that's just for sports, isn't it? I mean you don't go around beating up people."

"Not as a rule." Peter didn't smile. "If they would have hurt you, I would have hurt them badly. They have reason to be afraid."

"You're sweet, but you don't need to act tough. I love you the way you are. Will you be coming home soon?"

Peter shook his head. "I'm still a fugitive from the law. There are a few things I have to clear up, but hopefully soon I'll be able to come home. Don't tell anyone that you have talked to me. Okay?"

She dried her tears and kissed him. "Okay." She got up. "I have to go. Another shoot. See you soon."

At the door, she turned and blew him a kiss, and then she was gone.

Chapter Twenty

After his shower, Peter looked for the kitchen. Maureen wasn't anywhere to be found. An older black woman was busy at the sink. She looked up when he approached. "Good morning, sir," she said pleasantly. "I was told to make you breakfast."

While he waited for his eggs, bacon and coffee, he decided to phone Stella.

Someone answered, but it wasn't Stella. When he asked for her, there was a short pause and then a man's voice asked who was calling.

"Tell her it's Peter."

The voice on the other end chuckled. "Well, well, Mr. Hartmann. We've waited for your call."

"Who the hell is this?" Peter asked. "I want to talk to Stella."

"Your bitch is tied up for the moment. She is unharmed…but who knows for how long."

"She's not my bitch," Peter growled.

"You're fucking her. That makes her your bitch."

"You harm her, and I will find you, whoever you are," Peter said with what he hoped was a menacing tone.

"Now, now," the voice said pleasantly. "No need to become hostile. You don't have to come searching for her. I'll tell you where you can find your pussy, but don't wait too long."

After getting the address from the mystery man, Peter slammed down the receiver. "Fuck it!" he cursed.

The housekeeper gave him a look of disapproval but kept silent. Peter gulped down his breakfast, not enjoying it at all. Then he took a cab to the address he'd received.

It looked like an abandoned warehouse. Peter told the cab driver not to wait.

Two burly guys intercepted him at the entrance. They did a thorough body search. Peter could tell they were pros.

He didn't have any weapons with him.

"Go through that door," one of them told him with a voice that sounded like gravel spilling from a truck. "They're waiting for you."

The other one grinned. "Have fun."

Peter grunted and, silently, he walked toward the indicated door.

He wasn't prepared and, later, he cursed himself for being so stupid and careless. As soon as he walked through the door, they grabbed him, and before he could take any defensive action, someone jabbed a needle into his buttocks.

His strength ebbing from his legs, his vision already blurring, he sagged into a pair of strong arms. When he regained consciousness, he was securely tied to a chair.

"Welcome, Mr. Hartmann, or should I say McDiarmid?"

The voice dripped with sarcasm, a voice he recognized immediately.

"Shaw," he said, his tongue a little thick from the drug. "Forgive me if I don't say what a pleasant surprise."

"It's Colonel Shaw," the other one said. "Remember that, Lieutenant!"

"Call me Mr. Hartmann, because that is my legal name now."

"I don't give a fuck what you call yourself, Lieutenant. As far as I'm concerned, you're still working for the Company…now that you're back with the living."

Shaw put on some weight since Peter had seen him last. At five foot eleven, he had always looked gaunt, but now he appeared massive, beefy. His hair and mustache were touched with patches of gray, but Peter knew he wasn't that old. Possibly in his late forties.

"Frankly, I'm surprised you were taken so easily. I'm disappointed. That wouldn't have happened in the old days." Shaw chuckled gleefully. "But then you've always loved your pussy. I guess that hasn't changed. A buck in rut is easy prey."

"Where is Stella?" Peter asked.

"Stella? Oh, you mean Agent Chandler? You do seem to care for her. Well, that is good. Maybe she can persuade you to give us what we want."

177

"I have nothing you want." Peter tugged on his bonds. "This is not necessary."

Shaw smiled thinly. "I don't trust you, McDiarmid. You killed one of my best men, you know."

"If you're talking about Adam, he deserved it. He murdered his partner and would have killed me, too."

"Too bad about that other agent, but in every war there are always casualties."

"War?" Peter almost laughed. "We aren't in a war. You're involved with terrorists. You're a fucking traitor to this country."

"Watch your mouth, McDiarmid. Don't talk to me about patriotism or shit like that. Our government is the worst offender. When the Russians tried to invade Afghanistan, we sold the Afghans weapons. We even trained Osama bin Laden. We sold weapons to Saddam Hussein to help him in his war with Iran. Should I go on? Somebody always gets rich. It's nothing but business. That's really what it's all about. I love my country, the good old USA, the Land of the Free, where any man can reach his full potential if he's not afraid to take advantage of every opportunity. The sky's the limit, and I'm reaching for the sky."

"Just make sure you're wearing your parachute," Peter said sarcastically.

"What do you mean by that?"

"Eventually you'll fall from that sky you're reaching for. You can bet on that. Don't think you're untouchable, Shaw."

The Colonel laughed. "I work for the government. I am the Law. Nobody can touch me."

"Don't be too sure. People like you eventually trip up. You may be wearing a badge, and you yield a lot of power, but you are abusing that power. You're nothing but a fucking criminal. You belong behind bars, and the sooner the better."

Shaw came close to Peter, his face inches away. Peter could see the vein throbbing in his temple. "You are the one running from the law," Shaw said between clenched teeth. "Don't call me a criminal. And another thing…I am Colonel Shaw. You will address me as such, do you understand, Lieutenant McDiarmid?"

"Fuck you!" Peter cursed then flinched when Shaw backhanded him across the face.

The Colonel walked away, stiff legged. Then he turned and stared at Peter. "You're a fool. You know, if you would have been smarter, you could have made a lot of money back in Colombia. You should have worked with me."

Peter laughed. "You would have given me the same deal you gave McAllister. You set him up."

"McAllister was a stupid and greedy fool. He wanted too much." Colonel Shaw stared at Peter with narrow eyes. "How do you know about McAllister? He died in Colombia."

"You forget we were friends," Peter said. "He told me about the deal he made with you. I told him not to trust you, but as you say, he was a fool. That cost him his life."

Obviously, Shaw didn't know Donald was still alive, and Peter wasn't going to enlighten him and possibly put his friend in danger.

"Did Colonel Bender know?" Shaw asked.

Peter shook his head. "Colonel Bender was my superior, not my friend. I didn't tell him everything."

"He wasn't your friend, yet you carried him through snake-infested swamps and jungle to save his life."

"He was my superior officer. I did my duty, like any good soldier would have done."

"Like I said, you're a fool, Lieutenant." Shaw eyed him speculatively. "You could still work for me. I could use a man like you. You'd be smart to take my offer. I could make all the charges go away. You'd be a free man."

"Go suck your dick, Colonel. Now…where is Stella?"

Shaw shook his head. "Insulting me isn't going to help you, McDiarmid. As for your girlfriend, you'll see her soon. By the way, you know that I can't let you leave here alive, unless you change your mind about where your loyalties lie. Why don't you make it easy and tell me what you did with the material you took from the Liebman place. I promise Agent Chandler will be unharmed, and your death will be swift and painless."

"How are you going to explain my death to her?"

"If you give me what I want, she won't know you were ever here. There will be nothing to explain."

"Sounds good to me," Peter said, "except I have nothing to give you. I told Palmer and friends, and now I'm telling you."

"Palmer and friends, very aptly put." Colonel Shaw laughed without humor. "Those amateurs managed to screw up everything. When Robowich came to me for help, I arranged to have that Liebman woman eliminated. It would have been such a simple operation, but then your boss, Robert Palmer, had to meddle. He decided this was the perfect opportunity to rid himself of an irritating employee. Who knew you were that employee? I mean, what are the chances? You should have stayed dead and buried."

He came closer. "I'm asking you one more time. What did you do with the chip and disk? Are you by any chance dealing with someone else?"

"You must be deaf, Shaw," Peter said. "Let me tell you once more...I don't have anything."

"Very well. You leave me no choice." The Colonel pulled a phone out of his pocket and dialed. "Bring her down," he said into the phone.

A couple of minutes later a door opened, and Stella was pushed into the room, accompanied by two men.

One of them was Detective Slovik.

The big detective grinned when he saw Peter. "Nice to see you again, tough guy. You don't look so tough now. Let's see you get out of here this time."

Stella wanted to rush toward Peter, but they held her back. "I'm sorry, Peter," she said, her voice strained. "I screwed up. They took me by surprise. I didn't tell them anything."

Before Peter could reply, Shaw held up a hand. "In other words, there is something to tell. You'd better speak up now, McDiarmid, or else your pretty girlfriend here may not look so pretty anymore."

"You harm her, and I'll kill you, you son-of-a-bitch!" Peter growled.

The Colonel laughed. "Big words from a guy who is tied to a chair." He turned toward Slovik and nodded.

The detective took hold of Stella's blouse and ripped open the front. Then he pushed down her bra to expose her breasts. "Nice," he grinned, cupping one of them.

Stella cried out angrily and kicked the big man in the shin. He cursed and slapped her across the face. "You slut!" he hissed.

Peter tugged on his bonds. "Take your filthy hands off her!" he yelled.

"Do you have something to tell us?" Shaw asked.

When Peter glared at him, Shaw nodded again.

While the other man held Stella, Slovik began to pull down her skirt. Stella kicked and screamed. "Take your time, tough guy."

"Stop!" Peter shouted. "I'll talk."

"Too bad," Slovik said. "I think I would have enjoyed this."

"Let her go," Shaw said sharply and turned to Peter. "All right, talk."

"It's in a locker. But I don't have the key with me. I gave it to Stella."

"Is that true?" Shaw asked Stella.

She looked at Peter then back at Shaw. "Yes, he gave me a key, but I don't know what's in the locker. And I don't have the key either."

"Who has it? Where is it?" The Colonel sounded irritated.

Stella shrugged. "In a safe place."

"Where?"

"In my office, but you'll never find it. I have to get it myself."

"Then get it! Detective Slovik will accompany you. We wouldn't want you to get any strange ideas."

Stella pulled up her skirt. Slovik had ripped the button off her blouse, so she tied it around her waist.

"Look very carefully in the envelope," Peter called to her before she walked out of the door. "I'm sure you'll find what is needed."

Stella stopped, looked back at Peter, and smiled. "I'm sure I will. I'll be back. Don't worry."

When she was gone, Colonel Shaw stood in front of Peter and stared silently at him.

"Why do you hate me, Colonel Shaw?" Peter broke the silence.

"I don't hate you, McDiarmid."

"Then why do you want me dead?"

Shaw pursed his lips. "It's nothing personal," he said. "You're an obstacle that has to be removed, that's all. I can't have a man like you running around free, knowing the things you know about me. That's why McAllister had to die, and that's why you must die, too."

"What about Stella?" Peter knew the answer but asked anyway.

"Agent Chandler? She will be terminated."

Peter laughed. "Terminated! I like that. It makes death sound so official and impersonal. How are you going to do it?"

"It will be quick and painless, as I promised." He turned and looked at the opening door, at the woman who came stalking in.

"Hello, Edward," the woman said. She walked up to Peter. "Nice to see you again, Mr. Hartmann." Smiling, she stood wide-legged in front of him. She wore black tight-fitting pants that seemed like a second skin, showing off her long, muscular legs. A loose black sweatshirt covered her top and part of her lower torso.

"Hello, Mrs. Liebman," Peter said. "How goes the charity drive, and how is the Senator?"

Delta Liebman laughed. "My husband is fine, and the charity drive was successful. There are plenty of bleeding hearts out there who are more than willing to part with their money. How about you, Peter? How is dear Linda, your employer's wife? I hear you finally screwed her. You should have kept that pecker inside your pants. You might not be sitting here right now if you had."

She bent down and put her lips against his forehead. The scent of perfume rose up in his nostrils, mixed with a hint of alcohol when her breath washed across his face.

"I heard stories about you, Peter. Apparently you're quite a stud," she whispered into his ear.

"Stories." Peter grinned. "They're sometimes exaggerated."

She straightened up, turned away from him, giving him a close-up view of her round buttocks. Peter saw Shaw watching them, his expression stoic, unreadable.

"Tell me, how do you fit into the picture, Mrs. Liebman?" Peter asked.

She looked back at him over her shoulder, her blue eyes half-hidden behind her lowered long, blond lashes. "Edward is my half-brother, and I am a high official in the Order of the Scorpion." She turned toward Colonel Shaw. "I'd like to be alone with Mr. Hartmann for a while. Can you arrange that we'll be undisturbed?"

The Colonel hesitated. "Are you sure that's wise? He is a dangerous man."

Delta laughed. "Dear Eddie, I am not a helpless little schoolgirl. My sting can be quite lethal. Don't worry. I'll be fine."

Shaw left the room without a backwards glance. Delta walked to the door and locked it. When she walked back to Peter, her blue eyes were wide open, bright in her tanned face. She squatted in front of him and untied the ropes from his feet. Then she did the same to his hands and arms.

"Take off your clothes!" she commanded.

Peter rubbed his wrists and his legs. They tingled as the circulation rushed back into them. "Why?" he asked.

The woman laughed. "Don't pretend to be stupid, Peter. You know what I want."

"You want me to fuck you," he said bluntly.

She smiled. "No. I want to fuck you."

"I could kill you right now. You're taking quite a chance," Peter told her but began to remove his clothes.

"You're smart," Delta said. "Killing me wouldn't get you out of here. Not alive, anyway. And your death would be slow and painful." She chuckled. "Look at the bright side of this. One last glorious fuck for the condemned man. What better way to go? Better than any steak dinner."

When he stood naked, Delta studied him, approval in her eyes. Smiling, she ran her hands down his muscular chest, stroked his wide shoulders, and squeezed his bulging biceps.

"A He-man," she said with a suddenly husky voice. "I had a feeling you'd look like this." Her finger trailed the outline of the tattoo on his right arm. "The Cobra," she whispered. Bending forward, she ran her tongue down the length of his arm. Then she stepped back and pulled her sweatshirt over her head.

As Peter had suspected, she was nude underneath. Her breasts were small, but firm. She had wide shoulders. Her arms and body rippled with muscles that could put a man to shame. The image of a scorpion with its stinger raised was tattooed below her right breast.

She peeled off her tight pants, pulling her panties with them. Then she turned and stood naked in front of him, letting him look at her pronounced smooth Venus mound.

"Sit in the chair!" she told him.

He sat down, watching her. Delta looked at his rising penis and licked her lips. Then she straddled him and, without any preliminaries, she slid her creamy, moist sheath over his hard mast.

She moaned loudly as Peter slid deep into her. He fastened his teeth over her left nipple and bit down gently. She cried out and snapped her bottom back and forth. Peter grabbed her solid buttocks to steady her. It didn't take long before he felt her warm discharge.

After that she stopped moving, just sat in his lap, eyes closed, rippling her inner muscles gently across his deeply lodged penis.

"I don't love my husband," she said suddenly. "I married him only for convenience. I need his position to gain the power I crave for." She gasped, moved her lower body gently back and forth. "But I need more than that. Sometimes I need to fuck a real man and have my brains fucked out by a man."

She opened her eyes and pulled herself up. Then she dropped to her knees, knelt on the floor and looked back at Peter through half-lidded eyes. "Fuck me from behind. Hard!"

Peter got down behind her, cupped her body and pushed his penis between her round, muscular buttocks. He slid back into her warm, wet sheath. Moving fast and furious, he slammed his belly hard into her solid buttocks, entering her deep with every powerful thrust.

"Yess…" she cried out. "Yes…oh…yess!"

Peter put his hands over her taut breasts, rocked backwards until he lay on his back. She straightened her upper torso, moved up and down, her buttocks clenching every time she lifted up. Then she turned around and faced Peter. With her hands on his knees, she lifted herself up as high as she could without uncoupling. Then she sank back down into his lap. She had powerful, muscular legs and thighs and she stayed in that position for a long time.

Peter stared at her swollen mound, watched his penis being swallowed up over and over by her greedy pussy.

She gave him a tense smile.

"There is a very old legend in the country where I come from. It tells the story about a scorpion and a serpent. No, they didn't fall in love, but they had sexual intercourse anyway. Their union produced a great warrior, who later became the leader of a clan of deadly assassins."

"Is that what you're hoping for?" Peter asked between clenched teeth. He was trying hard not to come inside her. As long as he was fucking this woman, he was alive. However, he had to admit, even knowing he was almost certain to die, somehow it didn't diminish the fact that he was enjoying himself.

He had been in dangerous situations before and that had never stopped him. Besides, his hands and feet were free, and if he could help it, they would stay that way. He reached for the woman, pulled her down, and then he rolled over until she was underneath him. She struggled against him, but he held her down.

"You want to be fucked?" he grunted, "Then let me do it."

Her strong, muscular thighs fell open wide, releasing their tight grip.

The short pause gave Peter enough time to gain control over his urge to come, and now he began to move with strong, powerful strokes between her widespread thighs. He pushed hard and deep, making her cry out with every forceful thrust.

A steady moan came from her open mouth, her eyes were wide open, staring unseeing into his face as she came. Peter kept pounding away until she cried out for him to end it. "Come inside me now," she sobbed. "Don't stop without coming inside me."

He was getting tired and the pressure had been building up for a long time. Letting go, he lay inside her tight embrace. Her strong legs clamped around his, her lower body lifted high to receive his gift.

He came with a deep loud shout, and then he collapsed, cradled by her strong arms and thighs.

When their breathing had returned to normal, she opened her arms and eased up on the pressure of her thighs. He rolled onto his back, lay on the hard wooden floor.

She got up, stretched. Her muscles rippled over her entire body. Then she stood above him, put one foot onto his stomach. "You are some stud," she said. "No man has ever made me come like that."

"Why did you try to have me killed?" he asked.

"What?" she seemed startled by his unexpected question.

"You hired some hit man, a Theodore Ronald Barkin from Dallas, to take me out," he said.

"Oh, that." She shrugged. The gesture made her small breasts jiggle. "Yes, I did. Edward's attempt was unsuccessful, so I decided to take care of it. But my man obviously failed, too. Now I'm glad he did. It would have robbed me of an unforgettable experience."

"Were you involved in your sister-in-law's death?"

Delta spat. "That fat cow! I've always hated her. She was such a good and upstanding citizen. Always doing charity work, always wanting to do good. She was so horrified when she found out that her husband was involved in something illegal. She kept a journal with names and locations. She was a security risk."

"So you and Edward decided to get rid of her. How about J. J. Liebman, your husband's brother? Why did you have him killed?"

"He was too weak. Rhonda had too much influence over him. It was my decision to eliminate him, too. Besides, with him out of the way, my husband will inherit Liebman Electronics."

"Which will make you even richer and give you more power. You are a devious woman." Peter commented, casually putting a hand on her leg. "What's going to happen next?"

Delta smiled. "You still have to die, Peter." She shivered as he ran his finger up her thigh. "Stop that!" she said with a quaking voice.

His finger moved higher, touched her pussy. Gently, he pushed one finger into her.

She moaned, moved her foot off his belly. Squatting down, she took his member into her hands, stroked it. Then she lifted up, hovered for a moment above his now rigid penis and, holding it with one hand, lowered herself onto it.

Peter felt his mast sliding back into her warm, creamy interior.

She began to whip her pelvis back and forth, riding him with wild and careless abandon. She had shed her cool exterior. Now she was nothing but a ferocious female animal in heat.

Peter grabbed her furiously moving hips. Grunting, he pushed up. She took his pole deep into her with every thrust. Her blue eyes glazed over, rolled in their sockets as a quiver ran through her body.

Peter held her down, erupting inside her.

When they both were finished, she lifted up without a word, walked over to the chair and leaned against it, her breathing still ragged, almost sounding like someone sobbing. Her body shone slick with sweat. She kept her eyes closed. When she finally opened them, she stared at Peter, who lay propped up on his elbows, watching her.

Her merry laughter suddenly filled the room. "You're a son-of-a-bitch," she said, her voice husky, almost hoarse. "You think you can fuck me until I let you go?"

Peter grinned. "It's a thought."

She shook her head. "I'm almost inclined to do just that, but it is not my decision alone. There are other people involved."

As if on cue, someone began banging on the door.

"Open up!" a muffled but commanding voice came from the other side of the door.

"Give me a minute," Delta called, slipping into her clothes with feverish haste. Then she ran her fingers through her short blond hair and went to unlock the door.

The man who walked in was short and squat, oriental looking.

He stared at Delta Liebman and then at Peter and grunted, obviously disgusted with what he saw.

The woman smiled, trying to look composed. She couldn't hide her flushed face and puffed-up eyes.

"You're a slut!" the man spat. "Women do not belong in our organization." He spoke with a slight accent. He looked at Peter who was slowly getting off the floor.

"You!" the man said harshly, pointing a finger at Peter. "I am going to kill you now!"

Chapter Twenty-One

"One wrong move and I'll blow your head off!" Detective Slovik put a hand on the gun under his arm to back up his statement.

Stella shot him angry look but kept silent. Detective Slovic seemed to know his way around the FBI's offices. He had said hello to a couple of agents, shook hands with another one. Obviously, he was known there.

Stella wondered who the mole was who had leaked information out of the office. She made a mental note to check out the three agents with whom Slovic seemed so friendly. If she ever got the chance. So far, it seemed unlikely.

She retrieved the key Peter had given her, and then they were on their way to the bus depot.

"Someday you'll make a mistake, Slovik, and you'll fry for this," she said.

The big detective laughed. "Shut up, and keep your eyes on the road."

"You knew all along Hartmann was innocent, didn't you?" she asked, defiance in her voice.

Slovik sighed. "I knew, but he was marked to take the blame. I only followed orders."

"You were willing to let an innocent man go to prison? Possibly getting the chair?"

"That Hartmann fellow or whatever his name is, he's no innocent victim. I understand he used to kill people for The Company. He was a fucking assassin...don't tell me he's innocent!" He reached for the car's cigarette lighter, waited until it popped out, then he lit a cigarette.

Stella coughed when he blew smoke in her direction. "Do you mind blowing it somewhere else?" she said tersely.

"Go fuck yourself!" Slovik cursed. "I'll blow it anywhere I like."

He put a beefy hand on her thigh and squeezed. Stella jerked her foot off the gas pedal. The car veered to the left, a car horn blared beside her.

"You want us to have an accident?" she yelled.

Slovik laughed, dragged on his cigarette. "I think I'll fuck you before we get back. You've got a lot of fire. I bet you fuck real good."

"Only with guys I like, and you I don't like. You're an asshole," Stella hissed. "I'll rip off your prick before you put it inside me."

"As long as you use your cunt to do it with." Slovik shook with roaring laughter. "As soon as we get the stuff, we'll make a little detour. I know this little motel, very quiet. You'll find I'm not such a bad guy. You might even like it. I know your type. You always cry no, but once you've got that piece of meat inside you, you'll change your mind."

"Never!"

"We'll see. Now shut up, and let me enjoy my cigarette."

They drove the rest of the way in silence, but when they were near the bus depot, Slovic suddenly told her to drive into a side street.

Stella looked at him. His eyes seemed glazed over.

"You're stoned," she said. She had finally figured out what that sweet smell was.

Slovik was smoking dope.

He laughed and told her to stop in front of a sleazy rundown motel. "Listen," he said, "I don't really like to rape a woman. There isn't much enjoyment in it. I'll make you a deal. If you fuck me without struggling, I'll protect you from those guys. Maybe I'll even suggest to let your friend live. What do you say?"

At first, she was infuriated at his proposal but realized it may be a good idea if she cooperated. There might even be a chance she got out of this alive. A slight chance but better than nothing. She had screwed guys whom she didn't particularly like before. Pretending Slovik was one of those guys, she accepted the situation. However, she knew the anger would come later.

"Okay," she said. "I'll let you fuck me. I hope you have some honor inside you, Slovik."

"Don't worry, I'll keep my word."

She walked ahead of him into the motel office. Slovik put his arm around her as they walked toward the desk.

"We want a room," he said to the desk clerk. Grinning, he took the key from the clerk. "We are very tired, the Missis and I. We'll go for a little snooze."

The clerk, a skinny guy with a pockmarked face, grinned back, winked slyly. "I understand, sir. Have a good rest."

She walked with him to one of the rooms in the back. Opening the door, he pulled her inside.

She lay down on the wide bed.

Laughing, Slovik took off his jacket. Then he undid his pants, dropped them and stepped out of them.

"Get undressed!" he told her hoarsely.

Stella took the knot out of her blouse, stripped it off. Then she removed her bra.

The big detective licked his lips when her breasts tumbled out. "The skirt," he said. "Hurry."

She pushed down her skirt and panties. Naked, she lay on the bed, looking up at him. He still wore his briefs. Pushing them down, he bared himself.

Stella's eyes widened when she saw his huge penis.

Slovik noticed her surprise and laughed. He told her to kneel on the bed. When she did, he stepped behind her. She felt his big hands on her hips, then his hard pole slid between her thighs, touched the entrance to her vagina.

With one hand, he grabbed his penis and rubbed the slippery glans against her labia. He entered her partially but pulled back when he couldn't penetrate her.

"Come on, open up," he grunted.

She opened her thighs slightly, felt him enter again. "Take it easy," she said, biting her lips. "You're hurting me."

"Just relax," he said soothingly.

She closed her eyes, relaxing her belly. It's just part of the job, she told herself.

He didn't last long. He pulled out of her and sat down at the edge of the bed, his breath coming in great gasps. "That wasn't so bad, was it?" he said. "I'll bet you enjoyed that."

She rolled over onto her side, away from him. Her eyes were open, she wanted to cry, but no tears came. After all, she had given her consent. He had not raped her, in fact, he had been gentle enough, but still, she was angry and furious. He would pay for this.

The bed creaked as he got up. "Get dressed," he said. "We have work to do."

The clerk grimaced when they walked out the door. "Come back soon," he called after them, "when you get tired again."

Stella found the locker easily. Keeping her back to Slovik, she removed the envelope. It wasn't sealed. Reaching inside, she took out the gun, checked the clip, and put the envelope with the money back into the locker. Then she turned around.

Slovik saw the gun in her hand, cursed and went for his own weapon.

"Touch it, and you're dead, Slovik!" she hissed. "Turn around." Stepping behind him, she pushed her gun into the big detective's broad back. "Now...let's walk very slowly, without attracting too much attention."

"What are you going to do?" Slovik asked.

"Kill you if I have to," she answered coldly. "And right now I don't need much provocation. By the way...You're under arrest. You have the right to be silent...You know the rest, but I'll read it to you later. For now...get moving!"

"There is no need for this," he growled. "I gave you my promise. You're making a big mistake."

"Maybe, but I don't really trust you, Slovic," she said.

A lot of people were milling around in the waiting area of the depot. When Stella spotted a security guard leaning against a pillar, she pushed Slovik in his direction. The guard glanced at them as they approached, straightened a little when they got closer.

He looked older. Probably a retired cop, she thought.

"I need your help," Stella said to him. "I am FBI Agent Stella Chandler. This man is in my custody. I've just arrested him."

"Really," the guard said, his eyes narrowing. "Do you have any identification?"

"She's lying," Slovik broke in. "I am Detective Slovik, and this woman is nothing but a common hooker. By the way…she's got a gun poking into my back."

The guard stepped away from the pillar he had been leaning against, his hand moved toward his holster.

"Leave your gun where it is, sir," Stella warned him. "You have a phone. Call the FBI. They will identify me."

Taking another step back, the guard took out his phone. "Patch me through to the FBI," he said into the mouthpiece. After a short wait, he said, "This is Security guard Hopkins at the bus depot. I have a situation. A woman claiming to be an FBI agent. Her name's Chandler. She's holding a guy hostage. He says he is a detective." He looked at Slovik. "What was your name again?"

"Slovik," the big man said.

"His name's Slovic…yes…right…right…sure…you don't say…okay, thank you very much." He clipped his phone back onto his belt, and then he looked at Stella. "They told me you should wait here. They'll send a couple of agents to give you a hand. Meanwhile, why don't we go into my little office over there? We're already attracting some attention here."

Stella shook her head. "Here is just fine. By the way, who did you talk to?"

The guard shook his head. "Don't know. He didn't give his name."

"I see," Stella said. "I'll take my prisoner to my car outside. Thanks for you help." She pushed the gun deeper into the detective's back. "Let's go, Slovik."

The big detective didn't move. "I'm not going anywhere," he said defiantly. "You'll have to shoot me right here."

Stella had taken her eyes off the guard. When she looked back, he had his gun out, aimed at her.

"All right," he said. "I'm pretty good with this gun, but I'm a little nervous right now. So be a good girl and hand me your gun. Then you can explain what this is all about. Maybe I'll even let you go." He moved his finger. "Come on, give it to me. Nobody needs to get hurt."

"What did the guy on the phone say to you?" Stella asked.

"He doesn't know an Agent Chandler, but he knows Detective Slovik."

Stella sighed. "You must have talked to the mole. Too bad you didn't get his name. Listen," she said, almost pleading. "I really am an FBI agent. I'll give you a number to call, ask for Colonel Bender. He will verify my identity."

"Don't listen to her," Slovik barked. "This woman is a trained assassin. A deadly killer."

"Didn't you say she was a hooker?"

"She is, but that's just her cover."

"She may be a hooker and a killer, but that bit about an assassin, I don't know…" The guard kept his gun aimed at Stella. "We'll just wait now. So don't any of you make any sudden moves."

Stella noticed the crowd gathering. People had noticed the commotion. She also became aware of the sudden silence in the depot. "Does anyone have a cellular phone?" she called out.

"I do," a male voice said close to her.

"Then do me a favor, please. Call the police."

"I don't have the number."

"Then dial the operator, damn it!" Stella cursed.

"Did you say the FBI was coming?" Slovik asked the guard.

"That's what the guy told me," the guard answered. With his free hand, he wiped his forehead. He was perspiring profusely.

"What's your name?" Stella asked him.

"Hopkins. Jerry Hopkins."

"Hi Jerry. You used to be a cop?"

"Used to… Yes. Retired five years ago." He ran the back of his left hand over his nose.

Stella noticed the slight tremor in his gun-hand. "I'm not going to shoot you, Jerry, unless you make me. So just relax. I don't want that gun of yours going off accidentally. Tell me…were you a good cop? I mean honest?"

"You bet I was. I have no use for crooked cops."

"Well, Jerry, neither do I. But Detective Slovik here, he doesn't think like you and I. He is as crooked as they come."

Slovik chuckled. "You be careful, Jerry. Before you realize it, she'll have you lick her pussy. She's been trained for this kind of situation. Tell her to shut up."

"You both be quiet, please." The guard rubbed his forehead again. "I'm getting too old for this kind of shit. What happened to that damn air-conditioning?"

Stella heard the screeching of tires outside. Through the glass door, she saw two cruisers coming to a stop. Four uniformed cops came rushing through the door, guns out.

As soon as they entered the building, they spread.

"All right," one of them said, looking at the guard. "Put your gun down. On the ground. Safety on."

"The woman's got a gun, too." The guard put his weapon on the floor in front of him.

"Now...kick it over here. And you..." he looked at Stella. "You, too."

"I am Agent Chandler. FBI. I have arrested this man. His name is Slovik. Detective Slovic. You must take him into custody. He carries a gun. Concealed." She stepped away from Slovik, shook out the clip and threw the gun on the floor.

The four cops rushed in, their guns ready, their eyes wary. They cuffed Slovik and Stella then told Hopkins to come along.

* * * *

Stella was appalled when they released Slovik. The big man waved to her when he walked away.

"He was my prisoner," she protested.

The desk sergeant looked at her over his glasses. "He has ID. You don't. And you were the one who was pointing the gun," he told her.

"I want to make a call," Stella said.

"Later. For now you'll join the other working girls." He shook his head. "A good-looking broad like you shouldn't have to do that kind of work. You could be a model or even a movie star."

They took her picture, fingerprinted her, and put her into a cell. Most of the half dozen girls in the cell were underage.

She sat down on an empty seat and put her face into her hands.

"Damn!" she said under her breath. Peter gave her a chance, but she screwed up.

She figured thirty minutes had gone by when a couple of female guards came to get her. "You're being released," the desk sergeant told her. "You lawyer posted bail."

"I didn't call no lawyer," she said. "Remember, I didn't get my call."

He shrugged. "Well, someone posted bail, so don't complain. He's waiting for you at the front door."

She didn't recognize the man who approached her. "Who are you?" she asked.

The man smiled. "Thomas A. Turner. Attorney at Law," he said. "Let's go." He took her arm.

She shook him off. "I'm not going anywhere with you."

"I think you will," he said with a low voice. "I have a syringe in my pocket. You'll be dead before you can utter a scream." He pulled her through the door, toward a car with darkened windows parked on the other side of the street. A big, burly man waited beside it. He was looking in their direction.

She knew, once in the car, she'd be dead. She could identify Slovik and Shaw. She might even be able to flush out the mole in her department. They could not afford to let her live. Desperately looking for a way out, she saw it when a man and a woman crossed their path.

"Excuse me, sir," she said to the man. When he stopped for a second, Stella pushed Turner into the man's arms then she turned and began to run.

Taking a chance, she turned into an alley. As luck had it, a door opened in one of the buildings, and someone took something to a garbage bin. She ducked into the doorway, unseen. In a darkened hallway, she entered another door, to be confronted by a man wearing a chef's hat.

"Hey," he said, startled. "Where do you come from?"

"I was looking for the ladies' room," Stella said, a little out of breath. "Must have gotten lost."

"You sure must be in a hurry to get there," the man said, smiling. "Relax, and I'll show you the way."

She followed him through the kitchen, out another door and into a small restaurant.

He pointed. "Over there."

She nodded and gave him a big smile. "Thanks. Maybe I can make it up to you some day."

"If I were younger, I'd insist on a date." He winked. "Now I just cook. Tell your friends about this place. We have good food."

Stella found the ladies' room. She took some paper towels and wet them, and then she went into one of the stalls and gratefully sat down. Wiping herself, she felt a little cleaner. After that, she washed her face and armpits.

She looked at herself in the mirror. I need a shower, better yet, a long soaking in the tub.

There was a payphone by the front door, but she had no money. She had left her purse in her car, which still stood in the bus depot parking lot.

Walking over to the cashier, she said, "I need to make a call. Do you mind if I use your phone?"

The girl gave her an odd look. "There is a payphone right there."

"I know," Stella said, "but I have no quarters."

"I can give you change."

"Listen, sweetie," Stella said, trying to stay calm. "I have no time for chit-chat. I've just been robbed. They took my purse, my cell phone, my credit cards, my ID, and all of my money. I need to call my attorney. So can I, please, use your phone?"

"All right, but my boss won't like it."

"Screw your boss," Stella said under her breath. Then she smiled. "I don't mean that literally." She dialed Colonel Bender's number.

When he answered the phone, she let out a grateful breath. "Hi, it's me. Stella. I'm in trouble. Serious trouble...and so is Peter."

"Where are you?"

"What's this place called?" Stella asked the cashier.

"Ben's Eatery," the girl said. "How did you get in here?"

"I'm at Ben's Eatery. It's on Forty-second Street, close to the police station. And by the way...bring backup."

"Where's Peter?" Bender asked.

"Shaw is holding him in a warehouse in the old East Riverside district. I can take you there. Do me another favor. Call Inspector Burgess at the Thirty-seventh Precinct. He can be trusted. Fill him in and bring a S.W.A.T. team. Also, bring me a gun."

When she gave the phone back, the girl stared at her with large eyes.

"Who are you?" the girl asked. "The FBI?"

"You got it, sweetie. I am the FBI and in no mood for any shit."

"Wow!" the girl exclaimed. "Why didn't you say so? I never met a real live FBI agent. Wait till I tell my boyfriend."

"I'm sure he'll be thrilled," Stella said dryly.

Chapter Twenty-Two

"A long time ago you've taken something that belonged to me." The man's slanted eyes were tiny slits, but Peter could still see the angry glint in their darkness. When Peter didn't say anything, the man came closer. "You don't remember me, do you?" he asked.

Peter chuckled. "I remember you, Scorpion. You tried to kill me once before."

"Your friends saved you then, but this time you are alone. A prisoner. I heard they call you Cobra," the man said mockingly. "I also hear that a man called King Cobra will release those whores who belong to the Sisterhood of the Viper from the Scorpion's yoke. Are you that King Cobra?"

Peter looked relaxed, but mentally he prepared himself. "Some say I am," he said. "I've never claimed such a thing."

"But you wear the image of the cobra on your arm."

"It's a tattoo, nothing more."

The man took off his jacked and stripped off his shirt. He looked bigger and more muscular than Peter remembered.

On his deep chest, he displayed the tattoo of a scorpion. "I am Scorpion," he said proudly, "and I will prove to you that my stinger is more lethal than your puny poisoned fang."

Without warning, he launched himself at Peter, but Peter anticipated the attack. Dropping to the floor, he rolled away, barely avoiding the deadly kick.

"You're the one extorting money from Connie," he stated.

Crouching, ready to spring again, Scorpion glared at Peter. "She belonged to me before you spoiled her, and she still belongs to me," he hissed. "I only take what is mine."

"You're a common thief and a criminal." Peter fell into the swaying dance of the cobra, his left hand held high, fingers stiff, his right arm bent, closed fist against his hip.

When his opponent sprang at him again, he moved with lightening speed. His stiffened fingers raked Scorpion's chest, drawing blood. With his right fist, he delivered a blow against his adversary's head, but he didn't connect.

Scorpion was fast, agile. Peter was physically not at his best. The ordeal from the night before was telling, and he had just finished with Delta Liebman.

As Peter swung his foot in a roundhouse kick, Scorpion grabbed it and twisted. The only thing Peter could do was follow the direction of the twist. Landing on the floor, he kicked his free foot into his opponent's chest, hard.

He pulled free, rolled away, kicked up again as Scorpion followed, missed, rolled again. A blow like a sledgehammer smashed into his ribs. Grabbing an arm, he twisted, but let go, when stiffened fingers aimed for his eyes. Blocking the descending hand, he managed to twist his body out of the way, stood in a half-crouch.

Scorpion had not followed him. He stood with his arms hanging by his sides. Peter noted the blood on his chest.

"You're very good," Scorpion said gravely. "A worthy opponent. But now I must kill you." He spread his arms.

Peter saw the glitter of metal, saw the six-inch blades in his hands.

Slowly Scorpion advanced. His hands began weaving a deadly pattern.

Peter readied his mind and body for the fight of his life.

A sudden noise outside the room made his enemy stop and look at the door. It was flung open; a figure appeared in the doorway, entered.

Colonel Shaw.

Two more men entered with guns in their hands.

"What's going on?" Scorpion demanded to know.

Shaw ignored him. He stared at Peter. "I guess we've underestimated you and that bitch of yours." He lifted his gun, pointed it at Peter. "But I'm taking you down with me."

Reacting out of instinct, Peter dropped to the floor. He heard Shaw's gun go off once then the crack of a different gun, the sound of a body falling.

Looking up, he saw Shaw lying on the floor, another figure standing in the doorway, wearing a black, tight-fitting bodysuit.

Stella.

She held her gun aimed at Scorpion. "You move one tiny muscle and you'll join your friend," she said with an icy voice. "Same goes for you," she said, glancing at Delta Liebman and the other two men.

Behind her, another figure appeared, walked slowly into the room. "Hello, Peter," he said. "Looks like we've saved your ass just in time."

Peter grinned. "Hello, Colonel. Glad to see you." He walked over to the chair, retrieved his clothing and began to dress. Looking at Stella, he smiled. "What took you so long?"

She returned his smile and came up to him. A full dozen black-clad men filed into the room, spread out. They disarmed the two men, cuffed them. Cuffed Delta Liebman as well.

Scorpion had dropped his knives to the floor. He spat in Peter's direction. "This is not over," he said as they led him away.

Colonel Bender joined Peter and Stella. Beside him walked another man. "This is Inspector Burgess," the Colonel said. "He has evidence that will clear you of all the charges."

* * * *

"Scratch me between my shoulder blades." Stella looked back at him over her shoulder, blinking hot shower water out of her eyes.

Peter rubbed her back with one hand, the other one moved around her to cup her breast.

"Ah…that feels nice." She pushed her buttocks back against him.

Peter was already stiff. He put his erect penis between her fleshy cheeks. She arched her back more and spread her legs to capture his mast. With one hand, she reached down to touch him. "I need to feel that thing inside me," she breathed and turned around to face him.

Putting her arms around his neck, she pressed her body against his. The warm water from the shower ran down between their bodies, pooled in the cleavage of her breasts. She smiled and kissed him deeply, her tongue probing the cave of his mouth.

They broke apart, gasping for breath.

Peter put his hands under her buttocks and lifted her up. Her legs spread, encircled his hips. He slid easily into her and pushed her against the back of the shower stall. She clung to him while he moved lazily in and out of her.

Crying out, she pressed her thighs tightly against his hips. He pulled out. "Let's do it properly," he whispered into her ear.

Water dripping, they ran out of the shower and into the bedroom. They never made it to the bed. He took her on the carpet. Her thighs flew wide open as he moved between them. She was hot and moist; the short session in the shower had prepared her well.

"A dangerous assignment always makes me horny," she gasped as he entered her.

"You should be really horny now," Peter groaned.

Then their laboring breaths filled the bedroom as they moved against each other. When he came inside her, Stella whimpered and her belly worked as she milked him feverishly.

Then she relaxed under him.

Peter put his face on her full, soft breasts, inhaling the fragrance of her body. She stroked the back of his head, ran her fingers through his damp hair.

"What are you going to do now?" she asked.

"I don't know yet," he said. "Obviously, I won't go back to my old job at Computer Regeneration, unless Linda hires me. She'll most likely run the company if Robert goes to jail."

"You could always work for the Department," Stella suggested.

Peter chuckled. "I'm through with that kind of work."

"No, no," she said. "I mean you could work as an investigator."

"I don't know." Peter rolled onto his back, turned to lie on his side. Then he reached out to touch her cheek. "First, I have to get back home to Kathleen and make things right again. After that…we'll see."

"What will you do for a living?"

He smiled. "I have some money."

"Oh, I forgot." Stella sat up. "I still have your key from the deposit box. I put the envelope back. Your money is safe, and so is your wallet."

"Thanks." Peter pulled her down on top of him and kissed her. "You're beautiful."

She pulled free and shook her hair, still wet. "You're a liar. I must look awful." She got up. I'm going to finish my shower.

Peter lay on his back and, listening to the sound of the shower, he reflected on what had transpired these last few days.

Technically, he was still a fugitive at large, but it was just a matter of time now. Inspector Burgess had released him into Stella's custody until the paperwork went through.

He smiled. That Stella, she was a remarkable woman and a competent agent.

Someone had delivered a package to her office. The package contained the missing master chip and a CD, made by Rhonda Liebman. Stella turned the package over to Inspector Burgess.

It seems that a young man, an employee of Beta Research, took a briefcase from the Liebman residence by mistake. Peter remembered that young man, the one who had come upon the scene just after Rhonda Liebman suffered her heart attack.

The information on the CD was damaging and detailed enough to send a few people to prison. Delta Liebman admitted to having known about the plot to assassinate her brother-in-law and his wife Rhonda. She blamed it all on her half-brother Edward Shaw, who, according to her, masterminded the whole thing. Shaw was dead, of course, and he couldn't defend himself.

Peter sighed. She would go free. The government would give her amnesty in exchange for information.

Stella came out of the bathroom and shot him a quick once-over.

"Aren't you tired?" she asked. "It is late, you know, and it's been a long day."

"You're right. Where can I sleep?"

"You can sleep in the spare bedroom. My bed is wide enough for two, but neither of us would get any sleep." She smiled. "You know what I mean."

"You're probable right...again," Peter said. "Do you have some pajamas for me?"

Stella laughed. "I'm afraid not. You'll just have to go to bed naked. I do."

"Maybe I should sleep in your bed after all," he kidded.

"Not a chance. Come on, I'll turn down the bed for you."

He followed her into the other room, watched her pull back the covers and fluff the pillow. Sighing, he slipped under the covers.

Stella gave him a quick kiss on the lips, and then she left the room. The last image, before he closed his eyes, was a pair of round naked buttocks.

When he opened his eyes again, it was dark. He had the distinct impression he was not alone. In the darkness, he didn't see anything, but he heard a soft rustling beside his bed.

"It's me," whispered a soft voice.

A hand groped around, touched his shoulder, pulled on the covers. Then a warm, naked body pressed against his, rolled on top if him. Thighs parted, a moist slit rubbed against his semi-erect penis. It didn't take long for his penis to turn into an iron-hard rod.

A tight sheath slipped over his rod and took him deep inside.

"Ah...ah..." she moaned, throwing back the covers.

The darkness was so complete, he couldn't even see her shadow, but he knew she sat up. He moved his hands along the curves of her body and touched her ample soft breasts. Whipping her bottom with frenzied speed, she brought herself to a quick orgasm. She cried out softly when she doused him with her warm discharge.

He let her ride him for a while, listened to her moans and little cries, then he reached around her back and pulled her on top of him. He felt her soft warm breasts against his hard chest. Turning, without uncoupling, he found himself between her strong, widening thighs. With powerful, deep strokes, he thrust into her, made her squirm and writhe underneath him. Her fingernails raked his back as another powerful orgasm gripped her body.

"Don't stop for a long time," she whispered fiercely into his ear. "I'll tell you when I want you to come. I know you can do it."

"You do, don't you?" He chuckled. "You make it awfully hard for a guy not to come." He put his hands under her buttocks, pulled her against him. She bent her knees sharply and crossed her legs behind his back. He moved slowly now, pulling out as much as he could without slipping out completely, then he pushed back deep into her.

The warm interior of her vagina felt like a vessel filled with soft jelly, yet extremely tight.

Her arms tightly around his wide back, she bucked up against him. Her mouth searched frantically, wide-open lips glued to his, let his tongue enter. She moaned loudly into his mouth, and then she broke free, gasped for air. "Now!" she cried. "Now…!"

He had felt his own climax building up for a long time. Shouting, he thrust deep. His fingers dug into her buttocks as he crushed her to him. It burst out of him with tremendous force.

She bucked and cried, her pussy alive around his gushing penis.

His pleasure was exquisite and seemed to increase with every throb until, finally, there was nothing left in him. Her legs relaxed, stretched out on either side of him.

"That was heaven," she gasped and stroked his back. Then she pushed him away. "I'm going to clean up," she whispered.

He felt her slip from the bed, listened to her soft footsteps as she walked out of the room, heard the closing door.

Pulling the covers over his naked body, he drifted back to sleep.

* * * *

A ray of sunshine burst through the slits in the blind. Peter blinked the sleep out of his eyes, pushed away the covers. He felt rested, wondered briefly if he had dreamed of having sex in the middle of the night.

Getting out of bed, he stretched, and then he opened the door to go to the bathroom. When he peeked into Stella's bedroom, he saw her lying naked on top of the covers. She seemed to be sleeping.

Quietly he walked to the bathroom and took a quick shower. Walking past Stella's bedroom again, he took another peek and saw her still on her belly, one leg stretched out, the other one bent.

Between her plump buttocks, he could see the puffy lips of her pussy. A sudden throbbing in his groin made him walk into the room. He lay down beside her, cupped her body with his.

His penis was already stiff. Putting it below her soft cheeks, he rubbed his pole gently between her exposed pussy-lips. She sighed, moved back against him. He felt himself slide into her, grabbed her hips and pushed deep.

Lying on his side, he didn't have much freedom to move, but it was not necessary. The tight sheath holding him prisoner had come to life.

Soft walls rippled gently along his shaft. He reached around to cup a full breast, let his fingers play with the rigid nipple.

Pulling back her hair, he kissed her on the neck, moved around to her cheek, searched her mouth.

Light from the window suddenly touched her face.

Peter stopped moving and let out a suppressed curse.

"You're not Stella," he said.

The girl laughed and wiggled her bottom, exerting delicious pressure on his penis. "Never said I was. I'm her sister Mirabelle. Don't you remember me?"

"I remember you. I'm sorry."

"Sorry for what?" she asked.

"For this," he said, pulling out of her.

"It didn't seem to be a problem last night," Mirabelle said, turning around to look at him.

"Last night? That was you?"

She nodded, smiling mischievously. "Stella phoned me and told me you were here. She said if I wanted to make love to the greatest lover she's ever met I should come over. So I did." She ran her hand down his chest. "Don't be sorry. It was great." She chuckled. "Of course, I've already made love to you at that party. I remembered how good you were."

"It was great, then and last night, but you deceived me by pretending to be Stella."

"Well…yeah. I guess I did, but it added to the titillation." Her fingers circled his stiff mast and squeezed it. "Let's not waste this. Come, put it back in." She lay back, opening her legs wide.

Peter stared at her naked body, her large breasts, solid on her ribcage, her flat belly, her shaved Venus mound, and her beckoning pink slit. "You're so young," he sighed.

"Twenty, almost twenty-one." She smiled. "Old enough and no innocent virgin. Come on, I'm really turned on."

Shrugging, he moved between her spread thighs and let her pull him toward her inviting pussy. He felt himself glide in easily, heard her loud moan as she pushed up against him.

Then he was moving in and out of her glorious softness. He studied her lovely, young face. Soft shadows and sunlight played alternately across it as she writhed beneath him.

They moved together for a long time. When he came inside her, she cried out, milked him with fierce passion. Her warm nectar mixed with his cream, moistened his inner thighs.

Then they lay panting in each other's arms.

"Wow!" she finally exclaimed. "That was even better than last night."

After a while Peter got up. "I'm going to wash up," he said. "And then I'll need a huge breakfast. By the way, where is your big sister?"

"Stella left early for work. She told me to take care of your needs." Mirabelle stretched her lithe body and yawned. Then she chuckled. "How am I doing so far?"

Peter grinned. "Make me some breakfast and I'll tell you."

She pouted. "Men! You let them get their rocks off inside you and they think they own you." She rolled onto her stomach and pushed up her buttocks. Looking over her shoulder back at him, she said, "Maybe I'll command you to make love to me again. Then I'll tell you to make breakfast."

Peter walked back to the bed, gave her a gentle slap on her plump buttocks, laughed, and went to the bathroom.

Chapter Twenty-Three

"Tell me, what are you doing with your life when you're not screwing older men?" Peter asked, studying her profile. He had to admit, she was quite beautiful. Her sister Stella was an attractive and beautiful woman, but Mirabelle's features were more delicate, move refined.

She took her eyes away from the traffic and glanced at him. "I'm not really in the habit of screwing older men, Peter. In fact, I don't sleep around much."

"Sorry, I didn't mean it to sound the way it did," Peter apologized. "So why me?"

She smiled.

"You're special. But I don't have to tell you, you know that already."

Peter shrugged. "I love sex, and I'm good at it. I don't know if that makes me so special. I also love beautiful women, and I love screwing them, but all men do."

"Not all men can make a girl come like you do," she said bluntly. "A girl could die in your arms and never mind at all."

Peter sat silent for a moment. She had hit a raw nerve with that remark. His thoughts went to Rhonda Liebman who had done exactly that.

Wonder if she minded?

Mirabelle noticed his silence. "Did I say something wrong?"

"It's nothing," Peter said. "My mind just wandered for a moment. So what do you do in your spare time?"

"I'm studying to be a psychiatrist. I'd like to work for the FBI, like my sister, but not as an agent. Maybe as a profiler." She laughed. "I like excitement, you know, but Stella's job is a little too exciting for me."

"She meets a lot of interesting people, though," Peter commented.

"People like you, for instance? You never told me what you do for a living."

"Nothing that exciting, really. I'm just a computer salesman. At least I used to be."

"Used to be?"

"My company is going through some reorganizing right now. In addition, I've had some personal problems. I don't think I'm welcome there anymore."

"It happens." Mirabelle lifted her shoulders. "I'm sure you'll find another job." She gave him a sidelong glance. "I have an idea. Since you're not in a hurry to get anywhere, why don't you hang around with me for a while? We could make love all day long."

Peter chuckled. "I don't believe that is such a great idea. What would your parents say if they'd see you 'hanging out' with an older guy? Besides, I have to get home to Kathleen."

"You're married? I should have guessed. A good-looking guy like you would not be single. Too bad." Mirabelle sighed.

"She is not my wife."

"You're sister?"

He laughed. "No, not my sister. My girlfriend."

"Oh. You love her?"

"Yes, I do."

"Then how come you're screwing around on her?"

"Good question, honey. I don't have the answer."

"Is she ugly? Fat? A bitch?"

Peter laughed at her childlike curiosity. "No. She is very beautiful, and when I'm with her, I feel good."

"Well, then I don't understand you. Perhaps I can study you," Mirabelle said thoughtfully. "Maybe I should talk to your girlfriend. Does she know?"

"I don't believe so." Peter shook his head. "I'm very good at everything I do, even cheating. I think you'd better put this notion out of your mind. I have enough problems to deal with right now. All I need is to add more to them. By the way, that's my house over there."

Mirabelle pulled her car into the driveway. "Wow! What a house! You must be rich."

"I'm not rich," Peter said, "but comfortable."

"I'll say." Mirabelle walked up the steps to the front door.

Peter searched for his key and unlocked the door. He wondered if Kathleen was in, but he knew she wasn't the moment he walked into the vestibule. The air in the house felt warm. Kathleen always turned off the air conditioning when she left the house.

Mirabelle took off her black leather jacket and threw it over a chair in the living room. She flopped down on the chesterfield. "Nice." She ran her hand over the fine leather. "Your girlfriend has good taste."

"What makes you think she picked out the furniture?"

She shrugged. "Women always do. It's common knowledge." She looked at a picture standing on a shelf. A picture of Kathleen with her little red sports car.

"Hey, is that your girlfriend?" Mirabelle jumped up to take a closer look. "She really is beautiful."

"I told you, didn't I? Listen…make yourself comfortable. I want to check my messages."

The first message was from Kathleen. "Honey, I won't be there when you come home. Sorry. Had to do a last minute shoot, but I should be back tomorrow. Kisses. Kathleen."

The other message was his.

"Looks like you'll sleep alone tonight." Mirabelle smiled. "You want company? I'm free."

"I don't think it's a good idea."

Mirabelle laughed. "I think it'll be fun."

Peter watched her as she put a CD into the player. The raspy voice of Tom Jones suddenly filled the room.

She did a few dance steps. "I like that song," she said. "Who is that guy?"

"He's obviously from before your time." Peter smiled, watching her grind her hips.

She noticed his looks, threw back her head and laughed. Then she slipped off her sweater. She was naked underneath. Her breasts jiggled as she moved her shoulders to the rhythm of the music.

"You're a vixen." Peter walked up to her.

She peeled off her jeans and pulled down her lacy panties. Then she bent over one of the big chairs, her naked rump up, her pink slit exposed to Peter's view. He stepped behind her, pushed down his own pants, and entered her from behind. His penis sank deep into her welcoming love channel.

"You see, you need me after all," Mirabelle gasped, reached back to touch his pounding hips.

Peter put his hands on her arching back and watched his stiff mast moving between her white clenching buttocks. Slowly sliding his hands across her back, he let his spread fingers rest on her buttocks, barely touching the firm flesh. His fingertips tingled where they made contact with her smooth velvety skin.

She rotated her hips slowly, while jerking her bottom back and forth. Her tight pussy milked his throbbing penis as the silky, smooth walls of her sex-canal gently rippled down its full length.

He grabbed her hips, began to pound harder. Even though his mind concentrated on Mirabelle's young curvy body, he was still aware of his surroundings. He turned his head when he heard the creaking hinges of the opening door.

"Can we join the party?" asked a woman's voice. A familiar voice. He'd recognize her strange guttural accent anywhere.

Walking into the room, the woman threw off her cape, exposing her nude body, still covered with glittering scale. A mask hid her face, leaving only her lips visible.

Behind her, another figure walked in, undid her cape, and let it slide to the floor.

As the women came closer, Peter stared at their beautiful painted bodies.

"Well," the woman with the guttural accent said, "are we invited?"

"How did you get in?" Peter asked.

The woman dangled a key in front of him. "Kathleen is a good friend of mine." She chuckled. "I guess you didn't know that. She said we could spend the night here. Seems we came at a good time." Laughing, she walked in front of Mirabelle, bent down and planted a kiss on the young woman's lips.

Mirabelle hesitated at first, but then she returned the kiss. Her already tight pussy tightened even more around Peter's hard mast.

The painted woman broke the kiss and whispered something into the girl's ear. Mirabelle giggled and kissed the woman again.

"Okay, Lover," the snake-woman said with her guttural accent as she stood up, "Pull that big fat rod out of her and stick it into me. She likes watching. She'll be even hornier later."

She lay down on the carpet and spread her legs. The sunlight that came in through the window, played across her painted body, reflecting in the iridescent colored scales. Her pussy lay in shadows.

Peter pulled out of Mirabelle, moved between the inviting spread thighs of the snake-woman. She laughed, grabbed his stiff mast and rubbed the swollen head between her puffy labia. They were soft and moist. He felt the head entering her cleft and penetrating the tight entrance. Then he slid into the hot, soft, and creamy interior.

The woman cried out softly as he pushed deep into her. She closed her legs tightly against his hips. Then she began bucking beneath him, her arms tight around his waist, writhing like the serpent she represented. The nipples of her soft breasts felt hard against his chest. Her pussy contracted and expanded, moving over his hard organ like a tight-fitting silky sheath. Warm liquid gushed from her as she exploded with a loud cry.

Peter wanted to join her with his own climax, but he controlled the urge. He knew there was much more ahead.

Pushing himself up on his elbows, he looked into her masked face. Her dark eyes glittered mysteriously behind the slits of her mask. "You seem oddly familiar," he said. "I have a feeling I know you."

"Sure you do. We've done this before."

"I know we have, but I have this strange feeling…"

Soft hands touched his back; a warm female body straddled him. He could feel a moist pussy rubbing against his skin.

"I think my friend wants you," the woman underneath him said.

Peter shrugged, pushed one more time deep into her, and then he pulled out. The woman moved away. Peter turned and lay on his back. The silent woman straddled him and hovered above his stiff mast.

Slowly, she sank down. Peter watched his pole disappear inside her slippery pussy. She rotated her hips, and at the same time moved up and down. Her hands gripped his arms for support.

His eyes glued to her large, cone-shaped breast, Peter wondered what her face looked like under the dark latex mask. Even her eyes were hidden behind glittering round lenses.

She has to be beautiful. She can't be anything but, with a body like this.

She changed her rhythm, snapped her lower body back and forth, taking him deep into her with every forceful thrust. She moaned and let out a sharp hissing sound, true to her disguise, her fingers digging painfully into his forearms. Breathing hard and moaning loudly, she doused him with her discharge.

She rode him for a long time, her glittering snake eyes never leaving his face. After a series of orgasms, she lifted and pointed at Mirabelle who had been watching silently.

With a little whoop, the girl lay down on the floor, opening her thighs in invitation. Peter rolled on top of her, between her soft thighs. He entered her without a word, slid deep into her velvety pussy.

Gentle hands touched his clenching buttocks, moved around to grab his penis, held it while he buried it repeatedly in Mirabelle's tight sex-canal.

"Come inside her," whispered the woman with the guttural accent into his ear. "I want to feel your penis jump in my hand."

Peter was ready to comply, when he heard the sound of a scuffle and then a woman's scream.

"Don't stop on account of me. I like watching."

Hearing the voice, Peter froze. "Scorpion!" he cursed, still wrapped in Mirabelle's clutching embrace. "How did you get in here?"

"Through the door," the man said.

"I thought you were in jail."

"I'm a free man. They had nothing on me to keep me there." Scorpion laughed. He had one arm around the silent woman's waist, holding her tightly against him, like holding an old friend. Then Peter saw the knife digging into her throat.

"The great Peter McDiarmid," the man sneered. "Yes, I know about you. Apparently, you used to be this hotshot agent. The best, they told me. Look at you now! Reduced to an animal in heat and fucking whores. I bet you don't even know who you're fucking these days."

He took away the knife and slid it into a sheath on his belt. Then he pulled something out of his pocket and threw it on the chesterfield. "Play this for him!" he commanded the woman standing beside Peter.

She nodded, took the disk, and inserted it into the player.

Puzzled, Peter looked at the scene on the screen. Two men screwing the snake-women.

"You're not showing me anything I haven't seen before," he said.

Scorpion chuckled. "You haven't seen the next scene."

A man stepped behind one of the snake women and guided his erect pole into her as she knelt on the floor. Reaching around her head, he pulled off the woman's snake mask. Auburn hair spilled over her painted shoulders.

The camera changed angle, and Peter cursed loudly.

The face was that of Kathleen.

He looked at Scorpion. "You bastard!" he cursed.

Scorpion laughed. "Wait, there is more to show you."

Peter watched as Scorpion removed the mask from the silent woman's head. Auburn hair exploded from underneath the tight skullcap.

Large green eyes stared at Peter. He could see the pain in them.

"I'm sorry." Kathleen said with a choking voice. "I was going to tell you tonight."

Peter was still frozen inside Mirabelle's embrace, but he was barely aware of it.

"Your girlfriend is my biggest star. She's been making porno-movies for years. I had no idea she was living with an old friend of mine." Scorpion squeezed one of Kathleen's breasts. "She and I, we've had some good times together. I bet she never fucked you the way she fucks me. Remind me to send you one of our videos sometime. You'll see her in ways you've never seen her." He tightened his grip around her. "We must be going now. Say goodbye. You'll never see her again…at least not alive."

When he turned with Kathleen in his arms, she struggled, slipped out of his grasp, and ran toward the open front door.

Cursing, Scorpion followed her.

Peter came out of his frozen state. Freeing himself from Mirabelle, he ran after Kathleen and her captor. Outside, on his front lawn, he saw three people. Two of them faced each other in a classic martial arts stance.

The man who called himself Scorpion and a figure dressed in black.

A woman.

The tight bodysuit she wore left no doubt. A camouflage facemask hid her features.

"I have no quarrel with you," Peter heard Scorpion say, "but if you don't get out of my way, I'll kill you."

The woman stayed silent, but Peter saw her muscles tighten under the thin material of her suit.

Then she sprang.

Scorpion stepped aside in defense. She rolled passed him, landed on her feet like a cat and attacked again. She kicked him in the shoulder, sent him reeling.

Scorpion screamed and launched a counterattack, but the woman was fast, agile. She used techniques Peter had never seen before, confirming his suspicion as to her identity.

"You may not have a quarrel with me, but I have one with you," she said with a cold, impersonal voice. "I don't like when people screw up my assignments."

Laughing, Scorpion kicked up with his foot, aiming for her head. "Viper! I should have known. Another snake! I think I will de-fang you." He sprang from a standing position.

Viper didn't move.

They made contact. Together, they rolled across the lawn. Then they broke apart. Scorpion staggered, sank to his knees. His hand touched his neck.

"What did you do?" he said with a thick voice.

Viper stood wide-legged above him. The rays of the sun bathed her body with rainbow colors. Only now, Peter noticed the two stylized white snakes circling her ample breasts.

She laughed. "This viper has a poisonous fang."

Scorpion struggled to his feet but collapsed into a lifeless heap between her spread legs. When Viper touched him with one booted foot, he sprawled onto his back.

The woman looked at Peter. "Help me put him into his car. When the police find him, they'll think he died of a heart attack."

Peter walked up to her. Then he looked at Kathleen who crouched nearby. He held out his hand to her. She came into his arms and hugged him tightly. "I'm so sorry, Peter," she sobbed. "Please, forgive me."

He stroked her hair, touched her tearstained face. "I love you," he said. "Go back into the house. I'll be in shortly." He turned toward Viper. "Thank you, Maureen," he said. "What made you come here?"

"The man who called himself Scorpion was a dangerous man. I knew about him. I knew what he did to Connie and the other members of The Sisterhood. When I found out that Kathleen was your girlfriend it didn't take much brains to figure out what he was about to do. Besides, he meddled with my assignments." She chuckled. "There is a code of honor even among assassins. Come on, let's clean up this mess. I want to get home and out of this ridiculous outfit."

"It looks great on you," Peter said, letting his eyes roam over her voluptuous body. "Do you need assistance peeling it off?"

Viper laughed. "You're incorrigible, you know. Maybe another time."

They dragged Scorpion out to his car and placed him behind the wheel. It looked like a man taking a nap. Viper left in her sports car, and Peter walked slowly back to his house.

The women were waiting anxiously for him inside. Kathleen sat on the chesterfield, the other painted woman beside her. She had removed her mask. Slanted dark eyes sparkled in her exotic, beautiful face, half-covered by long black hair.

"Sue Lin," he said lamely. "Nice to see you."

The oriental girl smiled. "Nice to see you, too, Peter," she said, dropping that phony guttural accent.

Peter sank into the big easy chair and looked over to Mirabelle. "Sorry, kid."

"For what?"

"For dragging you into this mess." His voice came out hoarsely. He looked at Kathleen who was watching him silently. Smiling, he bent forward to touch her leg. "It's over," he said. "I'm out of jail, and you are free of him."

She nodded and looked at him with large, green eyes. "I should have told you long ago," she whispered. "Maybe none of this would have happened."

He got up, sat beside her. Then he turned her head and kissed her. "Nobody is to blame," he told her. "I'm no choirboy, either."

She smiled bravely, trailing the tattoo of the Cobra on his forearm with one finger.

"I know," she said. "King Cobra."

Chapter Twenty-Four

The ringing of the phone woke him from his deep sleep. He looked at the clock. 7:00 AM.

Kathleen stirred beside him but didn't wake up.

He picked up the phone before it rang again.

"Good morning. Did I wake you?" Stella's voice sounded cheery and wide-awake.

"You did, but that's all right," Peter said thickly. "I have to get up and go to work anyway."

He slipped out of bed, took the phone with him. "What's up?"

"I have the day off. How about you and I spending the day together?" Her voice became a soft whisper. "I bought a sexy outfit. Mostly lace and not much of it. The bottom is nothing but strings. You may want to take it off me with your teeth."

"Sounds tempting."

"You seem reluctant. Don't make me beg, Peter. Let me put it to you in plain words. I am extremely horny and I want to be fucked."

Peter laughed into the phone. "Why didn't you say so? In that case I guess I'll have to come to the rescue."

"See you in a bit."

Peter threw some water on his face, brushed his teeth. Padding back into the bedroom, he found Kathleen still asleep. He studied her silently. She was so beautiful. They had promised each other to change.

He picked up his clothes and dressed in the living room.

He would change, but not today.

It takes a while for a snake to shed its skin.